When No One Was Looking

Was Looking

Project Mnemosyne

Kim Frauli

CONTENTS

CHAPTER 1

"Julianna, it is imperative that you remember these numbers. If anything ever happens to me, you're the only one who will know how to find it," her father told her in a stern, no-nonsense tone. "Pay close attention."

A small Julianna focused intently on what her father was telling her. "This is the number for the box," he started to say. All of a sudden, the earth between them split wide open. Her father lost his footing and fell into the abyss.

"Daddy!" Julianna screamed.

Julianna shot upright in her bed. She waited a moment for her breathing to slow to normal before she slowly put her head back on her pillow. *Another one of those dreams*, she thought to herself. *What is wrong with me?* In a matter of minutes, her alarm would go off anyway, but she was happy to absorb the peace and quiet for a bit longer before starting her bustling day. If she did not enjoy her work so much, she might have found it exhausting.

When her alarm chimed its pleasant wake-up tone, she swung her legs to the floor and walked to her window. She peeled back her curtains and greeted the sunshine with a smile as the warmth kissed her face. She sighed contentedly. Strange dreams aside, she did lead a pretty good life, she told herself. She tried her best to brush aside the feelings of discontent which had been cropping up only recently. Then she set about the business of preparing for her day. She smoothed out the cadet blue bedding on her full size bed before sliding open the pocket door on her closet. Selecting clothing of the day was never a problem as she really only had her work uniforms from which to choose. The sensible uniform of cotton pants and a long-sleeved shirt, both in a cold gray color, was comfortable and utilitarian, and tailored to fit her petite five-foot-three, slender frame. While she was at work, the uniform often hid beneath her sterile white lab coat anyway. She removed a hanger that held a complete fresh set and got dressed. She sat at a small vanity in one corner to brush her long honey blonde hair and pinned it neatly away from her face with a basic, silver barrette.

She considered herself fortunate to have one of the nicer rooms in the Scholars Compound. She did have cream colored carpeting instead of a tiled floor, which was nice during the chilly Midwestern winters. She had her own bathroom, and she liked the blue tones in the fabrics in her room. She didn't even mind the grey color of the walls, though she preferred to call it silver. That seemed happier to her. She walked into her bathroom where she brushed her teeth and put on a layer of lip balm. Sometimes, she would pretend the lip balm was coloring her lips a pretty color, like the lipstick she used to watch her mother apply for nights out. Julianna had never used lipstick herself. Make-up was frowned upon in the Scholars Compound. It was unnecessary, and that which was unnecessary was not used even if it was not officially forbidden. None of the Scholars wanted to be seen as foolish or superficial. Sometimes she wondered, especially more recently, what her life would have been like if the attacks had never happened. But such thoughts really served no purpose, and she rarely allowed herself to entertain them. Her life was in the Scholars Compound, and she had a very nice room.

Of course, she did not spend a lot of time in her room. She spent most of her time in the lab, which is where she walked now, with almost a skip in her step, to meet Declan O'Connor. Life at the Compound would have been terribly lonely without Declan. She smiled at the thought of seeing her best friend. She and Declan had wiled many days away in their lab working on medical advancements that they hoped were improving the lives of people everywhere. When they were not in the lab, they usually could be found in the library, sitting next to each other in lounge chairs in quiet companionship as they worked their way through the massive amount of material available to them. Declan always teased Julianna about how she outpaced him so effortlessly with her gift for speed reading. The only thing more impressive, he liked to point out, was her ability to retain the information that she read.

When she walked into the lab, Declan greeted her with a bright smile. "Good morning, Sunshine!"

She returned the smile. "Good morning, Friend! I see you beat me here today."

"You act like that's a hard thing," he scoffed.

"I don't just wake up this beautiful, you know!" she retorted. "Guys have it so much easier than girls." She ruffled his short dark hair.

He ducked away from her. "Excuse me! You have no idea how long it took me to get my hair just right this morning. And now look at me," he kidded with a sigh.

"Don't worry about it. I'm the only one who has to look at you all day, and I don't mind."

Few girls would mind spending their days looking at Declan. His hair had a slight curl to it, and its dark color really brought out the bright green of his eyes. Since she had first met him, he had grown to his full height of 6 foot even, and he made excellent use of his leisure time in the gym to sculpt his body. Julianna often thought it was a shame that the lab uniform covered so much of it, but she did take in some good, long looks when they would swim laps at the Compound pool. Of course, Julianna thought his smile was his best feature. She sometimes made it her goal to see how many times a day she could make him flash that smile at her, by joking with him or extending a kindness his way. She remembered the first time he had ever given it to her. That smile had helped her convince herself that everything was going to be okay after it happened all those years ago, when she was brought to the Scholars Compound as an orphan child.

Declan was not an orphan, and Julianna sometimes wondered which was harder - to not have parents at all or to have a parent out there and not be able to see her or have contact with her. Granted, their work at the Compound was very important, and as their supervising guard liked to remind them, they might even be saving the life of a loved one with the medical advancements they were making. It wasn't a bad life, but sometimes it could be a lonely one. Julianna felt so fortunate to have someone like Declan with whom to spend her days, even if she did miss her sister Greta dearly. She never understood why Greta purposely had bombed her assessment. Greta could have been at the Scholars Compound with Julianna. She was plenty smart enough, but Greta had told her little sister that the Compound did not interest her in the least. She preferred to have at least the little shred of freedom that was given to the Workers.

Greta always had been more of a free spirit, more interested in arts and crafting than she ever was in studying. Their mother had encouraged Greta's creative side, but it had annoyed their father to no end. He thought time Greta spent making her own dress for the dance would have been better spent working on the computer or studying, activities for which Julianna had always made time because she truly enjoyed them. Greta never cared, and Julianna looked up to her and all the things she could do.

Her heart had broken when she realized that Greta was not coming to the Compound with her. She remembered sobbing into her hands as her sister put a comforting arm around her as they sat next to each other on the couch in their living room.

"Ask if you can retake the test," Julianna begged. "You're smart enough to be one of these Scholars."

"Julianna, sweetie," Greta consoled. "I don't *want* to be a Scholar."

"Why not? Don't you want to come with me?" Julianna asked with large, sad tears rolling down her face.

"Of course, I want you to be with me, but I can't go to the Compound. I want to live my life and be free." Greta gave her little sister a hug. "I know you're only ten, but please try to understand. I know life isn't ever going to be like it was before the attacks, but I want my life to be as normal as possible. You are exceptional. You always have been. You were always going to be someone great no matter what else happened in this world. You go and be a Scholar. Maybe you can make a difference in this world."

Julianna appreciated Greta's words, but still she cried her heart out. As if losing her parents in the attacks had not been bad enough, she also had to say goodbye to her only sister. Julianna had no one left to look out for her.

For her part, Greta knew there was no recourse for Julianna. She had done far too well on that test to get out of being sent away. The only thing she could do now is try to make Julianna feel as good about it as she possibly could. While she tried to convince her little sister that this would be a positive thing for her, Greta's hatred for the New Regime had begun to grow deep in her chest that day.

Julianna shook her head slightly to bring her mind back to the present and focus on Declan.

"Well, I'm still glad to see you," Declan exclaimed. "Our breakfast trays have been delivered, so yours is getting cold. Plus, I'm not getting too far working on this pill by myself."

"And which pill might that be?" Julianna asked hopefully.

"The nonsomnus navitas pill."

Julianna frowned. "I don't want to work on that one at all," she said as she lifted the lid on her breakfast tray. "I wanted to work on the heart medication again."

"I was told this morning that they decided that pill was going to trials. We're done with that for the time being," Declan informed her. "They haven't given us any new projects, other than the energy pill."

Julianna took a bite of eggs and looked around her cautiously. Declan knew this meant she was going to

7

say something controversial that the New Regime probably would not like. He started to get nervous before she even spoke.

"Why do they need it?" she questioned in a hushed tone.

"What do you mean?" Declan asked.

"Why do they need a pill to keep people awake? It doesn't make sense, and it's just not conducive to long-term health. I'm convinced of that without any trials. Why run the risk of health issues in order to keep people awake?"

Declan shrugged. "I think it's supposed to help people work longer. Like a truck driver who can keep driving to get where he's going without getting tired. It would help save people if it prevented an accident, right?"

Julianna smiled at him, pointing her fork in his direction before taking another bite. "You're ever the optimist, aren't you?" Declan returned her grin. "Just pointing out the obvious, which I'm sure your genius brain already deduced."

"I just wonder if what we're doing with this is really a positive thing, that's all," she replied. "I could see how it could cause some serious issues for people. Frankly, it makes me a little uncomfortable."

"No sense in worrying about it," Declan said with a wave of his hand. "It's not like we can do anything about it anyway. And you'd b etter stop talking like that unless you want to get booted from your suite. I, for one, do not want to return to the communal bathrooms and a cot in a room for six!"

Julianna picked up a nearby notebook and prepared to get to work. "I guess you're right. But you don't need to call it by that fancy schmancy Latin name. We haven't come up with a project name for it yet. I think we should call it Project Wired!"

Declan laughed. Julianna liked to amuse herself by assigning silly names to each of the projects they were assigned.

"And I promise I'll try to behave myself the rest of the day. I'm just out of sorts this morning," she admitted.

"Did you have another one of those dreams again?" Declan asked knowingly.

"Yes. I don't know where they're coming from, but I wish they would stop," she sighed. Then she perked up, "Hey, what should we do this afternoon? We're scheduled for some free time. Any ideas?"

"I think we should do something outdoors. I could really use some fresh air for a change. Maybe take a walk in the wooded area?" Declan hoped Julianna would agree. He loved nothing more than spending their free time together, even if he could never outwardly show much affection for her. The New Regime frowned upon emotional connections, especially of the romantic nature, between the Scholars. He always took special care to make sure his feelings for her did not shine through enough to arouse any suspicions. So far, any mistakes he had made had been overlooked.

"I agree. We definitely need to get out. It's sunny enough. Maybe if it's warm enough, we could even eat lunch outside."

"Great idea!" Declan exclaimed, hoping he did not sound overly enthusiastic.

While looking forward to lunch, Julianna and Declan set about working on their assigned project, despite Julianna's reservations, and the morning seemed to fly. When the lunch chime sounded in their lab, they were quick to head to the door. The cafeteria was located fairly close to the lab, and Declan held open the door for her. "Ladies first," he said with a gallant sweep of his arm.

Julianna giggled. "You just want me to go first and make sure it's good."

The food at the Compound usually amounted to standard cafeteria food, nothing too horrible nor too delicious, and she and Declan had grown accustomed to taking what they were given without question. They stood to gain nothing by making a scene about it. The Scholars were kept on a strict diet designed to maximize their brain activity. Their meals were not terrible, but they also usually weren't very fun. Some days, Julianna sorely missed the treats her mother used to bake her when she was a little girl. Alas, white sugar caused sluggishness and was to be avoided at all costs. She really could not have acquired any even if she had wanted. They had very little free time, and although some Scholars earned the right to travel a short distance outside of the Compound for very brief periods, she had not received such clearance. At this point, she had no idea what she could do to try to get the necessary clearance. She was one of the most successful Scholars in the Compound and had earned a plethora of other awards, recognitions and special privileges. She had earned everything from certificates presented at a general assembly to her very posh, by Scholars standards, room. Yet it seemed they simply refused to give her the right to leave the confines of the Compound, no matter how brief.

Once she got very excited that she had earned the right when she and Declan were taken to have the tracking devices implanted. Any Scholars who left the Compound were given these implants, tiny devices that were placed just under their skin. The New Regime could track the whereabouts of any Scholar by using these implants which emitted signals that could be tracked using a computer program. The devices prevented Scholars from getting any ideas about going where they were not allowed. Typically, the devices were not installed until a Scholar had earned the privilege to leave the Compound. After her device was installed, she waited with anticipation to receive the word that she had been granted a day pass for her hard work. When the day never came, Julianna assumed she was a victim of some type of clerical error. Every once in a while, she would notice the little bump on her forearm, knowing that device rested just beneath her skin, and she would scowl at the unfairness of it. She had endured a rather painful procedure for no good reason.

After Julianna and Declan had been handed their plates with their allotment of baked fish, brown rice, spinach, and some blueberries for dessert, he led the way to a small picnic table just outside the door. Although she normally was quite sociable in the cafeteria, Julianna preferred to be alone with Declan today, and he could sense this.

As he sat down, he asked, "Would you like to talk about it?"

"About what?"

"You know," he coaxed. "Your dream. Did you have another one about Greta?"

"No," she admitted. "It was my father. He was trying to tell me something that was very important. He said only I would know this, but then he suddenly fell into a giant hole before I could get all the information. At least that's the part that I can remember."

"You've never really told me much about your father," Declan said softly. "To be honest, I think I know more about him from reading his work than listening to you.

Aside from falling into a hole, do you think this is something that really happened?"

"I'm not sure. It's really frustrating for someone like me who remembers everything to suddenly be doubting that. Some of the other dreams seem more like memories. At least, I distinctly remember parts of them as memories. They help me recall certain events that actually happened," she explained. "Like I remember my mother taking me into the large church building we visited in the one dream. I don't remember specifically why we were there, but I knew I felt comforted and safe there. I remember a blanket that Greta had made for me in another dream. I used to snuggle up in it on my bed while I read. In another one, Greta is working on a painting of a place I know we had been. I think it was somewhere we had gone on a vacation. I just don't know why they are happening all of a sudden. Dreams about my past before the Compound used to be few and far between."

"Why does it bother you so much?" Declan asked with genuine concern. "Why aren't you just looking at it as some kind of nice trip down memory lane? Giant hole aside, of course. But it doesn't sound like your dreams about your mother and sister are nightmares."

"No, I wouldn't say they are nightmares," Julianna agreed. "It just feels like they're trying to tell me something, and I'm not getting the message. Like something is locked away in my brain somewhere, and

I can't shake it loose. I'm not exactly used to that feeling, you know!"

Declan chuckled. Julianna's eidetic memory was quite impressive and had always served them well in their work. "Maybe just relax and try not to worry about it too much. Then the answer might come to you when you least expect it."

"I suppose," Julianna said with a slight pout as she pushed the berries around on her plate with her fork.

"You'd better eat those, you know," Declan said. "You don't want to get in trouble."

"If you'd have told me 10 years ago that I'd still be worried about what the lunchroom monitor was going to make me eat by the time I hit 20, I'd have said you were ridiculous," Julianna said with a wry smile.

"What's with all the negativity lately, Missy?" Declan gently chided. "You'd better watch yourself before the wrong person overhears you."

Julianna rolled her eyes but did not reply. She had nothing to say; they both knew he was correct. But sometimes the worrywart side of Declan annoyed her.

"Perk up!" Declan encouraged. "We're almost to free time!"

When free time arrived, Julianna could not wait to ditch the lab. Even though she usually enjoyed her work, she did not care for this particular project and was itching to get outside and enjoy the beautiful spring day. Once they were outside, she stretched her arms and turned her face toward the sun with a blissful smile. Declan smiled at her. "There's something I've been missing today."

"What's that?" she asked.

"Your smile, Sunshine."

She giggled. Then she challenged, "Race you!"

She sprinted toward the wooded area to the east of the Compound. For Julianna, this was the outskirts of the world, the farthest she was allowed to go. Declan chased after her. When he caught up to her, he grabbed her around the waist and playfully flipped her around him before he continued running.

"Hey! That's cheating!" Julianna protested.

"You got a head start," he called over his shoulder. "It's perfectly fair."

They ran toward the back of the woods and found their favorite shady tree, the one that had an old log next to its trunk that made it easy to sit beneath the tree's branches. As she sat next to him among the pine needles and crumbly brown, deciduous leaves, Julianna savored the warm breeze that rustled through her hair and wondered what it would be like to be able to stay outside as much as she wanted. Was that the freedom Greta could not give up?

Still slightly out of breath, she asked, "What shall we talk about today?"

"Why you're so crabby," he answered. "Is it just the dreams or is there something more?"

"The dreams make me feel weird and unsettled," she said. "It's like I used to be perfectly happy with the way things were, and now all I can see is every little thing that's wrong."

"Maybe you need to watch a few refresher films," he suggested.

She turned her head toward him and arched an eyebrow. "Really? You think that's the cure for my life's problems? Propaganda films!"

Declan smirked. "No, I don't think cheesy cinema alone is the answer. I just meant maybe it would help if you remember why you're here."

"Maybe that's part of the problem. I really don't like this current project. I signed on to the medical wing to make sure I was doing something to help other people. I don't know that this is helping anybody. I just have suspicions about why they would need such a pill. What if they're planning on giving them to the Workers to force them to work more hours?"

"Julianna!" Declan exclaimed in shock. "You know no such thing! Why would you even suspect that?"

"I'm not sure," she admitted with a worried frown. "It's just something I've been thinking lately. Maybe it's all tied into the dreams. I just feel like there's something I should know, and I'm just not getting it." She looked straight into his eyes with a dead serious expression. "I don't like feeling stupid."

Declan threw his head back and laughed. "You, my dear, are anything but stupid."

Talking about it gave her no comfort, so she decided a change of subject was in order. "Enough about me. How about you? Anything been bothering you?"

Declan considered this for a moment. "Well, I'm a little concerned about the Genos List. That's coming up, you know. We may have finished schooling the same time, but I'm a couple years older than you. I don't think I'll escape the list again this year, but you might not either."

Julianna wrinkled her nose. "Don't remind me. Like I needed more negative thoughts. That being said, of course, I have been thinking about it. Do you think the name is derived from the Greek definition, which means to bear, conceive or beget? Or I remembered something else from my church days with my mom. Do you think it's a take on Genesis, the first book of the Bible? Do you think they're going with the literal meaning or are they implying that we're expected to create a new, superior group of people?" Julianna asked.

Declan smiled. "It sounds like you've been overthinking the whole thing or maybe not thinking about it enough. If your biggest concern about the Genos List is what the New Regime is implying with the name, maybe you haven't really thought about what it could mean for your future."

The dreaded Genos List came out each spring, in keeping with the season's theme of new life and renewal. Scholars were paired with each other as mates for the purpose of reproduction. The Scholars were expected to create the next generation to help lead the New Regime into a bright future in this new world, or so the propaganda films had explained. The whole process had its own unique set of rules which were very foreign to those who still clung to the old way of life before the attacks. While the rules were explained fully to the Scholars prior to their names ever appearing on the Genos List, Julianna thought some of the rules and procedures were insane. Particularly, she was troubled by the practice of aptitude testing the Scholars' children. If these children were not considered to be intelligent enough to become future Scholars, further resources were not wasted on them, and they would not be permitted to distract their parents from their important work. Instead they were shipped away from the Compound altogether to a willing family member on the outside.

"In either case, I'm going to guess you're down on the whole process altogether?"

"I think it's weird and wholly unnatural," Julianna ranted. "I don't like it at all. I never have. My mother and father may not have been perfect for each other, but they did love each other and chose to be together. I think that's how it should be. Why would you want to spend the rest of your life connected to a person you might not even like? And what would it be like if the qualities you didn't like about that person were handed down to your child? I'll tell you what that would be like. A veritable nightmare! And then to run the risk that you may have a child who gets sent away from the Compound. How are you supposed to bond with a child when you know he may be sent away eventually? And then what kind of life is that for the child? Oh, you're not good enough or smart enough. You're unexceptional, so you're exiled from your parents. It's cruel!"

Declan rubbed his chin and said, "Yes, but how do you *really* feel about it?"

"Well, we all know how babies get here. Can you imagine doing *that* with someone you barely know? Or what if you do know them and you don't like them? Or what if they're just not attractive? How do you even make *that* happen?"

"*That* doesn't have to happen, you know," Declan reminded her. "There are more scientific ways to make a baby. You have that option. You only do *that* if both parties agree that's the way they want to go."

"Don't get me started on the other options," Julianna continued. "That just doesn't seem right to me either. You don't even have to have a conversation, and you can have a baby together? Do you think that's right?" She turned to face him.

"It really doesn't matter what I think," Declan said honestly. "It's not like we have much say in the matter."

He was trying to get a read on whether she hoped they would be paired together, but he was not brave enough to ask her outright. Julianna seemed so put off by the entire idea that she did not seem to want a partner at all.

"I mean we're smart enough to do all this incredible stuff. We can invent all kinds of things, create new medicines and medical procedures, advance technology, solve some of society's problems, but we can't be deemed smart enough to pick our own partners? It's ridiculous. It's *maddening*!"

Declan asked with an amused smile, "Are you done?"

"Maybe," she replied.

"This is why I have to take you out so far into the woods. When you start talking like that, you need to be far enough away that nobody could possibly hear you."

"Oh, what difference does it make? Nobody cares what I think as long as we keep producing results," she stated.

"I know what you need. You need a little snack," he said. He handed her a small white cupcake from a pre-packaged twin pack.

Her eyes widened with delighted surprise. "Forget about what I'm saying. Where did you get that?"

"From a certain guard who likes to be nice to me," he replied. "And I like to be nice to you, so I'm willing to share."

"That's why you're the best!" She snatched the cake and took a small bite, rolling her eyes and sighing in bliss. "Delicious! I'm sure glad that Britta has the hots for you!"

Britta, one of the younger guards at the Compound, had taken a strong liking to Declan. Both Julianna and Declan knew that she was attracted to his good looks, and she flirted shamelessly with him. But neither Julianna nor Declan were offended since Britta was more than happy to oblige him with the occasional favor. Sometimes the treats were even homemade, and Declan always shared with Julianna. He knew how much she missed the sweets her mother used to make for her.

Julianna rested her head on his shoulder. "Thank you for sharing."

"Thank *you* for sharing," he replied. "I hope you got some of it out of you, and you're feeling better."

"I am," she said. Then she jumped, "Wait! You never told me what you think about the Genos List. How are you going to feel if you're on the list this year? Have you thought about what you will do?"

He shrugged. "I don't know. I guess it would depend on the identity of my partner, but I agree you make some valid points."

"I hope you're not on the list again, but if you are, I hope you're not paired with some jerk," she said.

"Back at you," he said with a laugh. "Okay, happy memory time."

Long ago, the pair had started a tradition of sharing with each other a happy memory from their former families and lives as a way to keep those memories alive and fresh in their minds. Neither of them wanted to forget their past, which for the most part, had been really happy.

"I remember my pretty blanket," Julianna said. "Our nice neighbor, Rose, made it for me. She liked to say I was her namesake because Rose is my middle name, even though my parents didn't know her until after I was born. My blanket was really soft, and it was very, very pretty. The fabric was printed with all kinds of flowers. Sometimes when I was supposed to be taking a nap, I had trouble falling asleep. So I would smooth out my pretty blanket and look at the flowers and pretend I was in a meadow and could smell them all."

"Even then, you had trouble turning off your brain?" he asked with a grin.

"I guess so," she giggled. "What's your happy memory today?"

"I remember I once had this super cool pedal fire engine. It even had little ladders hanging from the side and everything. I would pedal it really fast and pretend I was going to an emergency. Sometimes, I'd squirt the side of the house with the garden hose, pretending the house was on fire. The ladders weren't really big enough to climb, but I always wanted my cat to climb the tree. Then I could pretend to save him, but that darn cat never would climb the tree! Eventually, I got too big for it, and it was handed down to Colin. I was so jealous to watch him ride around in it, but I also was secretly glad that my favorite toy was at least still around, even if I couldn't really use it anymore."

"Did Colin like it as much as you?" Julianna asked.

"Personally, I don't think Colin could ever appreciate it quite as much as I did, but he did like it and used it quite a bit."

"I wonder if my blanket and your toy still exist somewhere out there in this world," Julianna said.

Declan sighed. "I guess we'll never know."

They continued to talk about happier things and enjoyed their break in the woods until they could no longer deny the time on their watches. They needed to head back to the Compound if they wanted to maintain their free period privileges the next time. Declan stood and offered Julianna his hand to help her up. "Shall we?" he asked. She took his hand as she reluctantly stood and unenthusiastically replied, "I suppose."

Julianna slept soundly and dreamlessly that night and woke up feeling more refreshed than she had in days. She breezed through her morning working with Declan and did not even complain too much about their current project and her disapproval of it. Lunch arrived quickly for her. Declan noticed she seemed to be acting more like her old self, smiling frequently and chatting amiably. They walked to the cafeteria together and got their trays. Since she was feeling more sociable today, they joined a table in the middle of the dining area action. Some Scholars their age already were seated around the table. Declan and Julianna sat across from each other and joined the conversation at the table.

Declan smiled as he watched Julianna chat with her friends. He had always considered Julianna to be lightning in a very pretty bottle. Her energy matched her intelligence, and she was always ready for the next challenge. Today she beamed radiance as she talked animatedly with the group. He always thought that, even if she had not been so pretty, he still would have been attracted to her magnetic personality, as were most of the other people in her orbit. Julianna usually brightened any room she entered. She was the one people wanted to be around because she was fun, friendly and energetic. Her light had dimmed in the past few weeks when her dreams had begun to disturb her, but today he was glad to see her acting more like her usual self again.

The Scholars Compound was divided into wings according to areas of specialty. Declan and Julianna belonged to the medical wing. Other wings included social justice, which focused on policy-making and social issues, technology, physics and sciences, engineering, economic development, and agriculture. The Scholars were encouraged to interact with those in other wings during their free time to hopefully find ways in which they could collaborate. Although Scholars often were assigned projects, the New Regime would entertain presentations made by Scholars for new concepts and projects dreamed up by the Scholars themselves. Declan was most proud of the projects for which he and Julianna had received approval following their presentations. The duo excelled at making these presentations.

On one occasion, they had made a presentation that involved collaboration with the technology wing to develop a new monitor to detect blood clots. A couple of those technology Scholars, Scott and Teagan Ross, sat at their table today. Scott and Teagan were twins who had been allowed to stay together and work as partners within the Compound. Julianna sometimes envied the siblings for maintaining at least a tiny part of their former family life while living in the Compound. "Working on any interesting projects?" Teagan asked Declan.

Declan hesitated momentarily, not wanting to sour Julianna's good mood by discussing the energy pill. He answered, "We've been assigned a new drug, but maybe we'll have to put our heads together to see if we can come up with a more inspired project. Any ideas?"

"We always have plenty of ideas in the tech wing," Scott answered. "The only problem is getting approval for them. The New Regime seems rather hesitant to approve our projects lately. They must be focusing on something other than tech right now."

"Really?" Julianna pondered. "That's curious. I wonder where the focus is."

"Certainly not in the social justice wing," Sarah Wrigley replied. "But then again, I don't think it ever is. We have a small budget by comparison to medicine or technology. Then again, we really don't need much by way of materials and experiments. Ours is a gentler science."

Since they really did not know Sarah well, Julianna held her tongue and did not mention that she did not consider social justice to be a science at all. Instead she said, "How about you, Sarah? Anything interesting happening in your wing?"

"Not particularly. We're anticipating the release of the Genos List, but then again, I suppose everyone is," Sarah responded. "Personally, I'm very nervous about it. I hope I'm not on the list until next year."

"Don't we all," muttered Julianna.

The group quieted a bit as Britta, one of the supervising guards, approached the table. "Happy lunch, Scholars," Britta greeted. She put a friendly hand on Declan's shoulder.

Some smiled politely at Britta, and some averted their eyes. "How are you, Britta?" Declan inquired.

"I'm just fine, thank you," she replied, giving his shoulder a little squeeze. "I'm looking for a volunteer this afternoon. Would anyone want a break from their usual duties?"

"That would depend on the volunteer position," Julianna answered cautiously.

"I need someone to show a Newbie Scholar around the Compound. We've got a new one who has just arrived this morning. Any takers?"

"Julianna and I will do it," Declan volunteered with a smile.

"I knew I could count on you!" Britta exclaimed, patting his shoulder. "That would be most perfect because this Scholar is interested in the medical wing.

I'll bring him by your lab immediately following lunch. The New Regime thanks you for your service." She caught Declan's eye and winked before strolling away.

Declan and Julianna exchanged an amused look. "Figured it was better than working on the pill," he told her.

"That's true," she replied.

Declan secretly hoped that showing a Newbie around the Compound would help Julianna remember everything that she enjoyed about being a Scholar.

CHAPTER 2

"Jonah, these are your tour guides, Declan O'Connor and Julianna Brenner," Britta stated. "And this is Newbie Jonah Preston."

Jonah appeared a bit timid as he politely extended his hand to his guides. "Pleased to meet you," he said. Jonah was just a bit taller than Julianna and slightly pudgy with a round, innocent face. His diet and training sessions at the Compound would take care of that in no time, Julianna thought. He pushed his rectangular-framed glasses further up, and Julianna guessed him to be around 12 or so.

"Thank you again for agreeing to help out today," Britta said, as she shook Declan's hand longer than necessary and passed off some lollipops in the process.

Declan quickly shoved them in his uniform pocket. Julianna, who had observed the whole thing, grinned at Declan with a look that told him she would be expecting her cut later. Then she turned to Jonah. "Since you're interested in the medical wing, why don't we start your tour right here in our lab?"

"Sounds good," Jonah said amiably.

"Enjoy yourselves," Britta said as she waved flirtatiously to Declan while she walked away.

They showed Jonah some of the features and amenities of their lab. "Of course, you might be working in a slightly different lab. They each are unique for the needs of that team," Declan explained. "But you won't have to worry about that for a while anyway until you're done with your education and training."

"Keep an open mind," Julianna suggested. "You may decide you would rather focus on one of the other wings the more we get into it."

"To be honest, I just thought the medical field would give me a greater chance of having a normal life. I was hoping to be a doctor who works on actual patients, not just research. That way I can still get out and interact with regular people, not just the smart kids," Jonah explained. Then he hurriedly added, "I mean no offense to you."

"None taken," Julianna giggled. "Unfortunately, that's not really how it works anyway. If you made it this far in the process, you won't be a standard physician. You see, they need bright minds to be doctors, true. But they need the brighter minds to develop innovations in the field. We have been chosen for that task. In other words, you tested right out of your freedoms!" Jonah looked at her with shock. Julianna playfully punched his shoulder. "It was just a joke, but seriously, once you've passed the test to be a Scholar, this is your life."

"But it's a really good life," Declan rushed to add, tossing Julianna a scolding look. "Especially as you find a little success. You'll be rewarded for your achievements with recognition and lifestyle upgrades. For example, right now, I'm assuming you've been assigned a cot in one of the group bedrooms, right?" Jonah nodded. "Once you complete your studies and achieve some goals, you'll be upgraded to your very own room. The more you accomplish, the nicer your room. Julianna has one of the nicest rooms in the Compound. Would you like to see it?"

Jonah nodded.

"Okay, the next stop on the tour will be the personal space quarters," Julianna said with a wave of her hand. "Follow me!"

They arrived at the men's quarters first. "Since Declan doesn't exactly live in squalor, I'll show you his room also."

Declan's room was nearly as nice as Julianna's, except it had a large blue braided rug covering the gray tile flooring rather than the plush carpeting Julianna preferred. His window overlooked the outdoor recreational area where Scholars were allowed to play basketball and such in their free time. Declan had challenged Julianna to a game of horse there every now and again, but usually he played on a team with some other young men. Jonah smiled when he saw the courts.

"Do you enjoy basketball?" Declan asked. "You could feel free to join my game sometime if you like. We'd be happy to have you."

"That's really nice of you. I enjoy playing, but I'm really not the best player. I hope you're not expecting much."

"Don't worry," Julianna retorted. "We're all the nerds. None of us are really athletic overachievers."

Declan gasped in offense. "Speak for yourself, Missy!"

Jonah smiled and seemed to lighten up a bit.

"Did you play much at home?" Julianna asked.

"My friends and I met for a regular game. Just for fun though. Nothing too high-stakes," Jonah answered.

"That's the way the game should be played," Julianna opined. "Shall we head to my room?"

"Lead the way," Declan invited.

As they walked, Julianna continued to kid around and chat with Jonah about his past.

"So what's your origin story, Jonah?" she asked.

"What do you mean?" he asked.

"Where do you come from? How did you wind up here? You know, what's your story?" Julianna clarified.

"Oh, I see," he said as he pushed his glasses further up his nose. "I live about two hours away from here. Or rather, I did. I lived with my parents, a brother and two sisters. I was the second kid. I was just going to school, minding my own business. I really didn't think I was anything super smart or special, and I really didn't try very hard at school. One day, they had everyone take these tests at school, and I tested as a Scholar. I really was not trying to do that. I was quite honestly a little surprised. I'm still trying to wrap my head around being here."

"I hope you weren't guessing on the test or making some kind of pattern," Julianna suggested. "You will be really regretting that in a couple of days when you get into your classes."

"Oh no!" Jonah protested. "I knew all the answers. I just didn't consider myself a Scholar. I wasn't anticipating being sent away from my family, and I'm not sure how I feel about being here."

Julianna gave him a flippant wave. "Don't spend too much time trying to figure it out. Your feelings about it really don't matter to anyone but you. We're here, and it is what it is." She pushed open the door to her own quarters. "Here we are."

"Wow, this is really nice," Jonah said. "How did you two both earn such nice rooms?"

"We learned at an accelerated pace. Then we were put to work in the lab where we came up with a couple of important innovations. Made some medical advancements that helped everyone from the Workers to the Warriors. That sort of thing," Declan said. Then he added, "Not that I'm bragging."

Julianna giggled. "Of course, we really had little else to do. You're only allowed so much free time. We may as well have come up with some successful projects. At least now I don't have to listen to Gina Sallaworth snore like I did back in my shared room. Ugh! I hope you're not dealing with any snoring or sleepwalking."

"Um, not that I've noticed, but I only arrived last night and I'm a pretty heavy sleeper," Jonah answered.

"How about we check out the pool area and workout room next?" Declan suggested.

"Let's go," Julianna agreed.

When they walked through the corridors again, Jonah asked, "So what are your origin stories?"

"We have both been here since the creation of the Scholars Compound," Declan said. "For the most part, we've been partners since day one. We were accepted during the initial rounds of aptitude testing."

"Are you from the area?"

"Yes, we both were. You typically get sent to the Compound in your region. In our case, we would've been sent here anyway because we have been told we are of special interest to the New Regime for some reason. Therefore, they want us located close to the headquarters," Julianna explained.

"Why are you of special interest?" Jonah inquired.

"That's so classified even we don't know," Julianna replied with a snort.

"I think it's because of Julianna's memory," Declan explained. "She has a very impressive eidetic memory."

"Stop, you're making me blush," Julianna said sarcastically. "Personally, I think it has more to do with my father. He was a well-known neurologist who happened to specialize in memory. They must think he performed some sort of voodoo on my brain, and I can carry on his work."

"Is he at the Scholars Compound as well?" Jonah asked.

"No," Julianna answered stoically. "Unfortunately, he died in the terror attacks."

"I'm sorry to hear that," Jonah said with a bowed head. "I can't imagine losing a parent."

"Thank you for your condolences. I lost both in the attacks, but I still have an older sister. She's now a Worker."

"How about your family?" Jonah asked Declan.

"Prior to the attacks and then aptitude testing, I lived with my mother. My parents had divorced, and my father had moved to the East coast for work. I really didn't get to see him often in those days, and eventually we learned he had died in the attacks. I had a younger brother, Colin, also."

"Is he at the Compound?"

"No, he actually was sent to be a Warrior. He became very upset when he was taken from my mother for the initial aptitude testing. Back then, anyone who was of appropriate age was tested in schools. They would test us for aptitude to determine if we were best suited to be a Scholar, a Worker or a Warrior. Colin became violent with the guards, and they were impressed with his strength at such a young age. I'm sure they didn't understand that his strength came from his anger. He basically was fighting for his life."

"Do you know where he is now?"

"No," Declan replied. "We really aren't supposed to keep contact with family on the outside. It's frowned upon and considered a distraction."

"Oh," Jonah said, suddenly becoming sad. "I wasn't aware of that. I was very young during the initial testing phase. I really didn't know that much about it, and I knew next to nothing about how the Scholars Compound worked before I got here. That's likely obvious to you two after listening to some of the things I've said today."

"Oh, sweetie," Julianna hugged his shoulder sympathetically. "You'll get used to it. It's not really a bad life, and once you start working, you can feel good about some of what you're contributing to humankind. You'll be proud of your accomplishments, and you'll make some friends here. It may seem very lonely right now, but it won't be that way forever."

They had arrived at the pool area. Chlorine stung their noses as they showed him the Olympic-sized pool which was used for recreation time as well as required workouts.

"Scholars are expected to maintain optimum physical condition to prolong your life and maintain good health," Declan said, sounding to Julianna a bit like one of the pamphlets they were provided about their recreation schedule for the month.

"If swimming isn't your thing, you can use the outside area, weather permitting, or you can use the gymnasium and workout facility," Julianna said. She was feeling empathetic toward Jonah adjusting to his new life, so she had decided to tone down her snarky attitude. "You have lots of choices. You can find something that works for you."

"If you both will excuse me, I think this is a good spot to take a restroom break before we head to the library and the classrooms," Declan said.

They both nodded and agreed to wait for him.

While they waited, Jonah surprised Julianna. "You don't seem like you really fit in here," Jonah observed.

Julianna smiled and shrugged. She had never really thought about if she fit in at the Scholars Compound. She really had never been given an option. If she did not fit in here, where on earth did she fit in?

"I get along just fine," Julianna said. "Despite my kidding, I know I've got it pretty well. I'm grateful for what I have."

"I'm sure you are," Jonah said. "I just mean you seem to have more of a personality. You're more of an individual than most of the people I've come across here so far. Everyone else seems to be parroting what they've been told. You seem to still hold your own opinions. I hope I'm able to hold onto that ability as I go through this program here. At least as long as it's going on."

"Thank you for the compliment," Julianna said. "But what do you mean as long as it's going on?"

"Just that there's some unrest out there with respect to the New Regime. "Not everyone is very happy with how things are going. There's a lot of grumbling about how the New Regime is no better than the old government. If something happens where the New Regime is no longer in power, I just wonder what would happen to this place."

"How do you know this?" Julianna asked, listening intently.

"I've observed some of it myself," he admitted. "I've heard other people talk. That sort of thing. Now, don't get me wrong. I don't believe that anyone in my living room was going to launch some kind of revolt, but if someone else started something, I don't think they would support the New Regime."

Julianna's mind was spinning, finding this information hard to fathom. "You mean, they do not appreciate all the advancements that the Scholars Compound has brought them?"

"I think people appreciate some of these advancements, definitely some of the medical and technological advancements. I don't think they have an issue with the Scholars at all, only with the policies of the New Regime."

Julianna was trying to process what Jonah was telling her and thinking of follow-up questions she needed to ask when Declan returned.

"Shall we continue to the learning center classrooms?" Declan suggested.

Julianna and Jonah both silently followed Declan. They finished the tour without much chatter. Julianna let Declan explain where to find things in the library, the best areas to study in silence, and the various classrooms where Jonah would be studying before long. After showing Jonah the cafeteria and explaining the rules of eating and the occasions when snacking was allowed, the meeting rooms were the only stop left on the tour. These rooms were where Scholars occasionally were summoned to meet with members of the New Regime about project proposals or to listen to a project idea the New Regime would like to see come to fruition. Declan explained in detail the procedure for developing a proposal, even though Jonah was years away from needing to know such information.

At the end of the tour, Jonah thanked both of them for their time and kindness. Julianna shook his hand. "If you ever need anything, you know where to find us. Join us for lunch sometime. We'll introduce you around."

As Julianna and Declan walked back to their lab, Julianna wondered whether she should say something to Declan about Jonah's observations about the New Regime. What would happen to the two of them if the New Regime were to fall from power? Where would they go? What kind of life would they lead? Would it be better or worse?

"You got awfully quiet," Declan observed.

"Hmm?" Julianna murmured, still lost in her thoughts. "Oh, I'm sorry. I was just thinking."

"That's sometimes dangerous. Are you dreaming up a new project for us?"

"Not really. My thoughts are more in the past today. Being with Jonah who is just starting out here brought back some memories of my time on the outside."

"I hope they were happy ones," Declan said as he patted her shoulder.

Julianna gave him a small smile as she opened the door to the lab.

CHAPTER 3

Julianna awoke in the early hours of the morning again. Her vivid dreams had returned to haunt her. She had decided it was not so much the content of the dreams that bothered her as the feeling with which they left her. She had begun to feel stupid, as if someone were trying to deliver a message to her, but Julianna could not decipher the code. The night grew intolerably long as she struggled to slumber again. When she finally fell asleep, her dreams focused on the terrorist attacks. She did not get much rest as her dreams put her back inside the worst moments of her life.

By the time she arose and trudged down to her lab, she was in a foul mood. Declan noticed the scowl as soon as she opened the door.

"Uh-oh," he said. "Long night again?"

"You have no idea," Julianna muttered.

As she slipped on her lab coat, she asked Declan, "Do you remember much about the terrorist attacks?"

Declan seemed a bit surprised by the question. They had covered this topic briefly when they were getting to know each other, but overall, it really never had been something discussed much at the Compound. No one wanted to dredge up bad memories for themselves or others, and chances were everyone there had had a bad story from the attacks. Hardly anyone had emerged unscathed. Declan knew Julianna's parents both had perished in the attacks, but he knew little other than that about the person who was closest to him in the world.

"I remember where I was and what I was doing, of course," he said.

"Where were you?"

"I was at school," Declan said. "It was absolute chaos because no one knew how to respond to an attack of that scale. I remember looking at the clock on the wall in my classroom and thinking it was almost time for lunch, and then everything that I knew changed just a moment later. They herded everyone into the gymnasium, and we just had to wait there and pray nothing hit us until someone from the outside could get to us and take us home. For some kids, nobody ever came. As it was, with all the roads closed down, most of us had to spend the night in the gym. We used our coats as pillows. If you were lucky, you got a place on a gym mat when we drew lots for the privilege each night. We were allowed to take turns going to eat in the cafeteria that first day. Then we ate even less for dinner. We were fortunate they had enough food to feed us, but they were trying to ration it by the evening since no one knew how long we'd be there. We basically were trapped in an unprecedented event, and no one knew the new rules. We could've stayed that way for days. My mother made it through, and she picked me up three days later. She had minor injuries and had been taken to a hospital during the attacks. Then she had to find a way to get home from the hospital and to her car before getting to us. Kids just kept waiting to be picked up, and I think everyone held their breath each time an administrator escorted a parent to the gym. We were just hoping the next parent was one of ours, not because we couldn't wait to get home, but because that meant they were alive. Even though we knew very little about what was going on in the outside world, my friends and I were old enough to know it was very serious to cause us to be held inside like we were. It was well into the second day before the administration decided it was safe enough to organize us into a couple of different activity groups, let us go to the library to hear a story, watch a movie in the cafeteria next to the gym, let kids make quick trips to their classrooms to grab their books or any food they may have. That sort of thing."

"What happened once your mother picked you up?" Julianna asked, trying her best not to be envious that he had had a mother to collect him.

"We returned to our home, and we didn't leave again for a week. I remember the strange route we had to take to get home to make our way around closed roads and collapsed buildings. I remember my mother being very weepy all the time. My last memories of her are of her crying or trying to pretend she wasn't crying. She had tried repeatedly to reach my father, but she hadn't heard from him. I think the worrying and dread were worse than actually hearing he really was dead."

"How long did it take for you to find out for sure?" Julianna asked.

"About five days," Declan said. "You have to understand that all the computers were down, so communication was very, very slow. It wasn't like they could just post the names of the victims online or anything, and with him being so far away geographically from where we were, we couldn't just go looking for him. We had to wait until some systems started working again when he didn't just call us or answer any of our calls. We tried to keep our hopes up since he might have been in a hospital and unable to reach us, but that was just false hope. Instead we basically locked ourselves in our house for a week and made it by with what we had on hand as far as food and supplies. We read books off my mom's bookshelves to entertain ourselves since my mom would not let us watch the tv. She was afraid of what we might see in the news broadcasts. She watched it for updates, but only ever very limited. There was no programming on for us anyway. All the networks had been shut down and the only things broadcast were necessary updates on what was being done for recovery efforts and any changes in the rules to martial law, which we really didn't need to know because Mom refused to even run out for milk. She wanted to keep us safe, but she also had very little cash on hand and with the banking systems down, she could not access any more money. Some were speculating that the money might all be gone anyway." He shook his head. "There were just so many different problems all at once. It was terrifying."

"That does sound scary," Julianna agreed.

"It wasn't scary for you?" Declan asked, a little bewildered by her response.

"I don't really remember much of anything at all about the attack. I was with my father. At least, I think that's where I was. To be honest, I was told that; it's not a real memory of my own. I was injured in an explosion in a building at the university where he worked. I was knocked out. Supposedly, rescue workers found me. When I awoke, I was in a hospital bed. Later, I was told both of my parents had died. My mother died in a car accident when a bridge collapsed. My father died in the explosion with me. My sister Greta, who had been in school, was the only one in my family to survive. Our family was very small, since both my parents were only children. One of my father's aunts came to the hospital. She's the one who took me home and stayed with Greta and me for a while. She's the one who packed me up and shipped me off to the Scholars Compound. I think she was glad to see me go. Now that I'm older, I think she felt duty-bound to care for us, but she really didn't *care* for us, if you know what I mean."

"Why weren't you in school?" Declan asked.

"I don't know. I can't remember," she said. "I just know it was very important that I go with him, but it's more of a feeling than anything specific that I remember. Does that make sense?"

Declan shrugged his shoulders. "I suppose."

"I am really struggling to put the pieces together these days, which is very annoying for someone who is supposed to have such a world-class memory. I would be such a disappointment if he were here today! The daughter of the world-renowned neurologist who specializes in memory and she can't even answer the one question everyone in the world can answer. 'Where were you when the attacks happened?'"

"That may have had something to do with the massive head trauma," Declan surmised. "Why are you being so hard on yourself?"

Julianna heaved a sigh. "I don't know. I just feel like I am forgetting something I'm supposed to know. I can't even remember my last moments with my father. It's awful."

"Did you get any part of it back from your sessions with Dr. Montegro?"

"Ugh! No, that was a complete and utter waste of my time."

"Did he help you feel better though? Maybe you should think about talking to him about your most recent dreams," Declan suggested.

Julianna pointed a pen at him. "Bite your tongue!" she exclaimed. "Don't even say such a thing! If anyone hears you, they'll make me do more time with Dr. Cuckoopants. I think he's got more issues than any of his 'patients' ever did." She used her fingers to make air quotes as she said patients.

A little over two years ago, Julianna finally had been granted permission to discontinue sessions with Dr. Montegro, a psychiatrist who worked with Scholars at the Compound. Julianna had been sent to him shortly after her arrival at the Compound. A leader of the New Regime had told her she was being provided this service as a courtesy, like all the other Scholars who were orphaned in the attacks. The New Regime was vested in their emotional well-being and wanted to make certain they were processing their loss in a healthy way. Declan and most of the other kids Julianna knew did not have to go to him. She assumed this was because they had at least one surviving parent somewhere in the world, for all the good it did them.

Julianna hated her time in these sessions. Not only were there dozens of things she would rather be doing on any given day, but Dr. Montegro insisted on talking about a day Julianna could not remember. He tried all sorts of psychological tricks to help spur her memory, including hypnosis, to no avail. The entire time,

Julianna kept wondering why on earth it was so important to this man that she remember what was surely a horrifying moment in her life. He also asked her many questions about her father and his work. She assumed this line of questioning was inspired by envy or admiration for her father who was famous among those who studied the human brain. Julianna found the whole process to be rather tedious at first, and then downright annoying when Dr. Montegro became frustrated with his inability to unlock the secrets of her mind and occasionally shouted at her for her lack of cooperation, as if she were doing it on purpose just to irritate him.

At one of her final sessions, Julianna confessed that so much about her father seemed cloudy to her, even then. Of course, she knew who her father had been. Her memories of her younger years seemed clearer to her than his final year or so. While she remembered him being her hero when she was a small child, she seemed to recall very little about the later period of time. She had heard people at the Scholars Compound talk about him. She had even read some of his research papers in the library, but she had trouble putting together a personal recollection. She knew he loved her, and she loved him. She thought she even aspired to be like him at one point. However, she could bring little else to mind. As for her mother and Greta, she had countless memories about them. She could have talked all day to Dr. Montegro about her mother and sister just to be able to think about them because doing so made her heart happy, despite her mother's fate and her endless separation from her sister.

Unfortunately, Dr. Montegro was not interested in these stories and would always try to redirect her to memories of her father. This endless cycle frustrated Julianna because she hated the fact that she was a failure at anything, and this seemed like such a stupid thing at which to fail - failing to remember anything concrete about her father.

At this particular session, Julianna snapped back when Dr. Montegro began criticizing her for not remembering. "I'm sorry you consider me to be the abject failure in this situation, Dr. Montegro. I, too, had hoped to remember more about my father. I know he was very important to me, and I wish I could remember something more substantial about him than a vague feeling of love. However, I am starting to be curious about why this seems to bother you more than it bothers me. Why is it so important to you that I remember something that apparently was painful enough for my mind to completely block it out? It really makes me wonder why you care about this one particular thing so very much. I apologize for frustrating you, but believe me, I am frustrated as well!"

Shortly after her little rebellious fit in his office, Julianna was excused from any more sessions. Her orders stated that regular sessions would no longer be of benefit to her. However, the option was always available to her should she ever have memories she would like to sort out. Even if these dreams really were memories, the last thing Julianna wanted was to be sent back to spend more time with this strange man. She would sort them out as best she could on her own.

Declan did not fully understand her dislike of Dr. Montegro and his professional ineptness because she had not shared much about her sessions with Declan. She found them to be emotionally exhausting, and the very last thing she wanted to do was rehash them when they were over. Declan thought they likely were of a private nature and usually did not ask many questions beyond a basic, polite, "How was your session?" upon her return. Julianna's reply usually was a noncommittal "fine." Typically, this was the extent of their exchange on the matter. When she was freed of the sessions and expressed her relief, Declan was surprised that she was anything less than pleased with Dr. Montegro.

"No! No Dr. Montegro. Nothing good can come of it," Julianna insisted.

"That's fine, but just remember, you can always talk to me about anything that's bothering you. Maybe a nice swim today will help you get your mind off your dreams. Shall we do that during our free time?"

"Works for me," she replied. "Anything to keep me moving. I'm so tired I might just fall asleep standing up!"

"Kind of ironic then that we're working on an energy pill right now," Declan observed.

"True. Maybe when we're finished, they'll crush this up and put it in our lunches," Julianna said sarcastically, holding up one of the prototype pills as she examined it. "Maybe we'll be the lab rats!"

Declan was horrified. He had heard rumors about what happened to the Scholars who seemed to question too much. In fact, he once even knew a boy from the Compound who, although extremely intelligent, persistently questioned the motives of the New Regime, and eventually he was told the boy had been sent away "for treatment." Declan was certain this treatment was being given at a mental asylum. The message was clear; people who questioned the motives of the New Regime must be mad and a threat to themselves and others. Declan took note and made sure to keep his head down, doing as he was told and never questioning anyone of authority out loud, even though he might occasionally think it in his head. The only thought that frightened him more than getting sent away himself was the idea that this could happen to Julianna. With the way she had been acting recently, Declan was becoming more and more concerned this could be a reality, and he wanted desperately to stop her. He was certain losing her would be the death of him.

"Don't say that!" he admonished.

Suddenly they were interrupted by Garron, their usual supervisor. As a guard, Garron really knew very little about what Julianna and Declan actually did to produce their results. He was just supposed to pop in on them from time to time to make sure they were not "lollygagging about," as he put it, instead of working hard. Usually, he moved efficiently among the different stations under his supervision, keeping the Scholars on their toes because they could never be certain when he might drop in. However, sometimes, he lurked in a corner, watching them. Sometimes, he yelled at them if he thought they were doing anything inappropriate, like the time he threatened to remove them from partnership when he thought they had a romantic interest in each other. Another time, he misunderstood something Julianna had said and thought she was speaking out against the New Regime. His presence now made Declan's heart quicken. He worried Garron had somehow heard Julianna questioning the energy pill. Declan did not know what he would do if the New Regime tried to punish Julianna in any way. He could not stand to see her hurt.

Garron came into the room and slowly walked around the lab, looking for anything out of place. He would be happy for any reason to admonish the pair he secretly called "the All-Stars" behind their backs. Guards were given credit and bragging rights whenever the Scholars under their supervision made achievements, even though this made little sense. Most of the time Garron had no idea what the Scholars were doing when he walked in the room, but somehow he was given accolades for their success. He would have rather received recognition for his own merits. Although he should have been happy that a team under his supervision had done so stunningly well, something about the pair rubbed him the wrong way. Maybe he was even a little jealous of their abilities. Whatever the reason, he was always willing to force them to tow the line even more than necessary. He would never dream of rewarding either of them with a treat like Britta. In fact, he would have taken Britta to task if he ever knew she did.

A little bead of sweat broke out on Declan's forehead. *Had he heard Julianna?* Declan wondered. What would he do to her if he had heard her make a joke at the expense of their current project or the New Regime? Would he take her away?

"Can we help you with something, Garron?" Julianna's voice made Declan pay attention to the present again.

"I was just checking on your latest project," Garron replied. "Almost done?"

"If you're referring to the energy pill, we've got some prototypes created. We need to produce some more. We're getting ready to start experimentation on the lab mice. Hopefully by the end of the week."

"Then you'll be ready for your next project?"

Julianna was chomping at the bit to work on something in which she could believe again. She would have loved a project to occupy her mind, not make her ask so many questions, but instead make her feel like her old self again. "Yes! Most certainly! Do you have a new assignment for us? We could easily start a new one in tandem with preliminary experiments on this one."

Garron was a little surprised by Julianna's enthusiasm. He assumed she usually was rolling her eyes behind his back every chance she got. "I shall have to get back to you," Garron replied. "I understand there is a new project in consideration, but I do not have any details at this time. I will let you know when I do."

"Fabulous!" Julianna exclaimed with a bright smile. "Thank you, Garron!"

Her amiability was making him uncomfortable and hard to dislike her, so he just nodded slightly and rushed out of the lab.

"Wow! You got rid of him in record time!" Declan complimented.

"I wasn't trying to get rid of him," she explained. "I'd just love a good project that would be exciting enough to keep my mind focused on it for a while instead of other things. Maybe then I could get some decent sleep!"

When their allotted free time arrived, Julianna and Declan headed for the pool area. Neither spoke much as they swam lap after lap. Julianna hoped she had exhausted herself well enough to sleep deeply that night. After bidding Declan a good night, she returned to her room. After changing into her night clothes, a pair of light cotton shorts and a t-shirt, she collapsed on the side of the bed. She did not even feel like reading for a bit tonight, which was her habit. Instead she turned off the bedside lamp, rolled over on her side and closed her eyes.

Julianna quickly drifted off to sleep after her long day, but it did not take long for the dreams to begin. Julianna could hear her mother's voice angrily saying, "Just because you *can* do it, doesn't mean you *should*!" She was not scolding Julianna though. Julianna was not even in the same room as her mother. She thought perhaps Greta was getting in trouble for something. Instead when Julianna peered around the corner, she saw her mother talking to her father. She was begging him to reconsider an idea he had. "It's not right what you're thinking about doing. I'm begging you to stop this. And just stop working with him altogether. I don't think he's a good man."

"Mnemosyne," her father said.

Suddenly, Julianna was standing with her mother and father and looking at a statue during their trip to Athens. Her father had had a speaking engagement, but the family had extended the opportunity into a family vacation. Julianna knew this trip had happened. She read the plaque in front of the statue and saw the word. Then her father began repeating the word, "Mnemosyne, Mnemosyne."

Julianna knew it was very important to her father, but she had never heard this before. When she awakened, she grabbed a small notebook from her nightstand and scribbled out the word. In the morning, she would figure out what Mnemosyne meant. She smiled as she drifted off to sleep. Maybe she was finally unlocking the secrets within her own brain.

Declan almost always beat Julianna to their lab, but this morning, he was certain she would be waiting on him, delighting in his tardiness. He was not sure what had caused him to be so tired and not wake up right away for his alarm. His evening workout had not been out of the ordinary for him, but now he was hustling down the hallway, hoping he would not get called out by one of the guards for being late. His mind was completely absorbed with these thoughts when he turned the corner and ran right into Garron. The stack of files Garron had been carrying floated through the air like giant confetti while Garron sat on the floor trying to focus on what had knocked him down. When his gaze landed on Declan, he scowled.

Declan immediately apologized profusely, "Please forgive me! I was in a hurry to get to my lab, and my mind was preoccupied with an experiment I hoped to try today," he fibbed. "I did not even see you coming around the corner. My humble apologies! I hope you are not injured." He offered Garron a hand.

Garron accepted Declan's assistance and got to his feet before bending over to gather his papers. Declan started grabbing at papers around him as well. As he bent over to pick up the loose sheets of paper, Declan noticed the words "Genos List: Draft One" on one sheet of paper. He deftly tucked it among his own notebook without Garron noticing and smiled as he handed the rest of the papers back to Garron. He knew that paper listed his future mate in a column. For a moment, he contemplated rushing to the lab to share his find with Julianna. They could learn their fates together. Then he changed his mind. Whatever the news may hold, he needed a chance to process it in private. He did not want to appear too eager or too disappointed to Julianna. After Garron scolded him for running in the hallway, Declan continued walking toward the lab for a beat until Garron was out of sight. Then he doubled back to his room.

Declan knew the day of being paired up for the purpose of producing what hopefully would be the next generation of Scholars was quickly approaching for him, and he had mixed feelings about it. On one hand, he would love nothing more than to be paired with Julianna. He knew they could have a lovely family together even within the limitations of the Compound. His fondest wish was that one day he could reveal the honest love he felt for her, and she would announce that she returned his feelings. If he were honest with himself, this would be made much easier if the New Regime had decreed she did not have the option of declining his affections. They could live happily together. He already considered her his family.

She had been his family almost since the day he had first met her when she walked into the meeting room at the original Scholars Compound, which had been old university buildings spared from the attacks while construction was beginning on their current facility. Declan already had a seat but no idea what to expect when the pretty little blonde walked into the room. He knew they were close in age, but she looked so tiny and frail, her china-doll face marred with sadness and worry, that he could not help but want to protect her. He forced a bright smile and invited her to take the empty chair next to him. Her large brown eyes stared at him with caution, but she slowly moved toward the chair.

Once she was seated, he extended his hand, careful not to move too quickly and scare her. At that point, he had had no idea what she may have been through during the attacks. "My name is Declan O'Connor."

She seemed to ease the slightest bit and took his hand, "I'm Julianna Brenner. Are you here alone too?"

"Yes," he answered.

"Would you like to be my friend?" she asked in a small, vulnerable voice.

He was pleasantly surprised by her straightforwardness. "I would," he answered with a friendly smile, and Julianna had made the truest ally she could have ever found.

In the next few weeks, they tried to stick as close to each other as much as possible. Declan had no idea that the New Regime had been watching them with particular interest and made sure that they were paired up as Julianna desired. At that stage, Julianna's comfort and earning her trust were of the utmost importance to the Regime. If Declan could help them achieve that goal, they were fine with letting him serve that purpose.

For the New Regime, their pairing happened to be a serendipitous victory. The two worked so well together that they excelled in their studies, learning at twice the pace at which they were expected. When it was time for them to head to the lab, they allowed them to stay together hoping for similar results, and the duo did not fail them. Their ability to work on medical advancements had been unsurpassed by any of the other Scholars.

But the Genos List was altogether different. The Scholars had been given a basic idea of what was expected of them from their pairings, but the New Regime had never been very particular on the policy. Declan assumed this was to allow them latitude in pairing under certain circumstances. He knew he and Julianna had been given special allowances in the past, and he hoped that would continue now. Declan believed the pairings had little to do with personality compatibility and much to do with IQ scores. The idea was to create the next generation of Scholars with maximum intelligence, so it made sense to pair the brightest Scholars together. In the event a child did not score highly enough, they would be removed at a certain age and sent to be either a Worker or a Warrior depending on the child's aptitude. While Declan was highly intelligent, he knew he fell short of Julianna's genius status. He was uncertain if anyone at the Compound was comparable to Julianna.

On the other hand, he could not even bear to think about Julianna being paired with anybody else. That would mean he had been paired with someone else as well, and he could not imagine being with anyone other than Julianna. As far as Declan was concerned, there was only one way for this to go. Any other way was simply unacceptable. His heart pounded as he walked swiftly back to his room.

CHAPTER 4

Once he was inside, he dropped all his other papers to the floor except for the list. He urgently scanned the list for his name and Julianna's name and found his name paired with Sarah Wrigley, a girl with whom he had barely interacted from the social justice wing. Even worse, Julianna was paired with Henders Costma, Guardian Costma's nephew. Declan read it three times, certain he had misread the columns. Then he barely could contain his rage. Henders Costma was not even a Scholar at all. He had been through Warriors training and was included in some of the innermost workings of the New Regime, but he was not a Scholar. Julianna never should have been paired with anyone so intellectually inferior. Declan saw this as nothing short of an outrage! Had Henders seen Julianna and taken a fancy to her? Or was Guardian Costma trying to plan for the next generation of New Regime leadership, making sure the Costma children were smart enough that power could be kept within the family? Declan found either answer to be unacceptable.

He dropped to the edge of his bed and sat quietly, trying to slow his breathing. He tried to wrap his mind around this new reality as he had done in the past. He had tried the same tactic when he first was brought to the Scholars Compound. Telling himself he had no choice but to accept this reality, he did a lot of slow breathing and meditation techniques to try to calm himself and understand that he had no choice but to accept this with a positive attitude. It was easier last time.

He did not want to go to the Scholars Compound. When his mother finally had let him return to school, he suspected she had done so partly to make sure the boys were receiving at least one square meal a day through the school's lunch program. She still was having trouble accessing her money and was not sure when it would run out. He had observed the look of worry when she had brought them with her to the nearby grocery store because she was afraid to leave them home alone even for a brief trip. Declan had noticed the weariness on her face as she had tried to run a tally in her head for each carefully selected item that was placed in the cart. The only time she had really shown any emotion other than sadness was when she had screamed at Colin for sneaking an afternoon snack without permission. "Do you want us all to starve?" she had yelled. Her reaction had frightened Colin and made him cry. Then of course, she had apologized profusely and hugged him tightly. However, neither Declan nor Colin made the mistake of ever taking a snack again. They were satisfied with the carefully allotted portions their mother divvied up at meal times.

Back at school, Declan had not been there but a couple weeks before officials of the New Regime marched into the school and required the school administration to hold an assembly. Declan had enjoyed school and had excelled at it easily, so when the officials announced that everyone was to take an aptitude test and the smartest children would be rewarded richly, Declan was excited. He knew he would do well on the test and thought he could relieve some of his mother's burdens by bringing home a prize for her. He would make her happy.

Taking the test was the only option, and the testing would last for several days. Students would not be permitted to leave the school building during this time. They would be provided with the necessities, and they were expected to focus solely on the tests being administered. This happened rather suddenly. His mother did not give permission for Declan or Colin to stay in the building, but she was not given a choice. The children noticed the armed guards at the building entrances. No one would be allowed to enter, and no one would be allowed to leave until testing was complete. Declan was not worried about the testing; he knew he could do well. However, he was a little surprised when part of their testing involved athletic prowess and physical strength.

Early on in the testing process, the children were divided by age levels, and Declan was separated from his younger brother. When the officials tried to remove Colin from Declan's side, Colin had pitched a spectacular fit, kicking, screaming and biting. Colin simply could not take any more trauma than he had already endured since the attacks. He had lost his father. He was told he would not be able to see his mother, and now he was being dragged away from his brother. Declan had stood rooted to the ground with his mouth agape, watching angry tears stream down his brother's face. He made no move to try to stop the men from taking Colin. He had done nothing to protect him, even though his stomach wretched as he watched them manhandle the child and listened to Colin's screams for help. He would never have dreamed of being disrespectful or questioning authority figures, but he had never felt the need until now. The feeling was so foreign to him, and he was not used to protecting himself, let alone someone else. He had always relied on his parents for that. Yet, he found himself standing in the hallway of his school, choking down the overwhelming guilt that threatened to drown him. He knew what was happening to his brother was wrong. He knew as the older brother he should have made some effort to defend Colin. Yet he had no idea what he should or could do, so he did nothing. And his inaction haunted him still.

Neither Declan nor Colin realized in that moment that Colin had sealed his fate as a Warrior. The might with which he had fought the adults trying to rule over him had impressed the officials. The officials had not troubled themselves with finishing Colin's scholastic testing. They moved him straight to the Warriors training facility. When Declan had asked where his brother had gone, he was told that Colin was a perfect example of what the New Regime wanted in a Warrior. At the time, the terms Warrior, Worker and

Scholar all were still foreign to Declan and the other children. He was told that it was an honor to be selected, and he should be proud of his brother. However, his brother no longer was in the school building.

Declan had not been extended the courtesy of saying goodbye to his younger brother. Neither had their mother. He had never seen Colin again after that terrible moment when he helplessly watched him being dragged away, and now he could not have Colin cross his mind without experiencing a nagging feeling of guilt. He had never confessed this to Julianna; he was too embarrassed to admit what kind of disappointing coward he had been. Julianna was not cowardly, and he admired her for it. Even when she spoke her mind and made him very nervous about the repercussions, he was impressed by her ability to say what she thought anyway. He was sure if Julianna had been in his place, she would have stepped up in defense of Colin.

Even though his last sight of Colin shook him to his core, he knew he had to press on and give his mother some reason to smile again. He continued to exceed on his testing in all subjects. When they ran his tests through the computer system and he learned he had ranked in the top five percent, he was thrilled. He knew his mother would be pleased with his reward.

Unfortunately, he had been wrong again. He had imagined his reward would be some type of cash prize that could help out his mother who had to continue trying to support their family without the aid of his father. The officials never mentioned that his reward was life in the Scholars Compound. After the initial testing, he was sent home with instructions to report to the temporary Scholars Compound in three weeks' time. If he did not have transportation, it would be provided for him. However not reporting at all was not an option. He would be allowed to take some personal belongings with him, but not much. The New Regime had provided a detailed list about what he was and was not allowed to bring to the Compound. He could only take as many belongings as would fit in the small foot locker he would be assigned. In the beginning, all of the male Scholars were given cots in a gymnasium. The girls were given cots in the library. Quarters were rather cramped while they waited for the construction of their current Compound. Of course, Declan later decided this worked to the New Regime's advantage. After living for a year in a crowded gymnasium, the Scholars thought their new living quarters were luxurious.

Rather than the smile for which he had hoped, Declan's mother looked aghast when he presented her with his "victory certificate." Declan was the only family she had left, and now he was being taken from her too. The letter to the parents explained that the children were to be in the Scholars Compound indefinitely with no visitors allowed to distract them from their important work for the common good. Declan spent his remaining time with his mother putting on a brave face while his nausea never subsided. His mother helped him give careful consideration to what he would take with him. He chose a few sets of his favorite clothing, some family photos and his baseball glove. His mother also insisted that he take his baseball bat with him. She wanted him to have some way to protect himself. It turned out he never had needed it, but he slept with it under his bed and within his reach, per his mother's instructions, until he finally earned a private room. Most of the other Scholars were just as shell-shocked as he was, and at some point, it seemed they had all silently agreed that they were in it together and actually were very supportive of each other.

His mother also had insisted on taking him to the drop-off point. Declan could not imagine anything being harder in that moment. His mother sobbed openly. The lump in Declan's throat seemed to grow as the car got closer to its destination. Declan could make hardly a sound as his mother hugged him, told him she loved him and bid him a happy farewell. Declan slowly walked into the Scholars Compound carrying a single bag of possessions and wearing his mother's tears on his shoulder.

He spent the first several days at the Scholars Compound trying hard to repress his own feelings, since it seemed ideally, according to the New Regime, Scholars would not have feelings anyway. He tried every method of meditation of which he had ever heard to attempt to calm himself down and try to get the anger out of him.

This morning had taken him right back there again. He was older now, and he refused to have such a major aspect of his life controlled by the New Regime again. Now, he just had to decide what he was going to do about it.

"Mnemosyne," Julianna muttered to herself as she wandered around the lab. "Mnemosyne." She could not wait for Declan to get to the lab. She checked the clock again and wondered if she should be concerned. Perhaps she should go look for him and make sure he was okay. What would she do if he was not? She shook her head to rid it of such unpleasant thoughts. When Declan walked through the lab door a few minutes later, she was flooded with relief and greeted him with a warm smile. "It's about time!" she kidded. "I was about to launch a search party, you know."

"Sorry," Declan muttered, seeming distracted.

Julianna gave him a funny look. These days, she was used to being the one out of sorts. "Are you feeling okay? You're not getting sick, are you?"

"No, I'm fine," he answered.

Julianna tilted her head and studied him with a frown creasing her brow. "What's wrong?"

"Nothing," he replied shortly without looking at her.

"For the record, I know that's not true, but if you don't want to talk about it right now, that's okay too."

Declan could not bring himself to discuss it with Julianna just yet. His wound was too fresh, and he was too embarrassed to tell Julianna why he found the whole list so offensive. Julianna found the whole idea to be unnatural and offensive, but it was not because she didn't have the right partner. He knew he should share the information, and he would. He just could not bring himself to have the conversation right now. He had barely been able to bring himself to walk down the hallway and be in the same room with her.

For her part, Julianna mostly stuck to work conversation and only when necessary. She respected Declan's right to have an off day. From time to time, they both had experienced days like those where they were just pensive or homesick and really did not feel like talking much. One of the nice things about being so close with someone is that she could pick up on his cues and simply leave him alone for a while. If something specific was bothering him, he would talk to her about it eventually. He always did.

In the meantime, they continued to plug away at their research and experimentation of Project Energy so she could put this project behind her and hopefully move on to one that actually inspired her and made her proud to be a Scholar.

When morning came the next day, Declan decided he needed to tell Julianna what he knew about the list. He had not rested peacefully with the burden of this secret on his mind, and he thought it only fair that Julianna have a warning as to what atrocity was heading her direction, specifically Henders Costma. Declan nearly wretched at the thought of the man.

When Julianna walked into the lab, she greeted him with a hopeful smile. He knew she had been understanding of him yesterday and thought he had just been out of sorts. Now she was hoping he had moved beyond whatever had caused his bad mood. He forced himself to return her smile and greeted her with, "Good morning, Sunshine."

"Phew,' Julianna sighed in relief. "I'm glad to see you're feeling better this morning. Ready to talk about it?"

He had always admired her ability to be so direct in her conversations, but he realized he was not ready to return the favor in that moment. "Oh, you know, just a culmination of things getting me down. I'd rather not dwell on it too much. I'm going to move on today."

Julianna shrugged. "Okay. Shall we then?" She grabbed a fresh lab coat and slipped it on.

They had not managed to get too far into their day when Garron appeared in the lab. Julianna braced for his usual attitude, but instead he surprised them.

"You have been summoned for a top-secret project," Garron reported in a formal tone. "You should report to the bottom floor expeditiously."

Julianna and Declan exchanged a surprised look. Julianna still held a beaker in her hand, and Declan stood in place in front of his microscope. They had been caught off guard so completely that neither one of them was sure what to do or expect. Garron was displeased that their reaction was anything short of pure elation at the honor. His pinched face turned a shade of red that bled into the top of his head, visible through his closely buzzed hair. "Did you not hear me? You must move! Immediately!"

CHAPTER 5

The duo dutifully set their work aside, washed up and followed Garron. Julianna knew in the past that leaders and the upper class members of society had preferred the top floors of buildings. Guardian Costma and upper-level members of the New Regime always held meetings in the underground level of the Scholars Compound, and she had heard the same was true for the government buildings. Guardian Costma preferred the safety of being underground in the event of another attack or even a natural disaster. While Julianna understood the reasoning behind this, she felt it must be sad and depressing to live a life that involved constantly being in the shadows. She thrived best when she could have an adequate amount of sunshine and natural lighting in her day, and she did not like the uneasy, nearly claustrophobic feeling she got as the basement door opened to a tunnel of a hallway.

Garron stepped out of the elevator first and motioned for them to follow him. He led them to a screening room, typical of others found around the compound, but this one was smaller in size. A projection screen was mounted on one wall, and two comfortable couches faced the screen. Garron motioned to the couches, and Declan and Julianna sat on one together, both being aware not to sit too close to each other to make Garron question their motives, as he was prone to do with them.

"You will receive orders on your project soon. In the meantime, you must view this," Garron said as he pushed a button and sent a picture beaming onto the screen. One of the usual propaganda films started. Julianna tried not to seem impertinent by rolling her eyes immediately. She was so tired of the propaganda films and found them a bit insulting, if she were being honest. Did the New Regime really think they could easily manipulate some of the most brilliant minds in the world by playing happy videos? All it did was lead her to question why they would be trying so hard to convince her and the other Scholars that everything in the country was perfect and going smoothly. She otherwise had no reason to doubt what she was being told by the leadership.

She pretended to watch the film while letting her mind wander to other matters as she usually did when she was bored. As she was thinking about a chemical compound she had been working on recently, her attention suddenly was drawn to the screen. A familiar face caused her to sit up straight and gawk at the screen. Declan noticed the change in her posture and expression.

Are you okay?" he asked.

Julianna still stared at the screen, mesmerized. She stood and walked toward the wall and stuck her hand out. She touched the face of the woman who smiled on the screen. Declan watched her closely. "Julianna? What is it?" He studied the woman on the screen. Her dark hair was styled differently, but her facial features bore a resemblance to Julianna. The woman appeared very congenial, smiling as she explained her duties at the hospital and how important they are to the country and mankind as a whole, but Julianna looked haunted.

Julianna turned to face him with tears brimming in her eyes. She motioned toward the woman with her hand as if the woman really were standing before them. "This is Greta, my sister," she whispered.

Declan's jaw dropped. "Really?" Then he smiled. "Well, that's wonderful! You get to see her, and you can see she's healthy and doing well." Declan could not say the same about his brother Colin. Oftentimes, he wondered if Colin had perished fighting the New Regime's cause.

"What exactly do you think you're doing?" a sharp voice questioned from the back of the room.

They both jumped and saw Garron's short but muscular frame in the shadows. "You're supposed to sit in that seat and watch the movie. That's all. Now sit down and shut up!"

Julianna obediently sat next to Declan. Her brain needed a moment to process anyway. The movie had continued, and the reporter now was interviewing another Worker. Once he was certain Garron had moved on and was not watching them at the moment, Declan softly put his hand on Julianna's leg. "She looks well," he said in a comforting tone.

"She's not happy," Julianna whispered. "She's not happy. I can see it in her eyes. Why didn't she do well on that test? I know she could've done better. Why didn't she come here with me? At least we'd be together." Her voice cracked. When she blinked, a tear escaped down her cheek. Declan realized he had never seen Julianna cry before, and he wanted to do everything he could to make her stop and take her pain away.

He wiped away the tear with the back of his finger. "It's okay. She looked happy to me, and I thought you said she chose to do poorly on the test because she did not want to be here. If that's the case, she certainly wouldn't be happy here. Especially if she felt strongly enough about it that she was willing to be separated from you."

The lights got brighter in the room, and Julianna sniffed and fought back the rest of her tears. "You're probably right," she replied. Then she added in a barely audible voice, "Maybe I'm the unhappy one."

Declan heard her anyway and flashed her a look of concern but did not get a chance to say anything before Garron returned.

"You shall now have an audience with Guardian Costma," he announced pompously. "I expect you to be on your best behavior."

"Guardian Costma?" Declan questioned. "We're meeting with the leader of the New Regime himself?"

"That is correct, and you shall be expected to act accordingly."

Julianna and Declan exchanged a look before following Garron down a corridor. Julianna had met Guardian Costma only once, when she first arrived at the Compound after the attack. She had assumed it was because she was one of the orphan Scholars as a result of the attack. Declan had never seen Guardian in person, only on the propaganda films.

Garron led them down a grand corridor decorated with marble and several pieces of fine art, including some paintings Julianna had once studied in a book. She assumed these were now being protected by the New Regime and therefore were kept in the heavily guarded Compound. *How have I lived here for all these years and never even knew this was here?* she thought. Julianna wanted to pause and admire the artwork, but she knew Garron would have a fit if she ever hesitated for more than a second. She was supposed to be experiencing feelings of pride or perhaps even nervousness at having been summoned to meet with Guardian Costma, the leader of the nation himself, but she was still too busy trying to grapple with the emotions of seeing Greta again to worry about any of that.

A set of Warriors pulled back two heavy doors that stretched from floor to ceiling, and Garron stopped and faced them. "You go from here on your own. Please don't embarrass yourselves or me," he warned before quickly walking away down the hall.

Julianna glanced at Declan from the corner of her eye and fought the urge to reach out for his hand. She had never experienced such a sense of foreboding as she did in that moment. Declan, however, seemed focused on the task at hand, so Julianna matched his steps as they walked into the meeting room. The guards shut the doors behind them as soon as they had made it past the threshold.

There's nowhere to escape now, Julianna thought.

Guardian Costma sat at the head of a long table. He silently motioned for the Scholars to sit on either side next to him, but Julianna could not bring herself to sit anywhere but right next to Declan. She was a bit embarrassed by her own behavior, but something about Guardian Costma made her skin crawl, though she could not explain why. She let Declan have the seat closest to Guardian and sat down next to Declan, doing her best to fight the sick feeling in the pit of her stomach.

Julianna felt he looked even more bizarre up close and in person than the times she had seen him from a distance or viewed photographs of him. He was in full make-up and costume. The costume was a deep purple robe with gold cords edging the material. A large gold button with ornate etchings pinned it together at his chest. All of his clothing underneath appeared to be black. He also wore a large headdress that appeared to balance on his head like an inverted pyramid. The headdress was the same purple as the robe, but the gold cords scrolled the letters NR across the front of the headdress. Julianna found the make-up to be most unsettling. His entire face was covered with a white grease make-up. He had a black paint on his eyelids and directly under his eyes, which Julianna thought gave him a skeletal, hollow appearance. He also wore a bright red lip coloring that went beyond the limits of his natural lip. She had been told that Guardian Costma preferred to wear the costume because he felt it commanded respect and set him apart. He wore the makeup to protect his true identity, enabling him to still interact with the public incognito if he so desired. Julianna did not think that would ever work on her. She would recognize those cold, steely eyes with or without the garish make-up.

"Greetings, Scholars," Guardian Costma began. "You have been summoned to me because I understand you are among the brightest Scholars in the medical wing, and you also have the best record with respect to successful projects done expeditiously. Therefore, I have called upon you for a task that is of utmost importance to this nation's security."

Declan glanced at Julianna who was staring rather blankly and silently at Guardian Costma, so he responded, "We are honored that you have selected us for a task of such importance. We shall do our best to be successful with whatever you request."

"As you know, the safety of this nation has been a top concern ever since the terror attacks. We cannot appear weak in the eyes of any other world leaders, of course, but also, we must establish ourselves as the foremost leaders of the global community. In order to do this, we must deal with any enemies of the New Regime swiftly and without mercy," Guardian Costma announced and pounded his fist on the table for emphasis. Julianna jumped slightly at the noise. "To that end, the New Regime has decided to commission the creation of a new biological weapon. You would be tasked with creating such a weapon."

Julianna suddenly snapped to attention. "Weapon?"

"Yes, you would be tasked with the creation of a weapon which would be used against countries who are enemies of the New Regime. Ideally, this weapon will be able to easily be disseminated among a large population at once. I will leave the method of delivery to your expertise. If you feel this would be best accomplished with a gas, so be it. Perhaps, you think a virus would be most effective. I would find that method agreeable provided we had some sort of vaccination available for our Warriors or any other friends of the New Regime who potentially may be exposed. I would prefer if we did not use any organism that would contaminate a water supply since that damage might be harder to repair in the long term."

"No," Julianna said, her voice barely a whisper.

"Excuse me, Miss Brenner?" Guardian replied. "I'm afraid I did not hear you." Julianna straightened her spine and stared bravely into the eyes she found so deeply disturbing. "No, I do not want to take part in such a project."

Anger flashed across Guardian's face. His voice was steady but firm. "I did not ask if you wished to take part in this project. I gave you the orders for the task of which you will be expected to successfully complete. Your desire is completely irrelevant to the matter. Am I clear, Miss Brenner?"

Julianna did not respond verbally, but she did not break her eye contact with him either. Declan was beginning to sweat, worried about Julianna's safety.

"We understand," Declan answered for both of them. "Of course. As I said earlier, we will do our best to fulfill this request. I will take on full responsibility for the success of this project."

Guardian turned to Declan only momentarily before he continued to study Julianna as he said, "I am glad you understand, Mr. O'Connor, but I need to make sure Miss Brenner understands as well."

"You are asking me to create a weapon that could be used to murder countless people, including innocent children," Julianna stated. "I would have a problem living with the deaths of innocents on my hands. Therefore, I need to be certain that such a weapon will only be used with great discretion. Could you please explain to me why you feel a need for such a weapon now at this point in time?"

"Miss Brenner, I do not feel that you have a need for any specific information at this time. Please understand the motive of the New Regime is to protect our way of life going forward, as well as the safety of our remaining people. Never again should this country suffer the loss of life that was claimed during the terror attacks. I would think that you, more than anyone, could understand this, given the substantial loss you sustained during the attacks with the deaths of both parents."

"Guardian Costma, this is exactly why I must ask the question," Julianna explained. "You are asking me to potentially orphan other children. I need to be assured that, if this is done, it is for a very valid reason."

"Miss Brenner, you need to understand that sometimes the sacrifice of a few is necessary to protect the common good. Will this weapon be used with discretion? Of course, that will be true. Does the New Regime feel some may pose an imminent threat to the safety of our people? Yes. Do you need any more specific knowledge than that in order to begin work on this project? I do not feel that is the case. You shall do as you have been requested by the New Regime because it is your duty. You have been given a gift, and you are obligated to use that gift to the fullest of your abilities."

"I feel that is what I have been doing here all along, Guardian Costma," Julianna replied. "I feel I can use my gift to help people."

Guardian Costma was beginning to lose patience. He slammed his palms on the table. "This is all I am asking of you. Use this gift to help *your* people! Help *your* country!"

Julianna lowered her eyes. She was done having this conversation, and she did not know how much longer she could stand to be in Guardian Costma's creepy presence. "I understand my calling," she told him. "I understand what I have to do. My apologies for questioning you. I meant no disrespect."

She could feel Declan's relief without looking at him. She knew her loyal friend was always worried about her getting herself into trouble.

"Then you both understand what you have to do?" Guardian Costma clarified. Both Declan and Julianna nodded. He continued, "Of course, your utmost discretion is required. You are not to speak of this project to anyone outside of me and the special project coordinator assigned to this task."

"Do you mean Garron?" Declan inquired.

"No," Guardian Costma answered. "Garron's security clearance does not permit him to supervise a task of this level. We will be bringing in another to supervise. Henders Costma now will be your supervising guard rather than Garron."

Declan felt his face flush with anger, but he tried to maintain his composure. He reminded himself that the name really should be of no significance to him. Julianna did not seem to flinch.

"Will Henders Costma be our supervisor on our other projects as well or just this task?" Julianna asked.

Guardian Costma gave her a look of annoyance. "Miss Brenner, there *is* no other project but this one. You will work exclusively on this project and this project alone. Am I clear?"

"Crystal," Julianna replied. "Will we be allowed the usual latitude to do what is necessary? Will we have any budgetary restrictions on purchasing materials for experimentation and the like?"

"Budget will not be of concern," Guardian Costma replied curtly. "You are free to experiment as you see fit. This is of the utmost importance and is a top priority for us. You shall not be hindered by inadequate resources."

"Wonderful," Julianna replied. "When will we be able to begin? And will Mr. Costma be assuming supervision duties immediately?"

"I would like you to give this concept some thought. You may spend the rest of the day out of the lab. You may go wherever you feel inspired. Perhaps that's the library. I would like you two to brainstorm together. Wonderful things seem to happen when you two think together," Guardian Costma said in a tone that led Julianna to think he believed he was being generous by offering them a compliment.

So she took advantage. "Outside! I feel most inspired and come up with my best ideas when I'm outside. May we spend the afternoon outside?"

Guardian Costma gave one sharp nod. "So be it. Henders will begin his supervision duties tomorrow morning. You may be dismissed."

They both stood and bowed courteously. "Thank you, Guardian," Declan said formally.

"Yes, thank you, Guardian," Julianna added.

Julianna tried to walk at a slow, steady pace as she left the room. She really wanted to break out in a run just to get away from him. She could not wait to make it to the other side of those looming doors. Once they were free from the shackles of that room and the door had closed firmly behind them, Julianna turned to Declan with a sly smile and said, "It's time to brainstorm."

Meanwhile, Guardian Costma stared at the closed doors and muttered to himself, "She is too much like her mother."

Julianna could hardly wait to get to their spot in the back of the woods and talk to Declan privately. Her skin had crawled when Guardian Costma had referenced the wonderful things she and Declan had done and implied that mass genocide would be one of those wonderful things. She knew, without a doubt, that she would never work on such a project.

Once they were far enough away, Declan said, "I have to say, I'm kind of surprised that you would be okay with this project."

Julianna looked around her cautiously before she spoke in a low voice. "Declan, I am anything *but* okay with this. I am not going to participate in this project in any way, shape or form. I am, however, going to let them believe that I am doing my best for the 'common good,'" she said, putting air quotes around the last two words.

"That's only going to work for so long," Declan replied. "Eventually, they're going to demand results from us."

"That's why we have to go."

CHAPTER 6

"Where?" Declan inquired.

"We have to leave here."

Declan was silent from a moment while he absorbed what she was trying to tell him. "You mean run away? To what? You forget we don't have families anymore. This is our home. If we're not here, where would we belong? What would we do? How would we take care of ourselves? Have you thought of all this?"

"I've thought of some of those things. I still need to work out the details, but I know that I cannot stay here any longer. I no longer believe that Guardian Costma is a good man. Do you?"

"I don't know what to think!" Declan exclaimed. "Do I want to create something that kills a bunch of people? No! I went into the medical wing of the Compound because I wanted to do good, and I thought that's where I could do the most good. Not because I wanted to murder people who disagree with us."

"Disagree with *us*?" Julianna questioned, still in a hushed tone. "Do you really think it's a matter of us? I think it's more them. Or perhaps even just him! What do we really know about any of these foreign relations? We know only what we're told. That's it.

Don't you remember when we were in our real homes? Don't you remember your parents maybe watching the news on the television? What do we get? We get what they want us to know. Or rather what they want us to believe. We can't even say for certain any of it is true!"

"I know you've been feeling this way about the New Regime for a while, but I'm just getting there. Give me a minute to catch up with you," Declan requested quietly as he sat down on a nearby log and put his head in his hands.

"I don't mean to pressure you, but you're going to need to catch up in a hurry because today is our chance to discuss it without prying ears," Julianna countered.

Declan sighed. "I know you're probably right. Given your initial reaction, I'm sure they're going to be keeping a close watch on you. I'm surprised we were even allotted this much time alone, if I'm being honest." He rubbed his eyes and then looked up at her. He saw the hope in those eyes he had come to trust. "How about this? I am not going to make any decisions for myself today. However, I will listen to everything you have to say and try to work out any kinks in your plan if I am able."

She rewarded him with a bright smile. "I'm not trying to talk you into a rash decision. I understand now that I've been toying around with this idea in my head for a while, even though I did not want to admit it to myself. I am just grateful that you're willing to hear me out and consider the possibility."

"So run the basics past me. What are you thinking?"

"I haven't really developed an entirely new life plan. I'm simply working on getting out of here right now. First and foremost, that's the most important thing right now. We cannot stay and take part in this project."

"You do understand that, if we both were out of the picture tomorrow, this task simply would be reassigned to another team of Scholars. You running away won't stop that."

"I know that," Julianna admitted. "But without trying to sound too cocky, I also believe that anyone else would take longer than we would to accomplish it. At least it buys a little time. I don't know what is happening outside these walls. I don't know how many lies have been told to us. Maybe it's all part of the plan. Maybe that's why they cut us off with all contact from the outside world. Why else would we not be able to visit your mother or my sister every now and again? What harm would that do? I have so many questions. Don't you?"

"I do have some questions about certain things. Just because I've always played by their rules does not mean that I have blindly agreed with everything they say. I just didn't see any other option," Declan explained. "I saw no advantage to rocking the boat and getting placed in a treatment facility."

"I know exactly what you mean. So here's my plan. I would like to get away from the Compound and try to head for our family, either your mother or my sister."

"But we don't even know for sure if they are still living in our old homes. They could be anywhere. Especially Greta once she was grown."

"I agree, which is why I think we should try to go to your mother first," Julianna said. "Once we located her, we can just take some time to figure out what is reality. We can learn about how life works outside of these walls. As for the project, I know we may not be able to prevent that indefinitely, but at the very least, we can refuse to participate. Maybe we'll accomplish nothing other than living normal lives, but we'll be free."

"How do you think you're going to get out of the Compound?" Declan asked. "You've never been given permission to leave before."

"I have questions about why that is the case, too. Why have I never been allowed to leave at all? I've been successful. I've earned every other reward and incentive except that. Why not?"

"I have no idea, but I do have something else to tell you." He paused while he got up the courage to speak about the Genos List. "I happened to run into Garron, literally, yesterday. He dropped a draft of the Genos List. We're both on the list. I saw our pairings."

Julianna gasped. "Don't keep me in suspense. I'm assuming from your tone we did not get paired with each other."

"No, I was paired with Sarah Wrigley. You were paired with … Henders Costma."

Julianna's jaw dropped, and she was silent for a moment before loudly exclaiming, "You have got to be kidding me! Henders Costma isn't even a Scholar. How can they pair me with him? That makes no sense."

"Perhaps he thought you were pretty," Declan said. "Or maybe they want you to help make the next generation of leadership smarter."

Julianna cried out in exasperation as she stomped her foot. "No! This, too, is unacceptable!" She looked at him, her face contorted with outrage. "Have you caught up yet?"

Declan was quiet for a moment. Then he softly replied, "Yes, I think I have."

"Ugh! I almost wish you hadn't have told me. Now I'll have to look at him tomorrow and try not to vomit. Just … unacceptable!" She shuddered at the thought of Henders and then shrugged her shoulders. "At least Sarah Wrigley is nice, I suppose."

"I think she's a bit too opinionated and self-important the couple of times our paths have crossed, if I'm being honest. I don't really know her that well, but she's not really someone I would've gone out of my way to try to get to know either."

Julianna shook her head. "Good grief! I would not have thought this was how my day was going to play out when I woke up this morning." Suddenly, she remembered her dream. She gasped and put her hand over her mouth. "I almost forgot! Do you know what Mnemosyne means? Does it mean anything to you? It's spelled with a silent M in front."

Declan wrinkled his brow. "Mnemosyne," he repeated as he tossed the word around in his brain, trying to see if he could make a connection. "Hmm, I don't think I've heard of it before. Why?"

Julianna waved her hand. "Just something from another dream. I remembered this word, but I don't know what it means. Or if it means anything."

"We can spend some of our free time looking it up in the library if you want," Declan offered.

"No, it's okay. I can always do that later while I pretend to research effective ways to mass murder people," Julianna retorted. "I think our time right now will be better spent working on our plan. Especially now that you've got me even more enraged than before! So back to your question, do you have any ideas on how we can get on the other side of these walls?"

"I'll have to think on that for a bit. More pressing though, I think we need to come up with some kind of code to be able to communicate with each other once we're under supervision again. I'm sure they'll be watching us very closely, given the nature of this project. If we have a system of communication, we have some time to work out the details and share ideas when we have them. We don't need to do everything all at once."

"Wonderful idea!" Julianna agreed. "I'm pretty sure they'd bust us if we went with pig Latin, so what other kind of code could we work out?"

"Maybe something using the computer? You're the little computer genius. Can you think of anything?"

A strange look crossed Julianna's face. "Do you know what I've decided? He wants us to *think* he's smarter than we are."

"Who?" Declan asked.

"Guardian wants us to think he's smarter than we are. If he's really so smart, why does he need us?" Julianna questioned. "I think he's secretly afraid of us. I think he's been lying and trying to control us, but it's really all a house of cards."

"Perhaps," Declan said. "Who knows what he's really thinking! Heck, we don't even know what he really looks like!"

"And I have a feeling that Henders is not going to be all that bright either." Julianna face suddenly brightened. "I have an idea for a code. It's just so simple, it might actually be brilliant!"

She lowered her voice and began explaining her latest idea to her friend.

Julianna's code seemed to work like a charm. All they had to do was move their fingers over one key on the keyboard and type words as if their fingers were on the correct keys. The messages were very simple for them to decode but looked like nonsense to anyone else. They spent the rest of the afternoon outside brainstorming ideas for their great escape plan, tossing around ideas from faking their own deaths in a lab accident to sneaking out with a delivery truck. After dinner, they practiced for a little bit in the library to make sure their code plan would work. They both found it very easy to send and decode messages, and Julianna focused on the next challenge she faced - looking at Henders without gagging and revealing what she knew.

The next morning, Julianna and Declan both arrived at the lab before Henders. They decided to work on their plan for faking some work on the biological weapon. Julianna fetched a legal pad and a pen.

"First things first, what kind of weapon should we be making?" Julianna asked. "I don't like the idea of even pretending to work on a virus. There is just absolutely no guaranteed way to control it."

"I think we should be focusing on some kind of toxic gas bomb," Declan stated. "That way it's much more targeted, and when it's gone, it's gone. I think that would be the best way to go about it with the least residual effect."

"You mean besides the mass deaths," Julianna added sarcastically.

Declan grinned. "Yes, besides that. Glad to see you still have your sense of humor." Julianna giggled. "You're probably the only person around here who is! Most just don't appreciate how funny I am."

The lab door swung open, and Henders Costma entered. Henders had unnaturally light blonde hair that bothered Julianna on sight. The girls in the Compound really were not allowed to wear makeup. It was not officially forbidden, but they simply had no access to obtain any of it past the initial supply a girl may have brought with her when she was a newbie. But the Costma family was able to slather on as many cosmetics as they chose, from the extreme amount Guardian Costma used, all the way down to his daughter Delilah. Julianna had never met Delilah, who was a couple years younger than she, but Delilah wore an amount of makeup of which Julianna knew her own mother would never have approved. Now, here stood Guardian's nephew before her, with his colored hair. His makeup was not as extreme as Guardian's, but Julianna thought it may have looked even more ridiculous. At least Guardian's rationale of disguising his true identity gave a more plausible reason for his application of makeup. Henders wore a lime green lip liner around his lips and filled it in with a matching lip color. He wore a similar shade of eye shadow and used thick black eye liner all around his eyes. His cheekbones were highlighted with a purplish hue that Julianna thought made it look like he was bruised. Julianna thought the overall effect was humorous at best.

Henders' presence solidified her resolve to escape from the Compound. She immediately decided any life in which she had to procreate with a man like this was not a life worth living. She was sure he was so dim-witted that any child from the match would be taken away when he or she failed to pass the Scholars test. Of course, then again, since the child would have Costma blood, maybe that rule would not apply here either. The entire situation was infuriating, and she felt dumber for having given it as much thought as she did.

Between the dreams and thinking about such nonsense, I have to get out of here soon before they suck every last ounce of intelligence out of me! Julianna thought.

Declan, meanwhile, also found it difficult to make eye contact with the man who thought he could take Julianna and make her his own without so much as even asking. He barely glanced up as Henders entered the room for fear of revealing his feelings.

Good morning, Scholars," Henders greeted in a loud, booming voice. "I am Henders Costma. I will be your guard and supervisor for the duration of this project."

Declan quickly glanced up again to give him a nod and a hello before lowering his head to see what else Julianna was scribbling on her legal pad. Declan and Julianna sat on stools next to each other with their heads bent over the same tablet. Julianna, who had looked him up and down when he walked in the room, did not smile when she said, "Okay then."

Henders seemed taken aback by this less than enthusiastic welcome. "I don't know if you're aware of this, but I'm Guardian Costma's nephew. That's why I'm on this project. Your other supervisor did not have the appropriate security clearance."

Julianna looked at him again, unimpressed "We're aware of Garron's genetics."

Henders had no idea how to respond to her. "Um, I assume that's what you're working on right now? The project?"

To prevent Julianna from making another snide remark, Declan chimed in. "Of course."

Henders was quiet for a moment as he observed the two of them. Finally, he spoke again. "Do you think it is appropriate for the two of you to be sitting that closely to each other?"

Julianna slapped the pen down on the table, and Declan braced himself for whatever she might say. She stared directly into Henders' eyes. "I don't know if *you* are aware of this, but your uncle chose us for this project because of our proven record of results. Do you really think you should walk into this lab and question our methods within the first minute? Do you really want to delay this project by requiring us to explain the simplest of things, like where we are sitting? How is he supposed to see what I'm writing on the notepad from across the room? Do you really think he wants you to change the way we function at the risk of hindering our progress?" She tilted her head and asked, "Do you have experience in being a project supervisor?"

Henders' eyes widened and he stuttered a bit when he gave his response. "No, I have not supervised projects before."

Declan put his head down again to hide the smirk he just could not repress. He picked up the pen and began drawing a doodle. "What do you think of this?" he asked Julianna.

Julianna gasped and brought a hand to her heart. "That's so crazy, it just might work!"

Henders shrunk back and leaned against the wall while they continued to take turns scribbling nonsense and rudimentary art on the notepad. After quite a while of this, Julianna drew an arrow to one of the drawings and wrote "research at library?" with the pen. Declan nodded.

"We are going to need to head to the library to research some things now. Are you planning on coming with us?" Julianna inquired of Henders, who had been standing like a statue against the wall the entire time. "Please don't feel as if you have to join us. Garron would only check on us a few times a day. I don't know if you really need to stay here the whole time. It must get terrifically boring for you."

"I suppose I could take a little break and find you in the library later," Henders decided, speaking slowly as if he were still considering as the words were coming out of his mouth.

"Very well then," Declan said. He put a hand on Julianna's back and urged her out of the door. "Enjoy your break."

As soon as they were out of his presence, Julianna heaved a huge sigh of relief. "Goodness, but that was awkward!"

"Perhaps the mating pairs may be changed now before the list is revealed," Declan suggested. "I think you scared him."

"Well, that needed to be nipped in the bud. No sense in dealing with that any more than necessary."

"Of course, if you stayed with him as a mate, he might be able to get you more sugar," Declan teased, gently nudging her with his elbow.

"I'd rather eat nothing but fish for the rest of my entire life!" Julianna declared.

Declan laughed as they walked into the library. "What was that word you needed to look up again?"

"Mnemosyne," she said.

"I think that should be our first order of business," he told her. "Let's see if we can solve at least one of your dream mysteries."

"That would be a lovely change of pace!" Julianna exclaimed.

They headed for the banks of computers. Julianna typed mnemosyne as a key word in the library's search engine and came up with a list of a few books. She sat back in the chair in surprise. "These are all books on mythology," she told Declan.

She and Declan split the list and retrieved the books. Declan found an entry on Mnemosyne first. "It would seem that word is a name - for the goddess of memory. She was one of the Titans. Now does that mean something to you?"

Julianna mulled it over for a moment and looked disappointed. "Oh. Maybe it was nothing more than a memory from a vacation. In the dream, my family and I were in Athens, looking at this statue. My father repeated that word. I must've just been recalling seeing this statue when I was young." Her lips turned into a pout. "Shoot! I was hoping it was something more than that. I still feel like I'm supposed to figure out something, and I just can't."

Declan put a hand on her shoulder. "Did you want to read any of the myths about her? Maybe that would trigger something else for you?"

She shrugged. "I suppose it wouldn't hurt." However, she did not get her hopes up.

It did not take Julianna long to read through the parts of the book that related to Mnemosyne, the goddess of memory and mother of the Muses, according to the stories. Declan read a few as well. When she was done, she felt no closer to an answer than when she had started.

"That didn't shake anything loose in my brain," she admitted. "Nothing. It must've just been a statue my father wanted us to see when we traveled to Athens, I suppose."

"Do you remember traveling to Athens?"

"I remember that trip to Europe. We visited several cities. Athens definitely was one of them because my father had a speaking engagement. That was the reason for the whole trip, but truthfully, I was small enough I really don't remember it all that well."

Declan laughed. "Hey! Maybe your dad wanted to name you Mnemosyne. That would've been appropriate given your incredible skills."

Julianna giggled. "I'm certainly glad he didn't."

"Do you think it could be possible that these dreams are just memories from times that happened when you were too young to have a very accurate conscious memory? Sort of like snapshots flashing through your mind while you sleep?"

"I suppose," Julianna said. "I just wish I knew why they were happening now and with such frequency. Why now? Why have I not had any dreams like this in all the years I've been here until now?"

"Is that what bothers you most?" Declan asked. "The timing aspect?"

Julianna shook her head. "To be honest, I don't even know."

Henders chose that moment to seek them out in the library. "Have you been making progress?" He picked up one of the books and read the spine. "Why are you reading mythology? What does that have to do with this project?" he asked suspiciously.

Julianna pursed her lips and then said sharply, "Don't you have any idea how many scientific advancements have come from ideas gleaned from mythological stories? These stories were created by people to try to explain the world around them. Haven't you ever heard the story of Icarus and his wings? Where do you think people first got the idea to attempt flight? If you want to effectively develop a scientific theory, you need to explore as many aspects about that idea as you possibly can. That is what we are doing here right now."

Henders' expression looked a little like a puppy in training who had been taken to task. "I was just asking a question," he muttered.

"I really think we're going to get along just fine, Henders. I don't mind explaining things to you," Julianna said with a slightly condescending tone. "If you have any more questions, you feel free to ask, and I'll continue to answer, just as I have." She gave him a sugary sweet smile. Henders clearly had no idea how to take Julianna. He gave a gruff nod and took a seat at a table nearby, grabbing a random book off a shelf along the way. Julianna's lips spread into a satisfied smile and whispered to Declan, "I can play him like a fiddle."

"So I've noticed," Declan replied with a grin. "Maybe he is better than Garron."

That evening, Henders walked into the private chambers of Guardian Costma. Guardian was awaiting dinner in his elaborate dining room at a large marble table which was lit by a crystal chandelier. His daughter Delilah sat to his right. Guardian motioned for Henders to take the seat at his left. Once he was seated, the waitstaff brought out fine china plates of prime rib served with baked potatoes and green beans. A basket of rolls was placed on the table, and one waiter poured their glasses full of water with lemon. Guardian Costma and Henders were brought glasses of red wine. Once the staff had finished scuttling about the table and disappeared again into the kitchen, Guardian turned to Henders.

"How did it go today?" he asked.

"They seemed to work hard on the project today, if that's what you mean," Henders answered. "But I would really appreciate it if I could find a different mate. I don't really care for her."

Guardian took a bite of his steak. "What about her do you not care for?"

"She's not very nice," Henders complained. "She acts like she's smarter than me."

Guardian rolled his eyes. Sometimes his brother's son was so dim. "She *is* smarter than you, Henders. That is why I paired her with you."

"I would prefer another Scholar."

"You are paired with Julianna Brenner, and that will not change," Guardian said firmly.

"Why is it so important that I be paired with this particular girl?" Henders challenged.

Guardian slammed a hand on the table in exasperation. "The future of the New Regime may depend on this pairing. All you need to do is have a child with the girl. You do not need to develop a deep, emotional attachment to her. You don't have to like her. She will give birth, and you will take custody of the child to be raised by the New Regime. Your affiliation with her ends there. Besides," he added, "you had no objection when you saw her from a distance."

"She's beautiful," Henders admitted. "But she's also very testy and condescending."

"When do I get to pick a Scholar, Daddy?" Delilah piped up.

Her father gave her a withering look. "You do not need to worry about that for some time, and you do not need to interrupt important conversation with silliness."

Delilah glared at her father but did not speak again. Guardian silently cursed his late wife for not providing him a son to be his heir. Instead he was left with his brother's son and a girl. He had entertained the idea of pairing a Scholar with himself, but he eventually discarded that idea. Such a child might not grow and be prepared in time to replace him, and he might wind up with another daughter. Perhaps he had been hasty in disposing of his wife during the attacks.

Guardian turned back to Henders. "Can you tell me about some of the work they did today? That would be useful."

"They did a lot of sketching and tossing ideas back and forth. Then they went to the library to research some things. They pulled a couple mythology books from the shelf."

"Mythology? Why would they need to be reading mythology to develop a biological weapon? That makes no sense."

"That's what I thought," Henders said. "Until she chewed me out about Icarus and many scientific advancements coming from ideas in myths."

"Hmm," Guardian murmured as he stabbed some green beans with a fork. "As long as you think they were being productive. I want you to keep your ears open while you're with them. If you hear her say anything about her father, I want you to make a very detailed note of it. Am I clear?"

Henders nodded. "Yes, Uncle."

Following dinner, Guardian Costma called one of the supervising guards who worked in the library. He asked her to look at any computers on which either

Declan O'Connor or Julianna Brenner had done searches for library materials. He requested that she provide him with a complete list of any key words searched on those machines. After reviewing the list of badge swipes on all the computers, she called Guardian with the list.

"Understand, I just know they used these computers at some point today. I am unable to pinpoint who exactly performed what search."

"Understood," Guardian replied impatiently.

She began reading down the long list of key words from that day. When she said Mnemosyne, Guardian stopped her. "Wait a minute! What did you say?"

"I'm not sure if I'm pronouncing that correctly, but it seems to be a proper noun. Let me spell it for you. M-n-e-m-o-s-y-n-e."

"That's what I thought you said. Please continue with the list," Guardian requested.

She continued to read down the remainder of the list, none of which seemed of any consequence to him. When she was done, he replied, "Thank you for your service. You have been most helpful." He hung up the phone with a wicked grin and said to himself, "She's finally starting to remember."

CHAPTER 7

The next morning, Julianna got to the lab early and began tapping on the computer keyboard. She had been inspired last night with an idea to possibly get them out of the Compound. She wanted to make sure she could get the message typed out to Declan before Henders arrived. She thought they might be able to make their escape inside one of the service trucks that delivered supplies to the Compound. They had tossed around a similar idea, but she had built a bit on it. Her plan was to hide in the back of one of the trucks and sneak out at the truck's next stop. Of course, this plan needed a little work. For one, they would have to be able to access the area where the trucks docked. Scholars typically were not allowed down there. Maybe they could request some special supply for an experiment and convince Henders that, due to the volatility of the chemicals, they must pick it up themselves. It would be dangerous for someone else to handle it. Once she was done typing, she stepped aside and pulled a chemistry book off a shelf. She sat on a stool and read while waiting for Declan to arrive.

When Declan opened the door, Henders followed closely behind. Declan had consciously kept several steps ahead of him to prevent the need for any interaction with Henders. Julianna picked up an apple off her breakfast tray and took a bite of it. She pointed casually to the computer while looking down at her book. "I worked out some stuff on the computer if you wanted to see what you think," she told Declan.

"Okay, thanks. I'll take a look."

Henders headed for his own breakfast tray, completely unaware. Julianna tried not to look his direction lest she encourage him to speak. Declan tapped away at the computer. After he had read Julianna's message, he replied back and suggested that he drive away one of the trucks.

"I like what you've got going there, and I added a bit to it," Declan told her.

She took another bite of her apple before rising from her stool. "Okay, let's see what you've got here."

She laughed when she read Declan's message. "Do you even know how to do that?" she asked him. "I didn't know you had experience with that."

"Who needs experience?" he asked with a jovial wink. "I think I could figure it out. I'm a pretty smart guy."

Julianna smiled. "I don't doubt it."

"What are you two working on?" Henders asked.

Julianna looked at him as if he was dumb. "We only have one project according to Guardian Costma. The same one we were working on yesterday."

Henders decided his ego could not take asking her to be more detailed, so he just shoved another bite of eggs in his mouth and left it alone. Declan suddenly sat up tall and hurried over to the computer. He typed only one word using the code. Julianna decoded it. It read, "Britta."

Julianna gave him a look of awe and whispered, "Brilliant!" She patted his back and said, "Do what you've gotta do."

"We've got time to work out the details. We'll think on it for a bit."

They went back to faking research under Henders' watchful eye.

Declan knew that, regardless of their plan in the end, he needed to get Britta on his side quickly. He knew he was going to have to return her flirting. Perhaps she would even help inspire the plan by providing him with information he did not already know about the deliveries and the truck dock. When her name had first come to mind, he had made a mental note to interact with her every chance he got.

Now, his first opportunity had arrived. Declan spotted her walking down the corridor in front of him as he was on his way to the pool for his free time. Julianna had decided to take a nap instead of swim. Declan assumed she had been having trouble with dreams again and needed the rest, so he did not protest to keep her company. Now that had turned out to be a stroke of luck! He called to Britta, "Hello there!" He smiled as brightly at her as if she were Julianna.

Britta looked back in surprise at the handsome, shirtless man with a towel draped around his neck. She waited for him to catch up to her and smiled in appreciation of the muscular frame. "Hello to you," she returned.

"Where are you headed?" he asked her.

"Oh, I was just getting ready to head home for the day."

"That's too bad," Declan said. "I was just about to go for a swim, and I was hoping for maybe a little company."

Britta tried not to look surprised at Declan's interest in her. "I would love to join you, but I have no swimwear with me."

"Too bad. An opportunity missed for me. Maybe we could do something else instead? I'm open to suggestions."

They both stopped walking. To go any further would put them in an area that likely would be much more populated than the hallway in which they stood. Britta tossed her dark hair over her shoulder and smiled flirtatiously at Declan's invitation. "Do you have a pass that you can get out of here for a while?"

Any opportunity that Declan would have had to leave the Compound on a pass went straight out the window when they were assigned to Project Much Death, as he and Julianna were calling it in private. Declan gave her a look of regret. "No, unfortunately, we've been assigned to a prestigious project that also has a high security clearance attached. I'm not going anywhere until that's done."

"Ooh, that sounds interesting," Britta cooed, putting a hand on his bare arm. "Maybe you could tell me about that?"

"Maybe we could sit down somewhere together and talk," Declan suggested. "You probably know this place better than I. Any suggestions?"

"Follow me," Britta led the way to a small library with books lining three of the walls. "This is one of the social justice libraries. Trust me, no one ever uses it." She walked over to a plush couch on the west side of the room and sat down. She patted the cushion next to her, inviting Declan to join her. Once Declan was sitting next to and turned facing her, she said, "Now, you were going to tell me about your special project?"

"I'm really not allowed to say much about it. It's so secret that Garron cannot be our guard while we work on it. Henders Costma is."

Britta snorted. "Henders Costma is lucky his uncle is in charge. He would never have made it to such a level on his own merit."

Declan chuckled. "I understand." He lightly touched her hand. "I can't really talk about that, but I just thought it might be nice to talk to you. You know, we see each other all the time, but I really don't know you all that well. Tell me a little about yourself. Did you always want to be a guard?"

Britta smiled. "No, that happened more out of necessity. Initially, I became a guard because guards were provided with a room at the Compound. I needed a place to stay. Now, I stay here because the work is not bad, and the pay is exceptional by comparison to most of the other jobs out there. Once you've proven your loyalty to the New Regime, it's a decent position to have."

Declan gave her a curious expression. "And how does one prove her loyalty to the New Regime?"

"It's more of a long-term test. During your initial employment, you are watched very carefully to make sure you are trustworthy. They want to make sure you don't spread secrets or talk about the business of the Compound among yourselves, that sort of thing. As you prove you can be trusted, your pay and your authority and positions continue to rise."

Declan nodded. "That makes sense. I guess the New Regime really has to have trust in the people who guard the Compound."

"Now, I've earned enough that I was able to purchase my own little house about five miles from here. It's an easy commute, and I have a space of my own. Plus, I still get access to all the advantages of the Compound. I could have gone swimming tonight if I was prepared and knew you needed company." She gently pushed his chest with her hand. "Hey! Where's your usual friend, by the way?"

"You mean Julianna?" Declan asked. Britta nodded. "She was tired and wanted to rest."

"What is going on with the two of you?" Britta asked suspiciously. "Don't get me wrong, I am enjoying spending a little time with you, but I just assumed there was something more between the two of you. I'm not an absolute idiot like Garron or Henders."

Declan hoped his little laugh did not sound too nervous. "There is nothing going on between Julianna and me other than friendship. I mean, I see her more than any other person in the world, so of course, we're close. But that's all."

Britta looked dubious. "Completely platonic?"

"Yes," Declan insisted.

"So," she moved closer to him. "You mean to tell me the two of you have never done this?" She leaned in slowly and kissed him very lightly on the lips; then she pulled away only slightly.

"No," Declan answered. "Never."

"Then you've never done this?" She kissed him harder and longer.

"No," he said, but he thought, *But I'm only kissing you now for her.*

Britta looked at him with narrowed eyes. "I don't know if I should believe you. How is it possible you've never gotten curious?"

"Because emotional attachments are discouraged among the Scholars. Because we are close enough friends that I would never want to do anything that would cause us to be separated. We keep each other sane in here! I can't risk losing that! But I suppose mostly because we knew there would be a list, and it wouldn't be up to us anyway. Why set yourself up for a fall?" he explained.

"Wow," Britta said softly. She found his story a little sad. As much as she was attracted to Declan, she knew the difference between lust and love. If what Declan told her was true, she knew he must have felt a great deal of love for Julianna to show such restraint.

Declan tried to redirect the conversation to more useful topics. "I am a curious guy though. I'm curious about all the places in here that I've never seen. Did you know, before we started this new project, we went before Guardian Costma? The meeting room was so grand! And the priceless artwork on the walls! I've lived here all these years and never even knew it existed. It got me wondering about all the places in this Compound that I've never seen. I'm sure there's plenty more places of which I don't know. Maybe you could give me the insider's tour sometime. I'm sure you as guards have to know this place inside and out."

"We're each assigned an area when we're on general detail. For example, you make sure no one comes in or goes out of a certain door. Nowadays, I do more of the project guarding, like Garron is for you. That's a little different. In that case, you basically check up on your Scholars wherever their work takes them that day, be it the library or their lab. My job is to make sure they reasonably stay on task and help facilitate their progress in any way I can be of assistance, such as ordering supplies and such."

"Really?" Declan questioned. "Garron never made it seem that way."

"Garron is a bit of a jerk, if I'm being honest. Garron is a little more concerned with self-promotion. He has his eye on eventually being brought in as a full-fledged member of the New Regime."

"That's not your goal?"

"That kind of power would be nice," she admitted. "Don't get me wrong! I just do not feel the need to treat people poorly to get there. I have been given a job to perform in the meantime, and if I do it properly and well, I will get what I deserve."

Declan found himself liking her more as he talked with her. "I like that philosophy."

Britta looked at her watch with regret. "I really should be going now. I'm supposed to be meeting friends later tonight." She and Declan rose from the sofa. She added in a low voice, "This has been fun though. Maybe I'll have to set you up with that private tour soon. I could show you lots of things."

She slipped her arms around his waist and kissed him again more deeply. She was no fool. He may have been in love with Julianna Brenner, but he still was an extremely attractive guy who had a lot to learn in the art of seduction. She would not mind playing the role of teacher for him. For his part, Declan was fine with her teaching him, but he had a different curriculum in mind. He was going to figure out the best way to get Julianna safely on the other side of the Compound walls. Britta sauntered away with a smile.

Declan waited a beat before continuing to the pool with a spring in his step and a song in his heart. He was going to get them out, and willingly or not, Britta was going to help him do it.

Julianna awoke with a sick feeling in the pit of her stomach. Then she remembered why. Today was the Genos Ceremony. Today, she would be called on the stage and matched with Henders Costma, and just the thought of pretending she was going to have a baby with that oaf was disgusting to her. Not to mention, she found it completely unjust. The match with Henders made no sense at all. She should have been paired with a highly intelligent Scholar, like Declan. If she was smart enough to create lifesaving cardiovascular advancements, she surely was smart enough to decide with whom she would like to have a baby. When Declan popped into her head again, she tried to push him aside. There was no point in thinking about such matters.

She got up and brushed her teeth, though it did little to remove the bitter taste in her mouth. She selected from her closet one of the few items that was not a uniform. At the Genos Ceremony, all of the Scholars who made the list that year were supposed to dress in their finest clothing. Each Scholar had at least one nice dress or suit which they were required to don on formal occasions, such as a media moment, one of the rare instances when a Worker was allowed within the Compound to report on an advancement or invention created by the Scholars. During media moments, Scholars were not to wear their uniforms. They also were able to wear the make-up provided for them by a member of the camera crew. Since most of them had outgrown the clothing they had brought with them, they were allowed to select new items from a catalog as needed. Their new clothes arrived in a package placed outside their rooms. Most recently, Julianna had ordered a lilac dress with a simple A-line. She liked the cheery pastel color because it provided a contrast to the rest of the basic uniforms in her closet, but the dress design was quite utilitarian at the same time. On the outside, she thought it would have been appropriate for any number of occasions.

Julianna slipped into her dress and thanked her lucky stars that Declan had seen an advanced copy of the list. If she had not been prepared for what was going to happen today, she had no idea how she would have responded. She might have just fainted dead away on the spot or maybe she would have burst into tears. Perhaps she would have even thrown an angry punch. At least now she was mentally prepared.

She had not even been too upset when one of the guards knocked on her private quarters door and handed her the purple and gold envelope which contained her invitation to the Genos Ceremony today. Had she not already known she had made the list, it could have been a moment for tears. She brushed out her long hair and twisted it into a loose bun. Then she set off for the assembly room.

When she arrived at her destination, she spotted Declan, who was already seated on a metal folding chair. When she caught his eye, he patted the empty seat next to him. She noticed how handsome he looked in his jacket and tie, and she gladly joined him. They could use each other's support this morning. "Are you ready for this?" Declan asked as she sat next to him.

"As ready as I'll ever be," she said, wrinkling her nose in distaste.

CHAPTER 8

The assembly room filled up quickly. The Scholars looked attractive and professional in their nicer clothing, but many also appeared apprehensive and nervous. No one seemed overly eager or happy to be participating in the Genos Ceremony. Julianna thought that she might have been hopeful about a pairing with Declan if she had not already known better. She wanted so badly to reach out and squeeze his hand and have his strength help her make it through this day. The Ceremony was one thing, but after the pairings had been announced, she would have to spend alone time with Henders. She was certain that would prove to be intolerable.

One of the leaders of the New Regime took the stage. Julianna had no idea which one he was. She only identified him as a member of the Regime from his hideous attire and over-the-top make-up. When he turned on the announcement system, the microphone made an ear-piercing noise. Julianna covered her ears until it stopped.

"Good morning, Scholars," the man said. "This morning, you will have the honor of being included on this year's Genos List. This is a great privilege. It means that you have been selected to carry on the next generation of great Scholars. We have high

123

expectations for these children, just as we have for their parents. So without further delay, let me introduce you to our illustrious leader, the man who will bring this country into a new era of prosperity and greatness. Please welcome Guardian Costma!" The man announced the name loudly with great flourish.

As expected of them, the Scholars rose to their feet with thunderous applause and cheering as Guardian Costma took the stage with Henders trailing behind and stepping off to the left of the podium, lining up with other members of the New Regime who stood at attention. Julianna wondered if the cheering Scholars were just being sheep, following along because they were too afraid not to participate, or if they really thought this man was as great as he proclaimed himself to be.

Julianna's thoughts drifted to the first time she had seen Guardian Costma. Shortly after she had arrived at the temporary Scholars Compound, Julianna had been brought to an auditorium similar to this room. Guardian Costma had taken the stage then as well. He smiled his shuddersome painted smile and welcomed them to their new home. Julianna remembered being horrified by his eerie appearance. He looked to her like something from a nightmare. He told them about how important they were and that, in this new world, their mission would be vital to the success of the nation. Their families and friends back home were depending on them, and they needed to focus and try their hardest at whatever task may be assigned to them. They need never worry about having all the resources they needed for their survival, education and later their work. They should consider themselves to be among the most fortunate people.

Although she found his appearance distracting, Julianna had listened to the speech as a ten-year-old child and had believed much of what he said. She believed she was in a place where she would be safe, and she believed she would play an important role going forward. Her mother and father had told her as much throughout her childhood. Even Greta had reminded her she was special. Without her parents to protect her and Greta being only fourteen, the Scholars Compound seemed like a safe alternative. Her only other choice was Auntie who did not give the impression she wanted Julianna around.

After the meeting, she was one of a handful of children who had been called to the side of the stage. She had timidly approached the stage and waited for instruction. A man in a funny costume had approached them and said, "Guardian Costma would like to meet each of you personally. Please form a line." Then the man grabbed Julianna gruffly by the shoulders and instructed the other children to "Get behind the blonde girl."

Julianna tried not to quake in her shoes. She was terrified at the thought of being so close to this nightmarish figure. A device on the man's belt beeped, and he announced, "He is ready for you." He pushed her forward, and a second man grabbed her hand and pulled her toward a small room. He shoved her inside and slammed the door with a thud that made Julianna jump. Sitting in a high-backed arm chair was the macabre man who smiled at her. She hoped he intended his smile to be comforting, but she thought it was ghastly.

"Hello, child," the man said. "What is your name?"

"My name is Julianna Rose Brenner," she answered in a shaky voice.

"Do you know who I am?"

"Of course," she replied. "You're the man who was just on the stage. You're in charge here."

His smile widened a bit. "Is today the first day you've happened to see me?"

She nodded. "It is."

"I understand that your parents both perished during the attacks. Can you tell me anything about them?"

"Their names were Jacob and Anne Brenner. They were married for a long time and had two children, me and my older sister Greta. We lived in a nice house in Springdale. My sister is still there with our Auntie."

"What did your father do for a living?"

"He was a famous doctor, a neurologist who specialized in the study of memory," she told him. "He had an office at the university building, and he worked on lots of stuff there. He did that and wrote books more often than surgery these days. He hardly ever does ... did surgery anymore."

"Ah, and how did he die?"

"His office building was hit during the attacks. He was inside."

"And you?"

"I was inside too. That's what they told me."

"You don't remember that?"

Julianna shook her head.

"Can you tell me about what he was working on most recently?"

"I ... I can't remember," she admitted, looking down at the floor.

"You can't remember? Or someone told you not to tell me?" he asked in a tone he hoped was gentle.

Julianna looked at him in surprise. "No, no one told me anything. I just can't remember."

"Was it something about computers?"

Julianna considered this and replied, "No, sir, I don't think so. His work focused on brains, not computers."

Guardian nodded thoughtfully. "Very well then. I am sorry for your loss. I hope you enjoy your new home. You are dismissed."

"Thank you, sir," Julianna said, hurrying to turn the door knob and rush out of the room. She could not get away from the man quickly enough.

Now on stage, Guardian Costma motioned with his hands for everyone to be seated, and Julianna focused her mind on the present.

"Thank you kindly for the warm welcome," Guardian greeted. "I am here today to read the Genos List. When your name is called, please approach the stage and greet your partner."

Julianna looked at Declan with a feeling of dread. *This is only temporary*, she tried to remind herself. Declan took a deep breath and exhaled slowly. The first several names Guardian read were of little consequence to the duo, but finally he read Declan's name. Declan rose slowly and walked toward the stage. Sarah Wrigley smiled broadly as she made her way to the front. Julianna rolled her eyes and tried to fight back the jealousy that was bubbling inside of her. Declan was *her* partner. Everybody knew this, but Sarah was acting like she had just won the grand prize in the greatest raffle of all time. Julianna narrowed her eyes as she watched Sarah approach Declan and stand next to him.

Several other Scholars were paired up, and before long, Julianna stood alone. She said a silent prayer that perhaps she had insulted Henders to such a degree that he had pulled strings to void their pairing. Perhaps she was no longer on the list, and they had just forgotten to remove her name from the invitation list. Her hope was dashed quickly. "And finally," Guardian Costma announced, "Julianna Brenner is paired with Henders Costma. Congratulations to you all. May your matches be amicable and fertile. You now may each retire to private quarters for your discussions."

Per tradition, each pair would go to one person's private quarters to get to know each other and discuss how they wanted to proceed. Some people would determine they could not tolerate each other and would count on science to create the babies the New Regime expected. Others would try their best to make a love match with varying degrees of success. Nothing needed to be decided today. Each pair had at least one month to spend time together and determine the best course of action for them. Julianna knew she did not need that much time. Even if she had not been planning her departure, she never would have consented to any kind of relationship with Henders.

When Henders approached her, she realized she had never bothered to walk to the stage. "You were supposed to walk up front," Henders said sharply.

"My apologies," she said sarcastically.

"Follow me," he instructed.

Julianna watched as Declan walked out the door with Sarah attached to his hip. She knew they were heading to his room. Suddenly her jealousy was replaced with worry. What if Declan made a love connection with Sarah? What if he decided he would rather stay in the Compound with Sarah than run away with her? She took a deep breath and shook her head. *No, he'd never do that to me.* But she could not stop the wave of nausea that washed over her as she blindly followed Henders.

She was still thinking about Declan and what he was doing when Henders shoved open the door to his private quarters. Of course, his room was far more opulent than any of the others she had seen. His flooring was gray ceramic tile with a large plush rug covering much of it. In violation of the rules everyone else had to follow, his room had an accent wall painted a maroon red. He sat down on the king bed and patted the plush comforter, inviting her to sit next to him. Julianna stayed near the door.

Julianna felt no need to placate him. "Listen, I think you and I both know how this is going to play out. We have the advantage of already knowing each other from working together at least. I don't think either one of us feels any kind of fondness for each other. Let's just agree to let science work its magic, and we can call it a day," Julianna decreed.

Anger flashed across Henders' face. "Listen, I don't necessarily care for you and your smart mouth either. But you were given to me. You have a job to do here, and I think you're going to do it." He walked over to her, picked her up by the waist and threw her onto the bed.

Julianna screamed and rolled off the bed as quickly as possible. "Stay away from me!" she warned. "You're out of your mind if you think I'm going to do anything with you. If I didn't despise you before, I do now, you awful cretan!"

She tried to head for the door again, but he threw his large body in front of her and blocked her. When she tried to move, he mirrored her movements. Just as she was thought her only chance was to attempt some self-defense maneuvers she had seen in a library book once, someone knocked on the door.

"Don't move," Henders warned through gritted teeth before turning to open the door.

Garron was on the other side of the door. Garron looked at Julianna's flushed face and tousled hair. He locked eyes with her and asked, "Is there anything wrong here?"

Julianna had never been happy to see Garron before now. She and Declan may have found him annoying, but he played by the rules. He was not a barbarian like Henders, and Julianna did not think Garron would approve of that behavior. Before Henders had a chance to speak, her quick wit kicked into high gear. "Actually, Garron, we were just finished here. We've already gotten to know each other. You know how guards get to know their charges, and he is one-on-one with us. There's really no connection between us, and I think we're just going to take advantage of the scientific method. I was just heading out."

"Very well then," Garron said, pushing the door open wider with his eyes glued to Henders. He waited for her to rush out the door before he gave Henders one last glare and shut the door firmly. "You should go back to your room right away," Garron instructed. "Would you like an escort?"

"No thank you," she said. "I'll head straight there."

Garron nodded and stood in front of Henders' door. He may not have been fond of her, but he also was not fond of those who did not work for what they had. Garron already had disliked Henders before his display today. He did not believe Julianna, or anyone, deserved to be treated like that. Julianna turned and sprinted toward her room. Once she found the safety of her room, she crumpled to the floor with her back to the door and sobbed. She hated this place. She hated having no control over her own life. Thinking about what Declan may be doing right now with that clingy little Sarah didn't help matters. Was he touching her?

Had she kissed him? She screamed in frustration and muttered, "I can't wait to get out of here."

Declan invited Sarah back to his room. She kept smiling at him, and he suspected that she was one of the people who had been excited about her pairing. While he found that flattering, he was beginning to feel guilty about leading her on. He had no intention of spending very much time with Sarah. Why waste his time getting to know her when he would be leaving, hopefully in a matter of days? For right now, however, he thought it would be best to play the part. He asked her how she liked her work at the Compound. He knew little about how the social justice wing functioned, so he actually learned a lot from the conversation. Then he asked her about her family before the Compound, where she was during the attacks and how she wound up at the Compound. Sarah asked similar questions of him.

After a couple of hours, Declan stood and said, "Well, I suppose we'd better head for lunch. Care to join me?"

Sarah stood and smoothed down her black sheath. She could not wait to get to the cafeteria with Declan O'Connor. She could hardly believe her ears when her name was called. Among all the girls to whom she spoke, Declan had been their top pairing choice. They all wanted to be paired with the handsome, talented man who was known around the Compound for his kindness.

Declan held the door open for her, and she slipped her arm through his as they walked to the cafeteria. When they walked into the cafeteria, Julianna already had a seat at a table. She poked at her food with a fork but did not bother to eat any of it. She looked up, and her eyes bulged a bit when she saw Sarah hanging from Declan's arm. Declan noticed her red, blotchy eyes. "Sarah, would you excuse me for a minute? I'll meet you in the line."

"Of course," Sarah said.

Declan approached Julianna and said softly into her ear, "Are you okay?"

"I'm fine. Just go get your food," she said glumly.

Declan did not believe her, but he joined Sarah in line and got his tray before he returned to the table. Julianna watched with dread as Sarah took a seat at their table right next to Declan who sat directly across from her. Declan gave her a questioning look.

"What happened?" Declan whispered.

"You don't want to know," Julianna whispered back. "But I'll tell you later."

Julianna thought her day could not get any worse, but she was proven wrong as she watched Sarah fawn all over Declan throughout lunch. Julianna thought Sarah seemed determined to rub her victory into the faces of the other girls at the table, especially Julianna.

"Are you heading back to work after lunch?" Julianna asked Declan.

"I can if you want," he replied.

"Good, I think we should. We have a lot of work to do on our special project."

"True," Declan said. "Sarah, I'll see you later?"

Sarah glared at Julianna, but said, "Certainly."

Sarah did not miss the very slight smile Julianna gave her as Julianna rose from the table. Sarah was bitter that, today of all days, Julianna had beckoned and Declan had agreed to go running.

Declan was relieved by Julianna's suggestion. He could hardly wait to get back to the lab and find out what was wrong with Julianna. "Now will you tell me what happened?" Declan demanded when he marched into the lab.

Julianna looked tired and sad. "I'd rather not talk about it."

"Something happened. What was it?"

"Henders is not only an idiot. He also is a caveman. When I tried to leave, he picked me up and threw me onto his bed. Then he wouldn't let me leave."

"Are you okay?" Declan asked as he rushed to her side. When he hugged her, she felt all the tension leave her body. She collapsed against him and held onto him.

"I'm fine. Garron actually came and got me out. He must've heard me scream."

"Don't worry, Sunshine," Declan said as he smoothed her hair. "It won't be much longer. It's all coming together."

"I know. But if you could please try to make sure I don't have to be alone with him, I would really appreciate it. He seems to believe I am now his personal property."

"Of course," Declan replied.

"So how did things go with Sarah?"

"What's it matter?" Declan asked. "She's nice enough, I suppose, but it doesn't matter. We'll be gone."

Julianna heaved a sigh of relief for more than one reason. "Let's see what we can do to make that happen," she said as she tapped away on the computer keyboard. Her encounter with Henders had inspired her to put her extensive knowledge of chemistry to good use. She had no plans to walk out into the outside world and be as completely defenseless as she had been in Henders' quarters. "I think Henders needs to order us some supplies."

Guardian Costma called Henders into his office when he arrived. He slammed the door shut behind Henders. "How dare you screw this up so splendidly!"

"What are you talking about?"

"I received a report that another guard had to set the Brenner girl free from your room after she was screaming. You tried to attack her?" he asked incredulously.

"She would not even consider speaking to me. Told me she wanted to take the science method without ever touching me. I did not find that acceptable."

"I don't find you forcing yourself on her to be acceptable. I have told you before that she is a very important component to our long-term goals. You need to be building her trust, not completely obliterating it, you buffoon!"

"I don't know what you want me to do about it now. She hated me before, and she hates me even more now."

"You are going to seek her out and apologize. You will make amends as best you can. You will bend over backward to please her and give her whatever she wants. Is that clear?"

"Fine," Henders muttered.

Britta was thoroughly enjoying her illicit relationship with Declan. Her life typically was not very exciting.

She was financially secure and had plenty of disposable income to go out with her friends, but she also lived alone and largely did the same routine day in and day out.

Sneaking off to find time alone with Declan provided her with a sense of danger. If she got caught fraternizing with a Scholar, she would be seriously reprimanded. Not that she was by any means the first guard to have gotten caught playing with a Scholar. Usually, it was the men taking advantage of the young girls. In those cases, the guards had been busted down in the ranks and sent back to door duty. The Scholars then were shipped away to a different Compound to prevent any further contact. Britta thought the men in those cases were disgusting. They usually preyed upon the younger and more naive of the girls who often did not think they had a choice other than to do as they were told.

However, Britta did not feel her situation with Declan was in any way similar to those cases. Declan was a mature adult who perfectly understood the risk involved in what they were doing. He also was quick enough, in the one case they were nearly caught by another guard, that he came up with a plausible explanation before Britta even had a chance to open her mouth. They were having fun together - nothing more and nothing less. Besides, the thrill was in the sneaking around. Their physical relationship had not advanced further than a little touching and kissing.

They had spent most of their time talking and tiptoeing around the Compound into various places they really should not have accessed. It gave her something to do and look forward to in a day. Plus, she truly liked Declan. Many of the Scholars were too buttoned up for Britta's taste, but Declan had a wonderful sense of humor and was willing to have a good time.

Today, he had suggested meeting her and sneaking into the truck docks, where the trucks that brought goods to the Scholars Compound unloaded, and some vehicles of the New Regime were stored. The members holding higher offices in the Regime had cars for official business and travel. A couple of emergency vehicles also were kept on hand in case a Scholar required medical treatment that was not available at the Compound. Declan had told her about how he had been fascinated with cars when he was a boy, but he had never been given an opportunity to drive one. Britta said she would let him check out the cars stored at the dock. He had smiled so brightly at her because he did not even know cars were stored at the docks.

"Hey! Over here!" Declan called and ducked back into the corner where he had hidden. Britta smiled wickedly and dashed the short distance to him. She greeted him with a hard kiss on the lips. "I've missed you."

"I bet you have," Declan replied, playing the role and smacking her bottom with the palm of his hand. "Now you need to make good on your promise."

"Right this way." She grabbed his hand and pulled him toward the dock.

She put her thumb over the keypad, and a low hum, followed by a thud, signaled the door unlocking. Britta jokingly bowed and swept her hand into a grand wave. "After you, sir."

Declan grinned broadly and walked through the threshold. He scanned the room and took in the wide selection of vehicles, most of which were high-quality, luxury cars. He took slow steps, taking in every detail he could. He could not help but think that Julianna and her photographic memory would have been more suited for this task, but he could not imagine Julianna would be very adept at flirting with a male guard. At some point, she would find them stupid and likely would let them know it. Declan snickered a little at the thought.

"See anything you like?" Britta asked.

Declan smiled at her. "Lots."

Declan never meant these double entendres as compliments or come-ons to her, but Britta chose to take them that way anyhow. Very few Scholars even knew this area existed, so the security once one was inside the docks was not very tight. The keys for all the vehicles were labeled and hanging from neat rows of hooks on the wall which seemed to coincide with the parking spots. The dock really was just one enormous garage with several bays on the north side for trucks to unload supplies. Declan walked up and down the rows of cars, admiring each and pointing out to Britta various qualities of this car or that one. She pretended to care.

"You're so lucky you get to drive one of these every day," Declan told her. "How do they even get these things out of here?" He turned in a circle trying to find the vehicle exit.

"It's right down that ramp," Britta explained. "All these doors over here are elevated for the semi trucks. But that ramp leads to a door that opens on the ground. You can just drive away from there."

Declan scoffed. "Sure, if you had the secret code."

"No secret code," Britta replied. "It's an automated door from the inside. Once a vehicle gets close enough, it just automatically opens. They tried having a code on it, but it wound up being a hassle, I guess. Now you only need the code to get in from the outside."

Declan shook his head wistfully. "What I wouldn't give to drive one!"

"Would you like to at least sit in one?" Britta offered.

Declan's jaw dropped. "Could I?" he asked.

"We've come this far. What's it going to hurt?" she replied, reaching for a set of keys on the wall. "Come here."

She led him to one of the luxury sedans parked nearest her. "This is probably one of the nicest ones," she said. She pushed a button on the key fob to unlock the doors and tossed Declan the keys. When she had slid into the passenger seat, Declan, who could hardly believe his luck, took the driver's seat.

"You'll have to walk me through what I would do if I wanted to drive this thing," Declan requested.

Britta gave him a quick driving tutorial on how to apply the brakes and the gas pedal, how to shift, where he would find the lights and windshield wipers and everything else she could tell him without actually starting the car or moving it.

"I wish I could really let you take it out for a spin, but I'm afraid that would most certainly be noticed," Britta said with regret.

"No worries," Declan replied. "I'm just glad I got to sit in the driver's seat. You made a dream come true for me today. Thank you!"

"You're welcome," Britta said seductively. "Now, do you want me to show you how to work the backseat?"

"No, thanks!" Declan said, trying to sound regretful but really moving away from her just a little too quickly. "I have to get back. I think Julianna is starting to get suspicious of where I've been spending my time, and the last thing I want is for you to get into any kind of trouble on my account. I told her I'd meet her in the library in about 10 minutes, so I'd better get moving."

Britta tried not to look too disappointed and instead walked her fingers up his chest until she tickled his chin. "Okay, when shall we meet again?"

"How about the same time, same place tomorrow?" He paused a second. "No! You know what? Make it an hour later. Then I should be able to stay longer. My time will be my own."

"Sounds delightful," she ran her fingers through his hair and pulled his face closer to hers. "I have so much more to show you." She gave him a long, lingering kiss. "Until then," she whispered as she pulled away.

Declan smiled nervously before he pulled the door handle and hopped out of the car. He gave her a little wave and then headed to the door. Britta had helped him more than he could have hoped. He knew how he was going to get them out of the Compound. He hustled to the library to share his news with Julianna.

When he walked into the library, he spotted her in a lounge chair, tapping away at a laptop keyboard. She looked up and asked quietly with a grin and a wink, "How'd your date go?"

"You're not going to believe my good fortune," Declan answered.

She shook her head. "I never doubted you and all your irresistible hotness for one second," she teased.

He gave her shoulder a good-natured shove. "You're just jealous I'm not using my powers of seduction on you." He flexed his biceps.

She laughed. "You caught me!"

"Let me see that," he said, taking the computer away from her.

He began typing away, using their secret code. He explained how he was going to meet Britta again tomorrow at the docks, and Julianna needed to be ready to leave then. He and Julianna had been secretly stockpiling supplies under the guise of materials needed for experimentation under Operation Much Death. Henders procured whatever they had requested, still trying to redeem himself following the Genos Ceremony. Henders could not stand her condescending attitude and had been doing everything he could to avoid interaction with her while still spending enough time with them that he had something to report back to his uncle, no matter how trivial or inconsequential a detail, and he gladly had given them any materials requested to try to appease her per his uncle's decree.

While Declan had been consorting with Britta, Julianna carefully had devised notes to leave behind for the next Scholars who would surely be assigned to finish the project. She had designed them to purposely mislead her replacements and cause serious delays in their progress. She knew she and Declan had a reputation around the medical wing, and her replacements likely would do their best to learn whatever they could from the work Declan and Julianna had already finished. They would be in too deep by the time they learned they had been bamboozled and would need to start again from scratch.

Julianna was in the process of decoding Declan's message when Henders entered the library. Julianna rolled her eyes, tossed her head back and groaned at the sight of him. Henders could not stand it anymore.

"Why?" he asked her sharply and too loudly. "Why are you always so mean? I don't like you either, but I'm not constantly mean to you. I suppose I could be, but I'm not. Maybe you would like me to be. Is that what you want?"

Several people in the library had turned to ogle the guard causing the commotion. Julianna wanted to scream at him at the top of her lungs about what he believed was the definition of mean. Had the way he treated her in his room been loving? Instead, she faked a look of surprise. "Henders, I simply was reacting to a failed idea that I thought might work for an aspect of this very important project. Your entrance at the same time was purely coincidental. Though I must say, I'm very hurt that you think I'm mean." She brought her hand to her heart. "I thought we were getting along just fine. I guess I'll have to make adjustments as I do not wish to hurt your feelings as you have just hurt mine." She sniffed her nose for effect.

Once again, Henders found himself staring at Julianna without any idea how to respond to her. Declan turned his head and walked away a few paces so no one would see his smirk. He knew Julianna was just messing with Henders for sport at this point. Declan was glad because he deserved a severe punishment for how he had treated her. If it had been Henders' idea to pair himself with Julianna, Declan was certain Henders regretted it now. When Julianna reached into her satchel and pulled out a tissue, Henders turned on his heel and just walked away.

As he retreated, Julianna said, "You know, there goes one of those guys that I looked at from a distance and thought he's really not that attractive. But then I got to know him a little better. Now every time he opens his mouth, I think he's *definitely* not attractive."

Declan smirked and raised an eyebrow. "Are you done?"

"Depends on if he comes back today," she answered honestly.

Declan took the seat next to her and whispered, "How are we on supplies? Are you ready for our biggest experiment yet?"

"Absolutely," she replied. She patted his face teasingly and said, "While you've been doing your part, I've been doing mine. Don't you worry about a thing."

CHAPTER 9

The following day, Declan's stomach turned somersaults for much of the morning, and it only worsened into the afternoon. "Last chance to turn back," he offered Julianna, although he knew it already was too late for that. Their reasons for leaving were sound. They needed to follow the plan now, even if the thought of executing it made him nauseous. Julianna, however, seemed as cool as a cucumber.

Julianna wanted Declan to believe she had full confidence in their plan because she knew he was extremely nervous about it, and she felt a little guilty about dragging him along with her. Even though he volunteered to go with her, she knew he never would have taken such drastic steps on his own.

When the hour finally came for them to put the plan in action, they both suffered from butterflies. Julianna checked and double-checked their supplies and carefully packed things into backpacks, using every last inch of space. She would head to the rendezvous point first in order to be hidden from sight before Britta arrived. As she walked out of the lab, she turned around and gave Declan an apprehensive look. She hoped she was doing the best thing for them, but things had deteriorated so much that she did not see how they could get any worse.

Julianna walked down the corridors toward the dock. She carefully positioned herself in a dimly lit alcove near the dock, certain to stay out of sight to any passersby. When she was settled, she reached into the front pocket of her backpack and pulled out a small syringe filled with saline. She had managed to do a little experiment with a tracking device from the supply room. When she injected saline into it, the device malfunctioned and would no longer emit a signal. She gritted her teeth as she carefully jabbed the needle under her skin, making sure that she got it in just the right place. She bit back her cry as a searing pain burned under her skin as the device went silent. Then she waited quietly for Declan and Britta to arrive. She hoped the pounding of her heart would not be audible when they arrived. Each minute was sweet agony. The anticipation of freedom was almost too much to bear.

Declan watched Julianna walk out of the door, knowing their lives going forward would never be the same. They were leaving the life and the place that they had known almost for as long as they had known each other, which was half of their lives. He had no idea what to expect on the other side of the walls. While he may not have always agreed with everything that happened inside the Compound, at least he had always felt safe here. He was sacrificing that peace of mind now. If he and Julianna would fail, he knew they would be shipped away to separate Compounds at best. She might wind up in California while he would be sent to the Eastern seaboard. He shook his head to get rid of the idea. They must not fail. He watched the clock diligently and was thankful that Julianna had made Henders uncomfortable enough to disappear again. Declan was not sure where he went when he left, and he assumed Guardian Costma had no clue about how often Henders left his dream team alone to their own devices. He had made pulling off their plan so much easier than if they had been under Garron's critical eye.

Declan pulled a saline-filled syringe out of a drawer. Julianna had instructed him on what to do right before he left the lab. He used the syringe to de-activate his tracker, just as she had done, and then he dropped the evidence into a sharps container on the wall.

When the proper minute arrived, Declan grabbed the backpack Julianna had left for him and walked to the door. He paused for a moment and looked back at their empty lab, feeling a sense of melancholy. He could not wrap his head around the fact that they would never work in there together again. Some of his best moments had been spent here with her. He sighed and pulled the door closed. He had somewhere else he needed to be. She was counting on him.

Just as he had planned, Declan ran into Britta in the hallway on the way to the docks.

"Hey, pretty girl," he said as he hurried to catch up with her.

She greeted him with a sly smile. "Hi there. Are you ready for your lesson on backseat driving?"

"As ready as I'll ever be," Declan returned.

When they arrived at the door, Britta placed her thumb on the keypad to unlock the door. She never saw Julianna sneak up behind her. Julianna had inserted the syringe into the skin of her neck and had injected the serum to render her unconscious before Britta even had focused on her. Confused and hurt, Britta looked at Declan who stood holding the door open. Because Julianna knew this part was agony for Declan, who had grown to like Britta in the moments she was not openly trying to seduce him, Julianna put on a hostile expression and said angrily, "Don't look at him. Look at me. Why would you try to take him away from me?"

"I ... I," Britta stuttered as she stumbled. She wanted to explain to Julianna that she had never planned to take Declan for keeps, but she could not form the words with her mouth.

Julianna grabbed the door while Declan caught Britta before she collapsed. He placed her gently on the floor. "Let's go!" Julianna urged.

Declan sprinted to the open door and grabbed the correct set of keys from the hook and popped the trunk. Julianna quickly hopped inside. They dropped the backpacks in the trunk as well. Then Declan slammed the lid shut. He felt a rush of adrenaline surge through his body as he sat in the driver's seat and turned the ignition key. Once the engine had revved, he cautiously applied a small bit of pressure to the gas pedal, and the car began to move slowly. He was careful to keep it slow as he learned to control the wheel. Finally, the moment of truth arrived. He approached the automated door at the bottom of the ramp and prayed Britta's information had been accurate.

He held his breath until the door slid open. Then he gunned the engine and drove as fast as he could, putting as much distance between them and the Compound as quickly as he could. As the scenery sped past him, he shouted in exhilaration. Driving a car had long been a favorite dream of his, and now he was living it. Now he just had to pay close attention to the signs on the road and make sure he followed the directions that Julianna had researched for him. At long last, he was going to go home.

They had a decent head start before Henders was coming to the sinking realization that his only charges had disappeared. He had searched the lab, the cafeteria, the library, the gym and the pool. He had searched the outside grounds, especially the wooded area for which they had a fondness. He had interrogated Teagan Ross and Jonah Preston because he had seen them dine together. He had grilled Declan's match, Sarah Wrigley, because she might have had insight into his way of thinking. He asked several other Scholars who had crossed his path if they had seen the famous medical wing whiz kids. Nobody had any idea where they might have gone. So now it was time to face the music. He was going to need reinforcements. He was going to have to confess to his uncle that he had lost them. His uncle took the news exactly as Henders had thought he would.

"I gave you one very simple job to do, you imbecile! How could you screw up this badly? You may very well be the death of us all," Guardian ranted. "Call tech headquarters and have them begin tracking procedures. They didn't just disappear."

"Yes, Uncle," Henders said.

Guardian picked up a cell phone resting on a nearby table and threw it at Henders' head. "Do it now!"

Henders flinched but managed to catch the phone, fumbling it but not dropping it to the ground. He punched the icon on the phone that indicated the tech headquarters and explained what he needed done. Although he was put on hold while the guard on duty pulled up their tracking numbers and booted up the system, Henders wore an intense expression and kept the phone firmly pressed to his ear, lest he have to listen to more of his uncle's verbal assault. He assumed Guardian should know that Scholars weren't tracked unless there was a reason to do it. Since none were off campus at the moment, tracking them would take a little bit of patience. Guardian paced off to the side of the room, occasionally mumbling to himself.

When the guard finally returned to the phone, Henders could tell something was wrong immediately from the tone of the guard's voice. "I'm very sorry, sir," the guard said. "I think there is something wrong with the system. We cannot seem to find them anywhere. I entered their numbers twice to make sure I had not typed a number incorrectly. Neither one shows up anywhere. It's as if the system cannot read their devices for some reason."

"Keep trying, will you?" Henders requested.

"Yes, sir," the guard vowed. "I'll do what I can."

He reluctantly ended the call and looked at his uncle.

"Well?" Guardian questioned. "Where are they?"

"They were not able to track them at this time. Their devices were not being read by the system for some reason."

"Is the system down?" Guardian asked incredulously.

"I don't think he really knows what the problem is right now, but he's looking into it and will let me know," Henders explained.

"And just what exactly are we supposed to do in the meantime?" Guardian asked.

Henders was spared momentarily when Guardian's phone rang. He grabbed the phone and angrily asked,

"What?" Then he got very quiet and listened carefully. "Is she okay? … Hmm … very well then. If that's the case, she must have intentionally deactivated her tracking device somehow… We shall need to enlist the services of the Warriors, yes. However, I think we should hold off on using the media just yet. They can't have gotten far, and the Warriors may be able to pin them down rather quickly." He listened again for a moment. Then his voice grew loud with rage. "What do you mean they stole my car? They must be found. She *must* be found!"

He knew she was extremely smart, but Henders still found himself wondering what exactly his uncle found so important about that obnoxious, conceited girl. If not for his uncle's fascination with the girl, he most definitely would have been thinking, "Good riddance!"

Meanwhile, Britta had been taken to a bed in the infirmary. Once she had begun to regain consciousness, she found herself surrounded by members of the New Regime waiting to grill her about what had happened. Britta had enough wherewithal to keep her mouth firmly shut until she had regained her wits. Now, after working out a plausible story in her head, she told them she was ready to speak.

"What was going on?" one of the men grilled. "Why were you down by the docks in the first place?"

"I had gone to the docks area because I was on my break. There is a small alcove that is out of the way and very quiet. I had a headache and I hoped to use my time to sit in a dimly lit, quiet area and rest in the hopes that my head would start to feel better."

"And then what happened?" another prompted.

"I saw Declan O'Connor. I'm not sure what he was doing, but he struck up a conversation with me. We spoke for a few minutes. Then out of nowhere, his jealous partner came and stabbed me in the neck with a needle. I don't know what she injected into me, but I remember everything going woozy before I collapsed on the floor. I think he may have caught me, but I'm not certain."

"Why were you on the floor several feet from the alcove then?"

"I do believe I stomped about the floor, trying to get away." She decided to add a tidbit that she had picked up from conversations around her. She borrowed one of the nurse's theories and said, "The only other thing I can think of is that they dragged me to use my fingerprint to open the door."

The men looked at each other as if they had expected as much too.

"Thank you for your cooperation, Miss," one of them said. "We will let you know your new assignment in the future."

Britta sat up further in the bed. "New assignment?"

"Of course, you must be reassigned as punishment for succumbing to an attack," he replied matter-of-factly.

Britta felt herself get hot with anger and tried to open her eyelids, still heavy with the drugs, even further to express her outrage. "I was attacked from behind, and your response is to bust me in the ranks? How is that fair? How would any of you fare if an armed person jumped you from behind?"

"That's enough!" the first man decreed. "We shall hear no more of this. You have served your usefulness. If you want to continue to argue, you may seek employment elsewhere."

Britta dropped her head to her pillow but continued to wear a look of disgust. She was glad Declan and Julianna had escaped. She hoped they could be happy together somewhere, and she was not even angry at them for using her. They deserved better, and so did she. She waited until she had been left alone before she shed a few tears as silently as she could manage.

As he drove into the night, Declan hoped that Britta was safe and had not gotten into any trouble because of the events that had transpired. He had suggested injecting Britta because it would make it easy for them to get away, but also because it would give her an excuse. If they made it look like she had been attacked, he thought it less likely that she would be punished for their actions. Britta had always been kind to him, and he did not want her to be collateral damage for his own selfish purposes. He hoped she would use the excuse that they drugged her and used her fingerprint to unlock the door. At least, it had been his plan for her.

He knew the time had come that he would need to get rid of the car because the Warriors most certainly would be dispatched soon, and they would be searching for the missing car. As he came upon the sign for Whispering Pines Park, he knew he did not have that much farther to go. Soon, he was exiting the freeway and traveling down a quiet road, following the signs to the park. This was part of their plan. Julianna had told him of the old deserted Scouts camp. She had explained that she had amused herself by memorizing the majority of their journey from the temporary facility to the new Scholars Compound. On the bus ride to their newly constructed home, Julianna had made note of every exit and attraction along the way. Whispering Pines had once been home to young campers in the summer, but it had been deserted after the attacks. Perhaps those who still had their children wanted to keep them close, or parents were unable to access enough money after the banking collapse to afford a luxury like summer camp. Whatever the reason, Julianna knew the place had been abandoned when they had been taken to the new Compound. Both of them were hoping that was still the case. Even if new campers now used the facility, they likely would not be there this early in the spring.

As Declan drove down the winding gravel road that led to the camp, it appeared Julianna was right. He did not see a soul in sight as he traveled deeper into the woods. When he came upon the lake, he stopped the car and popped the trunk. Julianna had made the trip in the trunk because Declan had thought it made more sense for her to be hidden. If he got caught making the escape, she did not necessarily have to go down with him. She had not been thrilled with the idea, but she eventually had conceded at Declan's insistence. Now, she looked at him with wide eyes that flooded with relief when she saw his face instead of that of a Warrior or someone else. He offered her a hand and she climbed out of the car.

Julianna looked at her surroundings and breathed the fresh, cool air. She heard nothing but the crickets chirping in the trees. She looked at Declan's handsome face lit by the stars and the moon. She turned around and saw nothing but trees, some rock structures and a small cabin in the distance. Overwhelmed, Julianna stood shivering and racked with sobs. She could hardly believe they had succeeded. Declan took off his jacket and draped it over her shoulders. She wiped away a tear with a shaking hand. She had just changed her life forever. Everything that she had known for half of her life now was gone, and going back to it was not an option. And she had dragged Declan with her. She hoped she had made the right choice. Declan watched her with a look of pain. Her face reminded him so much of the scared little girl he had first met that it nearly broke his heart. Instead, he put on a determined expression before she looked his way, and he gently grabbed her shoulders.

He turned her to face him and looked into her eyes. Julianna momentarily forgot her other worries when she thought he was about to kiss her. Her breath caught in her throat, unsure of how she should feel. He leaned his head toward hers and softly kissed her forehead. "I promise you I will always do everything I can to make sure you're okay," he vowed.

She did not want to admit even to herself that she was disappointed he had only kissed her forehead, so instead, she said nothing and threw herself into his arms, crying against his chest. Declan closed his eyes and enjoyed the warmth of her body against his, with no one watching them or telling them they should not touch. He held her tightly without saying a word until she seemed to have exhausted herself. Only then did he pull back slightly.

"I think we need to follow through on our plan to get rid of the car."

Julianna nodded. She reached into the trunk to grab the backpacks. Then she and Declan searched the rest of the car for anything they might be able to use, finding a small amount of the New Regime currency in the glove box.

"Something is better than nothing," Declan said as he stuffed the bills into one of the backpacks.

Then they looked around for a stone large enough to place on the gas pedal.

"This is just a shame," he told her with a shake of his head. He started the engine again and used the stone to push down the gas pedal. He hesitated only a second, then he shoved the gear into drive, moving his arm quickly to get out of the way. The car jerked forward and plunged into the water. With the driver's door open, the sedan quickly filled with the murky water and bobbed a bit before slipping beneath the surface. When the pond once returned to looking like glass reflecting the full moon, Declan turned to Julianna. "Looks like we were never here."

She gave him a weak smile, and he pulled her into another hug.

"How about we try to get some rest?" he asked her. "I think that cabin is too obvious, but I saw a small cave over that way as we were driving to the lake. Follow me."

He took her hand and led her to the mouth of a small cave. He pulled a flashlight out of one of the bags and used it to check the cave for signs of any other life. When he was sure they were alone and free of bats or other creatures, he waved her to follow him a little deeper into the structure. "I think we're good in here. Nobody will come looking for us if we stay quiet and in the shadows until morning."

She nodded. The cave was even cooler than the spring evening air. He moved toward one of his backpacks and pulled out a blanket. "I thought the pillows would've been too bulky to bring, so I figured we could just wad up our jackets," he explained.

"I'm just grateful we have a blanket," she whispered as she handed him back his jacket.

After making their makeshift bed, Declan slipped his arm under her jacket to give her more cushion. She put her head on his arm, snuggled up closely to him, and closed her eyes. She sniffed and said, "I hope you don't regret this."

He gave her a little squeeze and replied, "I've never regretted being with you, Sunshine. I wouldn't want to be anywhere without you."

She intertwined her fingers with his as she drifted off to sleep.

When Julianna awoke the next morning, she could see sunlight peeping in through the end of the cave as she slowly opened her eyes. Suddenly, she panicked as she realized Declan was no longer beside her. She sat up and slapped her hand on the spot where he had slept. She looked from one side to another as a feeling of dread crept across her entire body. Then she recoiled against the wall in fear as she heard the sound of approaching footsteps. She tried to make herself as small as possible as the footsteps got closer and closer. When a shadow fell across the mouth of the cave, she

CHAPTER 10

"Good morning, Sunshine," she heard.

She opened her eyes and sighed in relief as every muscle in her body relaxed. "You scared me! Where were you?"

"I thought you might be hungry when you awoke," he answered as he held out a small container with fresh strawberries in it. "I saw some wild ones growing nearby, so I thought I'd pick them for you. These too." He held out a bouquet of wildflowers. "I remember my mom always liked flowers, and I thought you'd probably never had any before."

"I haven't. Thank you!" she said as she accepted the bouquet and held it to her nose.

"I figured as long as we're free, we may as well enjoy all that the world has to offer," he said with a shrug. "I know driving that car yesterday is now one dream I can cross off my list. And as far as the berries go, you can eat as little or as much as you want. No one is keeping track anymore, remember?" He winked.

She smiled brightly. "Yippee! Imagine eating just because and not to optimize brain function! What a concept!" She popped a berry in her mouth.

Declan returned her smile, glad she was feeling more like herself this morning after being so overwhelmed with emotions. "So how do you wish to proceed today?" Declan asked. "Should we walk a ways and then try to somehow rent a car or hitch a ride?"

"I think we can walk to a truck stop," Julianna said. "Then we can pretend that we had car trouble or something and need a ride to get home. Hopefully some truck driver who isn't crazy will take pity on us and get us at least part of the way. It's too far to just walk to Linwood. We need to try and scam rides wherever we can. I don't think renting a car is an option. How would we do it without revealing ourselves?"

Declan flashed an identification card that bore a name she had never heard before, but it had Declan's badge photo. He also held a currency card with the same name on it. "Where did you get that?"

"I played around a bit on the computer in some free time and went to the office supply room to laminate it. No one ever questioned me."

"Well, that still doesn't solve the problem of how to pay for it. We have very little currency," Julianna sighed. "I don't want to scam someone and cheat them out of their due."

"I appreciate that about you, Sunshine, but we also are at a point where we have to do what we need to do for our own survival. We can use this currency card as often as necessary."

"Promise me that we'll try to do this as much as possible without going against our conscience. I didn't run away from doing wrong to be set free in this world to do other wrongs."

"Forgive me, but I'm not comfortable with you approaching strangers for free rides and hoping they aren't going to kill you somewhere along the way," Declan replied.

"I'm not worried about that. I'm armed," she explained. "And once someone has tried to kill me, I won't feel guilty about stealing their car."

"What on earth do you mean?"

She pulled a syringe out of the front pouch of her travel bag. "I have plenty of these. Just like the one I used on Britta, these will render anyone unconscious long enough for us to get away." She gave him an admonishing look. "You might be surprised with what else I have in this bag, too. You didn't really think I would leave without taking advantage of the full arsenal of supplies we had in the medical research center, did you? Heck, most of this stuff Henders procured for me. I just mixed some things together to make sure we'd be safe on the outside."

Declan grinned. "I always knew you were smarter than me."

Julianna giggled. "But speaking of supplies, I have something I need you to do for me." She reached back into the bag and dug around for a moment before pulling out a pair of scissors and a container. "I would do this myself, but I have a feeling it would look horrible. Could you please help me with my disguise?"

"Sure, what do you need me to do?"

"Cut my hair, and then I can dye it."

"You want me to what?"

She held the scissors out to him and nodded. "I need your help. If I tried to do it alone without a mirror, I might have nothing left before I get it evened out."

"I don't want to cut your hair. I don't think you need to do that."

"My guess is Guardian is going to be flashing around a photo of a long-haired blonde. If I dye my hair dark, I'll be able to blend better. Hopefully go unnoticed." She grabbed his hand and pressed the scissors into them. "Come on, please? I don't want to get caught and go back. Who knows what will happen to us then. If it makes you feel any better, I brought a little disguise for you, too." She reached back into the bag and pulled out a baseball cap and a pair of glasses. She slipped the glasses onto his nose. He could tell they had no corrective lenses in them. "There! Now you look very Clark Kent. You'd better make good use of them. I swiped the baseball cap from a guard at the pool when he wasn't looking. The glasses came from Scott Ross. I asked him if he had an old pair I could use. I was even nice enough to punch out the lenses for you."

"I guess you've thought of everything," he said, still not happy with the idea but relenting. "Fine, but you can't be mad at me if you don't like it."

She smiled at him more confidently than she felt and turned around. He sighed at the sight of her golden hair. "How short do you want it?"

She made a motion just above her shoulders. "Right about here should be fine."

"That seems kind of short," he countered.

"It'll be fine," she insisted.

He gathered her hair into his left hand and opened the scissors before dropping them back to his side. "Are you sure this is necessary?"

She twisted back to look at him. "Look, there's no rental place for miles from here. We'll need to get a ride from someone, and if Guardian has people out looking for us, they'll be looking for a female with long, blonde hair." She touched his hand. "It'll grow back. I promise you really can't hurt me by doing this. You'll only help me."

"All right, all right." He grasped her hair again. Once he could not see her face, she bit her lip and squeezed her eyes shut tight. A good portion of her hair fell to the floor of the cave with one quick chop of the scissors. With that much done, he set about evening out the ends until her hair no longer skimmed her shoulders.

She turned around once he announced he was done. "How's it look?" she asked hopefully.

He gave her a small smile. "Still as pretty as ever," he replied.

"Now I have another favor to ask. Can you go to the pond and get me some water so I can rinse this stuff out after I use it to dye my hair?" she asked as she held up the container.

"More supplies from the arsenal?" Declan asked.

"Just a little something I concocted when Henders thought I was working to kill people," she said with a wink as she removed the lid.

Declan chuckled. "Okay, I'll be right back."

By the time Julianna was done, her hair was much shorter and a dark chocolate brown that matched her eyes. "Are you ready to head out of this cave?" she asked Declan.

He pulled a GPS device, which he had stripped from the car, from his pocket. "I will try to keep us off the main roads as much as possible while we're walking to the nearest truck stop. It will decrease the likelihood of someone noticing us."

"Let's go!" Julianna exclaimed with all the enthusiasm she could muster.

They walked along in companionable silence as they cut through the park area and back toward the main road. Then they walked parallel to the main road without getting close enough to draw much attention from passersby. After about an hour, they stopped to take a break in another wooded area. Julianna gladly dropped to a bench and heaved a sigh of relief, thankful that their Scholars uniforms had demanded the use of sensible shoes.

Declan smiled at her knowingly. "I bet right about now you're glad that they decreed you could not eat all the cake you wanted and were forced to work out regularly."

"Truly, their bossiness of me turned out to be their own downfall," Julianna kidded. "I could walk a hundred more miles."

Declan laughed. While they were talking, they were oblivious to the strange man who had started lurking around them before they even decided to sit on the bench. "If you'll excuse me, I need a moment to myself," Declan told her as he stood.

Julianna looked at him, slightly alarmed.

Declan laughed, embarrassed. "I just need to use the bathroom."

"Oh!" Julianna giggled nervously as she blushed a little at the awkward moment.

"I'm going into that wooded area right over there," Declan mumbled. "Back in a few." He walked into the woods without looking back at her.

Julianna leaned her head back to look at the prettiness of the blue sky, which was punctuated by a few harmless, puffy clouds. She closed her eyes and took a deep breath of the fresh air and smiled at the thought that she was outside without a time limit and thankful that her first day of freedom had been a beautiful one of perfect temperature. When she tilted her head forward and opened her eyes, she was taken aback at the face of the man who now stood right in front of her.

The vagrant wore a long ponytail of mostly gray hair and clothes that looked as if they had not been washed in weeks. When he opened his mouth into a menacing grimace, some teeth were yellow and jagged. Others were missing altogether. His weathered face contorted into a threatening expression, and he mumbled for Julianna to hand over her backpacks.

Julianna realized that they had more to worry about in this outside world than just the Warriors or the New

Regime hunting them. She looked at the older man and figured she could stand a good chance of overpowering him. "No, I will give you nothing," she said firmly. "Please go away."

The man grew angrier, and he reached out to help himself to one of the bags. Without rising from the bench, Julianna stretched out one of her tired yet toned legs and kicked him sharply in the gut. He groaned and staggered backward momentarily. Then he flew at her in a fit of rage and charged toward her. This time, Julianna used a couple moves she had picked up in a kickboxing class at the gym. The New Regime may have been interested in increasing the life span of its Scholars when they set up the class, but she was grateful for the small measure of self-defense it allotted her now. While the man was catching his breath, she pulled a small ball from her backpack. She threw it to the ground right in front of him with all of her might, creating a cloud of smoke that enveloped the man. Julianna held her breath as she grabbed their meager belongings and ran into the woods. Declan was on his way out, and she nearly knocked him over when she blindly plowed right into him.

She grabbed his wrist and cried, "We have to go! We have to go!" He matched her steps, and the duo sprinted through the woods. When she had finally run out of adrenaline, she slowed, bent over and put her hands on her knees, trying desperately to catch her breath.

"What is going on?" Declan panted.

"This strange old man accosted me," Julianna said. "He looked like a homeless vagrant. He certainly was not a Warrior, but he tried to take our bags. I got away by using a few kickboxing moves and one of my weapons in my backpack."

"One of your weapons?"

"I have a few smoke bombs," she said, pulling one from her backpack for a visual aid. "You should know this anyhow. If someone is after you, you can throw one of these on the ground really hard, and it will release a cloud of smoke and fumes that will temporarily knock out a person. It's a little easier than trying to do one of the injections like we used on Britta, but it doesn't last as long. That's why I wanted to put some good distance between us."

Declan looked very concerned. "Well, I'd like to put even more distance between us," he said, grabbing Julianna's hand. "Let's see if we can't hurry and find a ride and get a lot farther from here."

They continued walking at a more hurried, purposeful pace and finally arrived at the nearby truck stop. They held back a moment and looked at the building.

"How do you want to play this?" Declan asked.

"How about if we say our car broke down, and we're trying to get home. We don't have enough money on us to get it fixed. We'll just ask if anyone is going in our general direction and can help get us part of the way."

"Okay," Declan said, not sounding very confident.

Julianna swatted his arm. "Oh relax. Just hang back and let me take the lead. All you've got to do is play along."

Declan followed a pace behind her as she walked toward the parking lot. Julianna did a quick scan of the parking lot and its occupants. She noticed an older truck driver who looked kind and seemed harmless. She could tell his age from his receding hairline, and his wiry frame did not hold much muscle. She reasoned they would be able to overpower him should the need arise. After choosing her target, she put on a smile and made her approach.

She stopped the man just as he was opening the door to the cab of his truck. "Excuse me, sir. Our car broke down, and we don't have enough cash on us to fix it. I was wondering if you might be so kind as to give us a ride for a while. We really need to get home and get some money to bring back." She did her best to sound pitiable.

The man scratched his head and thought for a moment. "It might be kind of close quarters in the cab, but I suppose I can do that if you're heading my way. Are you trying to head north?"

"Yes, sir. We're heading for Linwood. Do you think you could get us near there? We'd be grateful for any closer you could get us."

"Well, I can take you as far as Leland before I have to head farther west. How's that sound?" the man asked.

"Oh, that sounds perfect!" Julianna exclaimed. "Thank you so much!"

"Get on in," the man invited, motioning to the passenger side.

Declan walked around and opened the door, inviting Julianna to step up first.

Once everyone was seated in the cab, the man asked, "What's your names?"

"I'm Rose, and this is Connor," Julianna improvised, using her middle name and modifying his last name.

"Nice to meet you," he said with a nod. "My name's Hank." The man skillfully maneuvered the semi truck onto the highway. "You said your car broke down? What happened?"

"We had a transmission issue," Declan improvised. "Nothing cheap, of course."

Hank chuckled. "It never is. You two from Linwood then?"

"Yes," Julianna said. "We're trying to get home so we can get the money for the repairs and get a ride from someone back to the station then." She sighed. "Our car is getting old. It finally got us good, and now our whole day has turned into an adventure."

"Well, really, what are you to do in this day and age?" Hank mused. "You're lucky you have any kind of car. With this economy and all." He shook his head. "Nothing like the good old days. That's for darn sure."

Julianna cast a sideways glance at Declan who returned her smile. They could get some valuable information out of their newfound friend. "I keep hoping this economy is going to turn around, but who knows when," she said.

"Likely no time soon. The New Regime can't be having us Workers make too much money. Have to keep us under Costma's thumb. We're all just working for him now." He gave them a look. "You're probably too young to really remember how it used to be. Before the classifications, before the attacks, a man could make an honest living doing whatever he chose to do."

"I remember that, but not very well," Julianna said. "Were you a truck driver back then too?"

"I was. I owned my own trucking business. A few other fellas and me all drove trucks that I owned. My wife ran the office and handled all the logistics and the billing."

"You don't do that now?" Declan inquired.

"I really miss those days, but they're long gone. My wife died in the attacks. She was trapped inside a building when it collapsed. She was alive for a while, but they weren't able to get to her in time. It was slow going, moving the debris, trying to keep from making a bad situation worse. She lost too much blood from her initial injuries. As for the other trucks, two were out on the road and totaled in accidents that day. A third one was stolen from my lot. I guess someone thought that would be a good way to try to make their escape from the chaos. Poor fool actually thought there was someplace to escape to, I suppose. The only one to make it through was Old Trusty here." He patted the dashboard.

"Very sorry to hear about the loss of your wife," Julianna said. She paused for a minute then asked, "You didn't buy new trucks after the attacks?"

"With what money? None of the insurance companies honored any of those attack claims. With the computer hacking on top of the attacks, it was all one big mess. Nobody could get any money. Then the New Regime came in and started controlling the transportation prices, so it would be nearly impossible for me to get back to that same level I was beforehand. I'd just never make enough to buy a second truck. I had to let all my other drivers go. They understood, of course, but it was still tough."

"That's terrible," Julianna said.

"Yep," Hank agreed. "But not really much I can do about it. It's not like I'm the only one. There's a million stories like mine."

Julianna gave Declan a shocked look. This information was in stark contrast to the stories they had been fed in the New Regime's propaganda films.

Hank shook his head again. "It's true what they say. You just don't appreciate what you have until it's gone."

For the rest of the ride, Julianna was careful to direct the conversation toward Hank's history and his plans for the immediate future. She thought that was safer than she and Declan trying to concoct fictitious lives on the fly.

At one point, Hank mentioned, "At least as Workers, we still have some more freedom than those poor kids who were dragged away to be Scholars or Warriors."

"Sure," Julianna agreed with a grin. "We do have more freedom."

The ride to Leland passed by rather quickly, and soon Hank was dropping them off at the outskirts of town. "Do you have enough cash on you to get yourselves something to eat?" Hank asked them as Declan opened the cab door.

"No, but we'll be okay," Julianna answered.

"Now, there's no sense in you going hungry." He took a bill out of his wallet and handed it to them. "Here you go. That should be plenty for the diner right across the street there."

Julianna gave him a grateful smile. "Thank you so much! Both for lunch and the ride."

Declan helped Julianna down the step of the truck. She hopped to the ground, and they set off for the small cafe with a neon open sign lit in the window. A bell chimed over the door when they walked inside. A waitress turned around from behind the counter and invited them to take a seat anywhere they liked. When they had selected a booth out of the way, the waitress brought them each a menu. "Can I get you something to drink?" she asked them.

"I'll just take a water," Declan replied.

Julianna suddenly smiled and tapped his leg with her foot under the table. "What have you got?"

The waitress ran down an extensive list of sodas, juices and lemonades.

"I'll have the pink lemonade!" she said, trying her best not to sound weirdly happy and overexcited about lemonade.

"Coming right up," the waitress said before strolling away.

Declan leaned across the table. "Is it sad that it never even occurred to me to order something other than water?"

Julianna nodded. "Definitely! It's very sad. Would you like me to call her back and get you a cola?"

"No, it's okay," Declan smiled. "Just remind me the next time."

"You got it," Julianna said as she opened her menu to study it.

"Don't forget we're on a budget here," Declan reminded her. "You can't order a whole pie or anything."

Julianna laughed. "Of course. I don't want to overdose on the sugar yet anyway. I need to stay sharp at least until we get where we're going."

Declan asked her, "Hey, do you suppose there would be a bus that runs from here to Linwood? And if so, how much do you think it would cost?"

"As far as costs, I have no idea. From the little that I've seen, prices seem a bit skewed from what I remember. Maybe someone here could answer that question."

When the waitress returned with their glasses, Declan asked her his question. "Sure, the bus stops just down the block."

"How much does it cost?"

"I'm not sure what you mean," she replied.

"How much for a bus ticket?"

She gave him a funny look.

CHAPTER 11

"You don't have to pay for bus tickets. It's public transportation. Where are you from that they make you pay for bus tickets? Someone's been taking you for a ride in more ways than one, honey!"

Julianna and Declan exchanged a look of joy. Neither could believe their luck. Apparently, the New Regime provided public transportation services to Workers at no cost. They each placed their dinner order before the waitress walked away.

"I suppose that's one way to make sure no one has the excuse of not being able to get to work," Julianna said.

"Who cares about the why!" Declan exclaimed. "I'm just glad it works out in our favor."

"Thank you, Guardian," Julianna said sarcastically.

They enjoyed their lunch without worrying about sparing enough money for bus fees. When the waitress returned with their check, she told them, "You had better skedaddle if you don't want to miss the next bus." She turned her wrist to look at a watch. "It's due in about 15 minutes."

Julianna picked up the check and headed to the cash register to pay. The waitress took her money and said,

"Now you're going to want to head to the corner of Elm and Church Streets." She pointed in the direction they would need to head. She gave Declan a sympathetic look. "And seriously, honey, if you have someone who has been charging you to ride a bus, you might want to report them. That's just not right."

Declan nodded. "Thank you, ma'am."

Julianna handed her some money back for a tip. "Safe travels," the woman waved as they walked out the door with the tinkering bell.

As they walked down the street, Julianna reached over and took Declan's hand. "Have I told you just how happy I am that you decided to join me on this crazy adventure? I would never be having this much fun if I were all by myself."

"And I would never be having this much fun if I were sitting in a lab all by myself, so I guess we're stuck with each other." He gave her hand a little squeeze.

They made it to the bus stop with time to sit on the bench under a shade tree and wait. When the large bus braked to a stop in front of them, the doors parted and a bus driver greeted them. "Need a ride?"

"Yes, sir," Julianna said as she hopped to her feet.

"We're going to Linwood," Declan explained.

"Lucky for you, that's where this bus is headed," the driver said with no emotion. "Get in."

They got on the bus and walked a few rows back before taking a seat. While there were a few riders here and there, the bus was largely empty, which Julianna found to be a relief. She thought that the fewer people they encountered, the less their chance of being recognized and possibly caught. She was certain that the New Regime eventually would utilize the media, hoping to enlist the Workers in the search for them if the Warriors had not succeeded. Yet, she was not really too worried because she was having too much fun relishing the simple pleasures of her newfound freedom to worry about when or how it might end. She also could take comfort in the fact that so far no one had even given them much of a second look. She looked out the window at the blue sky and the trees flying past and smiled peacefully. Even if it all ended tomorrow, this time was worth it to her. She thought she would never take for granted the ability to walk around wherever she liked. She could not imagine ever being forced to return to the Scholars Compound.

She sighed contentedly and rested her head on Declan's shoulder. She had not slept well in the cave and the soothing sway of the bus was beginning to make her feel the effects of a restless night. Declan looked down at her and smiled. He was so happy he had decided to take this chance with her. He knew this extreme measure was something on which he never would have embarked on his own, but Julianna had made it seem like a possibility. Now he was being richly rewarded for taking the risk.

When the bus rolled into Linwood, Declan gently nudged Julianna to wake her. "I'm home," he whispered with a hint of excitement.

Julianna opened her eyes and blinked a few times. She looked out the window as the sun was sinking lower to the horizon and glowing a soft pink. The bus drove through a residential neighborhood with houses nestled on green lawns in neat rows. The bus headed toward the heart of the town and stopped in the middle of a street lined with small shops and offices. The bus driver opened the door and announced, "Main Street of Linwood. Only Linwood stop for this bus."

Declan and Julianna rose and walked to the door. "Thank you, sir," Declan said to the bus driver as they disembarked.

Once they were standing on Main Street, Declan smiled and slowly looked up and down the block. He sighed. Julianna smiled up at him. "Good to be home?" she asked.

He put an arm around her shoulder and hugged her to him. "More than you know."

"Which way home?" Julianna asked.

He put his hands on her shoulders and pointed her south. "This way," he said.

Julianna skipped down the street. "I can't wait to meet your mother," she said. "Oh my gosh! I bet she will be so surprised and happy to see you. What do you think she'll do?"

"Smile and hug me, I hope," he said with a laugh.

"How far away is your house?"

"Not much farther now. We're a couple blocks away. I used to walk to the shops downtown when I was a kid to get candy. Colin and I liked to go there whenever we got a few dollars from our grandpa or something like that."

When they reached a block with a park, Declan took her hand and pulled her toward the center. "If we cut straight across the park, we'll get there faster," he explained.

"Too bad we're in such a hurry or we could stop and swing for a bit," Julianna said. "Don't you want to swing again?"

Declan chuckled. "I wouldn't have said it was on my short list of things I wanted to do, but I'd give you a few pushes."

"Even better," she smiled.

Before long, they were standing in front of a cute white brick ranch home. "This is it," Declan announced. "This is my house."

He took one deep breath and ran to the front door. Julianna tagged along close behind. Declan pushed the doorbell, listened to make sure it chimed inside the house and then tapped his foot impatiently as he waited for someone to come to the door. An older gentleman with a balding head answered the door. He wore a navy sweater and pushed his glasses farther up on his nose as he looked at the couple on his doorstep with an expectant smile. "Hello," he greeted.

"Hello," Declan replied, somewhat taken aback by the man. Julianna could tell immediately that Declan did not recognize him from his past. "We're looking for Kate O'Connor. Does she still live here?"

The man's smile faded. "Oh my, are you relation of hers?"

"Yes," Declan replied without getting specific.

"Well, do come inside," the man invited as he pushed the door open wider. "My name is Pastor Rollins. I met Kate at when she attended my church. Please have a seat." He followed them into the living room and motioned to the sofa while he took a seat in an armchair. Declan could not help but notice he recognized none of this furniture.

"You said you were relation of Kate's. Are you her niece or nephew?"

Declan glanced at Julianna and answered, "I'm her nephew. This is my friend, Rose. I'm Matthew." He held his hand out to the pastor. When the pastor shook Declan's hand, Julianna followed suit.

"Well, Matthew, I'm sorry to be the bearer of bad news, but ..." The man hesitated, and Declan's breath caught in his throat. "Your aunt is not here. She is in Shady Oaks nursing home in a town about 15 minutes west of here, Oakland. Are you familiar with it?"

Declan was silent for a moment as he absorbed the fact that at least his mother was still alive. Yet, obviously, something was very wrong with her. He blinked a few times and tried to bring himself fully back to the conversation. "Yes, I'm familiar with Oakland. Not really Shady Oaks. Why is she in Shady Oaks? Forgive me, but I haven't heard anything about this."

"No, you wouldn't have. We didn't know she had any family left. We knew her ex-husband had perished in the attacks, and then both of her sons were removed when the New Regime launched the initial aptitude testing. I was unaware that she had any other relation, so we at the church did not notify anyone."

"What happened to her?" Julianna prompted again as she put a comforting hand on Declan's knee.

"She began to suffer from early onset Alzheimer's disease. She got pretty bad at an alarming rate. She had put me down as an emergency contact on some form at her doctor's office at one point, so they would call the church on the occasions when she would wander off and the police would find her lost somewhere without knowing how to get home. Some of the ladies from the church's women's group would take turns coming here each day to make sure she had taken care of herself. They made sure she had something to eat, tidied up, took her to appointments as needed, made sure she took her medicine, that sort of thing."

"Thank you for that!" Declan said. "Please thank them all for me."

"Of course, but then one day, one of the ladies came here and smelled gas. Kate had left a burner on the stove on with a kitchen towel very, very close to the flames. It's only by the grace of God that this entire place did not catch fire."

Julianna gasped. She could not imagine how heartbroken Declan would have been to find a burnt out shell where his home had been, with his mother nowhere in sight and no one to offer an explanation.

"You understand after that point, we thought it best to put her in a facility where she would be supervised and get the care she needs," the pastor explained. "If you would like to visit her, I can show you how to get there. I'll even give you a ride tomorrow, but I don't know if she'll remember you or be able to talk to you much. Do you know what I'm saying?" he asked gently.

"I do," Declan answered. "But I'd still like to see her just the same, if you would be so kind as to take me. We took the bus to Linwood and walked here."

"Most definitely," the pastor answered. "I was just about to get myself some dinner. Would you like to join me?"

Julianna smiled. "That would be wonderful! You're so kind to ask."

Declan and Julianna joined the pastor in the dining area of the kitchen while he served them each a generous portion of chicken and noodles from an aluminum pan. "The church ladies still make sure I have plenty to eat too, since my wife passed on," the pastor explained, motioning to the disposable cookware.

"Oh, we're sorry to hear about your wife," Julianna said. She felt awful about having to say that for a second time that day.

"Thank you for your condolences, but she was very sick and suffered much. She's in a better place now," the pastor said.

Julianna was curious, so she asked, "How did you wind up living here, Pastor?"

"When Kate got sick, the church board decided to sell the old parsonage. I was fine with that because I had too many memories there. I wanted a fresh start. They decided to rent this house from Kate and use the rent money to pay for her care at Shady Oaks. It seemed like an ideal solution for everyone."

"Thank you for that," Declan said, near tears. "Thank you for taking care of my … my aunt."

"Not a problem at all. I enjoy this house. Not as many steps as my old house, and at my age, that's got to count for something!" He took a bite of chicken before he asked, "You mentioned you took the bus here. Do you have a place to stay the night?"

"No, we don't," Declan admitted. "We had planned on staying with Aunt Kate."

"I insist you stay here then," the pastor offered. "There are two extra bedrooms, and the furniture in those rooms are as Kate left them. They belonged to her sons, and she left them the same in case either of them ever returned. I certainly didn't need the space, and I didn't have the heart to do anything else with them. They are yours for as long as you need them."

"Thank you so much!" Julianna exclaimed. She could tell Declan was too emotional to speak.

"To tell you the truth, I don't think she fought the memory loss," the pastor said. "I think she had just experienced too much pain. Perhaps the good Lord did her the favor of erasing some of those painful memories."

Julianna nodded sympathetically while Declan concentrated very hard on the casserole on his dinner plate.

When they had finished eating, Julianna helped the pastor clean away the dishes and offered to wash them. Declan said he would dry if the pastor would put away the dishes. They finished the task in no time.

"You must be tired from your journey, and you've learned a lot of unfortunate news today. Let me show you to your rooms," the pastor offered.

Declan and Julianna followed him down the hall. The pastor opened the door to Colin's old room first. Julianna could tell because his name was spelled with block letters painted in primary colors that adorned the wall above the twin bed. The room was decorated with images of old superheroes. A stack of comic books sat on the dresser. The closet door was slightly ajar and filled with clothes that would surely be much too small for Colin today. "Here's one room."

"I'll take this one," Julianna offered as she dropped her backpack on the floor near his small desk.

Declan followed the pastor to a door just a little way across the hall. The pastor pushed that door open and said, "Here's the other."

Declan took a deep breath as he looked into his old familiar bedroom and took in the sight he thought he would never have seen again. He could not believe he was here, and he silently reminded himself to thank Julianna again for bringing him with her. He needed to thank her for suggesting that they come to Linwood and the O'Connor residence first when she could have said she was heading straight for Greta. It may be for only one night, but he was going to spend the night at home, in his own bed. For that, he would be forever grateful to Julianna. He took a step into the room and was overcome with emotion and memories.

He remembered being a child in his room and his father getting down on the floor with him and running toy cars around on the rug. He remembered sitting at the desk and doing his homework, and his mom would ruffle his hair, give him a kiss on the head and tell him what a good boy he was when she came with his clean laundry. He remembered playing around and roughhousing with Colin on the floor. He remembered reading under the covers with a flashlight after his mother had told him it was bedtime. This room had been his haven. It had been where he went when he needed a break and wanted to relax, when he needed time to think about things, and when he was sad or angry and just needed to get away from everyone else.

This room was probably his most favorite place in the whole world.

"I'll let the two of you rest. I'll be in the study reading for a while if you need anything. The bathroom's down the hallway. Fresh towels are in the cabinet if you would like to shower," the pastor said as he walked away.

Julianna gave Declan a moment alone before she appeared in his doorway. She leaned against the door frame and looked around the room. Declan's room was decorated in a sports car theme. The comforter was decorated with lots of fast-looking red cars. Several posters of cars from Ferraris to Porsches dotted the cornflower blue walls. A square wooden unit with several tiny cubbies held an assortment of metal toy cars. When Declan still had not turned around to look at her after a minute, she softly asked, "Are you okay?"

Declan's eyes brimmed with tears when he turned to meet her eyes. She crossed the room in a few quick steps and engulfed him in a tight hug. He hugged her back and finally let his tears flow. "I can't believe I'm here," he whispered to her when he was finally able to speak.

"I'm so sorry about your mom," she whispered back, hugging him a little tighter.

"I'm just so happy she's alive. When he started talking tonight, I thought for sure he was going to tell me she had died. I'm so glad she had people to look out for her and care for her when I couldn't be here." Declan pulled away and held her by her shoulders so he could look into her eyes. "Thank you. From the bottom of my heart, thank you for bringing me back here. Thank you for letting me come with you. I didn't know how much it meant to me until I was back here in this room."

Julianna smiled modestly as her own eyes misted. "Now you're going to make me cry. You do know I would've never left without you, right?"

He did not really believe that, but he smiled back anyway.

She glanced around the room again. "I must say, I had no idea you were so into cars."

Declan shrugged. "Really wasn't any point when we were in the Compound. It wasn't like I was ever going to have the opportunity to drive any of them."

"True," Julianna agreed. "Still, I'm surprised you didn't lean more toward the engineering wing if you enjoyed cars so much."

"I just wanted to drive them fast. I didn't want to build them," Declan explained.

Julianna touched his arm. "Well, I should let you get some rest. You have a big day ahead of you tomorrow."

He pulled her into another hug before she walked out of the room. "I really, truly mean it. Thank you so much."

She reached out and gently wiped a lingering teardrop from his cheek before she returned to Colin's room. Once she had shut the door and put on her pajamas, she decided to explore the room for a bit. She thumbed through the comic books on the dresser and rifled through the small clothes hanging in the closet. Then she pulled open the desk drawer. She found a notebook that had some childlike drawings in it. One of them featured two stick figure boys with large heads, wearing what appeared to be baseball caps and with their little stick arms around each other's shoulders. Julianna imagined the boys were Colin and Declan. In a smaller drawer, she found a few photographs.

For the first time ever, she saw what Declan's family looked like as Declan liked to remember. This was the family she had grown to know from his Happy Memories. One photo featured the entire family, mother, father and children, standing at the entrance to a zoo, all of them smiling happily for the camera. Another photo featured Colin with his father. A third one featured Mr. O'Connor flanked by his two sons, both wearing baseball uniforms. Julianna surmised that Colin had been given the snapshots after his father had left.

Declan did not really talk very much about his parents' divorce. Julianna knew his father had lost his job when his employer went out of business, which caused stress on the family. Then his father had accepted a position at another company on the East coast. Mrs. O'Connor had been opposed to him accepting the position because she did not want to move the children and disrupt their lives. Mr. O'Connor was more concerned with being able to financially provide for his family and could not fathom turning down the job offer. He agreed to move without the family at first. Declan thought it was just going to be on a trial basis, but eventually his parents decided it would be best to divorce. Julianna thought there might have been something else going on with his parents' relationship for them to take such a drastic step, but she would never suggest that to Declan. According to Declan, his parents did not display much animosity; the distance had come between them.

She examined the two photos with Declan more closely. Declan had been an adorable child. In one of the photos, his grin displayed a large gap where his two front teeth should have been. It would have been easy to guess he would grow up to be a handsome man, but even at this young age, the physical differences between Declan and Colin were evident. Declan's tall, wiry frame was a stark contrast to Colin's more solid build. As she placed the photos back inside the desk drawer, she wondered where Colin was today and if he would ever get to experience a homecoming like his older brother.

As Julianna crawled underneath the covers of the twin bed, she smiled as she closed her eyes, proud of herself and her decision to leave the Compound. She slept peacefully and deeply that night.

The sunlight already streamed through the bright green bedroom curtains when Julianna awoke the next morning. The kind pastor had set out a couple boxes of cereal on the kitchen counter.

"I'm afraid I'm not much in the kitchen," he admitted. "I have some instant oatmeal also, if you would prefer that."

Julianna picked up a box of sugared flakes and smiled. "No, this will do just fine. Actually, I can't think of anything I'd rather eat right now. I really love these things." She shook the box for emphasis and made a mental note to try to put her sugar glee in check so as not to appear weird to everyone who had been able to eat sugar whenever they wanted for all these years. She was afraid this might reveal herself as a Scholar, but then again, she wondered, maybe the Workers had been fed the same propaganda about how wonderful life is as a Scholar. Surely they would have to think there was some advantage to it if people continued to allow their children to be taken away years after the initial shock of the life-altering attacks had subsided.

Meanwhile, Declan was finding it difficult to leave his bedroom. He wanted to drag out the moment as long as possible and relish every last second. Finally, he decided to head for the shower down the hallway. He knew it was likely just his imagination, but he thought the water was warmer and more soothing than any shower he had ever taken at the Compound. As he was drying off, he caught a glimpse of himself in the mirror over the sink. He studied the face staring back at him. He had changed vastly since the last time he had looked at himself in that mirror. Gone was the boy who was unsure of himself, the boy who did not know who he was or where he wanted to end up in life. Now he was a man who still may not always be completely confident in everything he did, but he was willing to take chances, and while he may not know even where this day would take him, he knew what was important to him now.

Julianna popped a spoonful of cereal in her mouth when he finally walked into the kitchen. "Good morning," she greeted him cheerfully.

"Good morning," he returned.

The pastor smiled at him. "Good morning, Matthew. Would you like to get started right away for Oakland? I'm free until this evening. I have a meeting later, but I'm all yours for most of the day."

Declan's face broke out into a wide smile at the thought of seeing his mother again, even if her condition was compromised. "I'd like to head out as soon as possible."

"Very well then," the pastor agreed. "We'll head out as soon as you've had a bite to eat."

CHAPTER 12

Julianna sat in the back seat of Pastor Rollins' small economy car, giving Declan's tall frame more leg room in the front seat next to the pastor. She did not mind at all; she was relieved they would not be walking or hitchhiking to Oakland. She watched Declan affectionately and could tell his body was tense with anticipation. She was overjoyed for him. She knew how much it would have meant to her to see her own mother again, and she was glad she was able to do that for her beloved friend.

The friends and the pastor engaged in amiable conversation as they drove the highway toward Oakland. "Pastor, do you have any children?" Julianna asked.

"No, my wife and I never were blessed with a child of our own, but we both were very involved with the youth ministry once upon a time," he answered.

"But no longer?" she inquired.

"I'm afraid we pulled away from that work after the attacks. It just became too painful, especially for my wife. We would bond with and grow attached to children who would be taken away and never heard from again. To be perfectly honest, I was kind of glad that we never did have children. I could not imagine living through the pain that someone like Kate experienced."

Julianna was careful in how she worded her next question. "Do you suppose most people feel that way?"

"Most of the people I know are horrified at the prospect of the aptitude testing. Perhaps there are some who think having a child named a Scholar or a Warrior is some sort of status symbol, but I would think they are few and far between. Having your own flesh and blood present in your life is far more important," he explained. "When the New Regime begins their testing each year, you certainly have a lot of worried parents. The problem now is in how they conduct the tests."

"How so?" Declan asked. "It's been a long time since we took our tests. We're not really familiar with what goes on in schools now."

"Well, I think the New Regime caught on to people who told their children not to do well on the aptitude testing for fear of losing them. Instead, the New Regime will work in random testing at some point in the school year on various assignments. The students do not know this is the aptitude test until they have completed it."

"Wow," Julianna said. "I had no idea that's what goes on now."

"It's a very scary thing for parents and children both, as you can imagine."

Julianna decided to be bold. "Why do you suppose no one does anything about it? Why do parents just accept it?"

"They really don't have a choice. The New Regime is the law of the land. They have all the power. If a parent were to deny the New Regime their child, it would accomplish nothing but getting the parent thrown in jail and the child removed anyway. There's no way to win."

"Surely, though, the people could work together to stop this kind of thing."

"If people would have worked together and not given in to fear, the New Regime would have never come into power. But unfortunately, that's not the case. People looked the other way as their liberties were chipped away little by little. Everyone expected someone else to do something about it. But no one did. That's how we wound up in this situation, in my opinion."

Oakland was a bigger town than Linwood, and Julianna had learned many people in Linwood made frequent trips to Oakland for goods and services. Nowadays, they often took advantage of the free busing provided by the New Regime. In the course of his conversation, Pastor Rollins was very careful to not be overly critical of the New Regime, but he also never sang their praises. He seemed to make every effort to remain perfectly neutral.

Finally, they pulled up in front of Shady Oaks, a pleasant-looking facility with well-kept grounds. As he stepped out of the car, Declan thought his heart might burst with excitement. He followed the lead of Pastor Rollins as they entered the building. Pastor Rollins wrote his name in the guest log, and Julianna and Declan followed suit, scribbling their aliases in barely legible penmanship. They followed the pastor down the west corridor until he stopped at room 145. Pastor Rollins knocked tentatively on the door and paused before he walked inside.

"Good morning, Kate," he greeted.

Kate O'Connor turned to look at the man expectantly.

"I've brought a special visitor for you," the pastor continued and held his arm inviting Declan to enter.

Declan walked slowly into the room, careful not to frighten her, while he was fighting back his own tears and reminding himself he was supposed to be only her nephew. Kate's face lit up with recognition as she brought a shaking hand to her face. "Declan!" she said. "I thought I'd never see you again."

She held out her arms to him, and Declan rushed toward her.

To cover the moment, Julianna whispered to the pastor, "Matthew looks a lot like her oldest son, Declan."

The pastor nodded sympathetically. "It's probably best that he plays along for now. We don't want to upset her," he said loudly enough for Declan to hear.

Declan looked at him and nodded, grateful to Julianna once again for her brilliance. He had been so consumed with thoughts of seeing his mother again that he had never bothered to think what would happen if she called him by name.

"We'll leave you two alone for a while," Julianna suggested. The pastor followed her lead, and they headed for a recreation area.

Julianna picked up a magazine and looked forward to reading about a world she no longer fully understood. She wanted to see the world that the Workers saw because the Workers were the closest classification to the people and world in which she had grown up, and she wanted that world back.

Declan, meanwhile, was enjoying his reunion with his mother, who was quite lucid for the moment.

How have you been?" Declan asked her.

"I've been better, of course," she replied. "Some well-meaning people put me in here because they think I can't take care of myself anymore. I didn't argue with them because I'm not so sure that I can."

"I'm sorry I couldn't be there for you," he said.

"That was hardly your fault!" she cried. "Those monsters stole you away, and I let them. Have they at least treated you well?"

"Yes, Mom. I've been treated well. The Compound actually is a very nice facility. We have a pool, gym, basketball courts, a nice wooded area, and I have my own bedroom. Plus, I really enjoy my work." He was determined to make the Compound sound like a glorious place so that his mother did not have to feel an ounce of guilt or sadness about his lot in life.

"What do you do there?" she asked.

"I work in the medical wing," he explained. "I help them develop new medicines and treatments for various health conditions. I work with the most wonderful girl. Her name is," he paused and decided to say, "Rose. She's brilliant. She can speed read, and she has the most amazing memory. She never forgets a thing!"

"It sounds like you really like her," Kate smiled knowingly.

"She's my best friend. We do nearly everything together. When we first arrived at the Compound, she asked if I wanted to be her friend, and we've been together ever since."

"What about Colin?" Kate asked. "Do you ever see Colin?"

That same image of Colin being dragged away down the school hallway flashed across Declan's mind. "No," he said, lowering his head. "I haven't seen Colin since the school."

Kate looked down for a moment before looking up with a smile again. "But I have you now. You're here." She thought for a second and then asked, "How are you here?"

Declan smiled sadly. "I'm only here for a moment. I can't stay. I'm not supposed to be here, and I have to keep moving."

"Are you in danger?" his mother asked with concern.

"No, I'm not in danger," he fibbed. "I just came to see you, but I'm not allowed to stay for long."

His mother sighed with relief. "Do you think they'll let Colin visit me someday too?"

"Maybe, Mom," he said with false hope.

"I want you to tell me all about your work. What have you been doing since I left you at the Scholars Compound. And I want to hear all about your friend, Rose."

Declan smiled and spent the rest of the afternoon catching up with his mother, even though he knew she likely would retain none of it tomorrow.

Once they returned to Linwood, Pastor Rollins had encouraged them to spend another night in the home. He had a meeting to attend at his church that evening, but he invited them to use his laundry room and help themselves to one of the church ladies' casseroles for their dinner. He warned them he might be late since the chairperson of this particular committee tended to be a little long-winded.

While Julianna started a load of their laundry, Declan warmed up some spaghetti pie for their dinner, knowing that Julianna was still enjoying the carb loading that would have never been permitted at the Compound. After they had finished dinner, Declan invited her to go for a walk around the nearby park they had passed on their way to the house.

"Did you used to play here?" Julianna asked him.

"Yes," Declan answered. "We had a small swing set in the backyard, but going to the park was a treat. It usually was our reward for doing something well or behaving when my mom really wanted us to be nice." He walked her to the swings and bowed before offering her a seat on one. "Would you like a push?"

She curtsied back and took the swing. Declan pushed her while she stuck her feet straight out to avoid accidentally kicking him. When Declan pushed her and ran underneath her swing, she squealed in joy. Declan took the seat next to her, and they both pumped their legs, trying to see who could swing higher. When they had had enough, they gradually stopped their swings. Julianna grabbed onto Declan's chain to bring herself to a complete stop.

"Did you enjoy today?" she asked him.

"I really, really did," he answered.

She smiled. "I'm glad. I wasn't sure if it might also be a bit difficult for you. To see your mom in that condition."

"I was lucky that she was very lucid today. For the majority of our conversation, she seemed to keep her wits about her. She had a few slips here and there, but I feel like I got her back for a day."

"Good!"

"As I was talking to her though, I did get a little angry," Declan admitted.

"About what?"

"I started thinking that if we were allowed any kind of contact with the outside world, I might have known she was suffering from Alzheimer's. Think of all the time we spent working on heart disease." He looked at Julianna and put up a hand. "Don't get me wrong! I've always been proud of all the work we've done as far as the advancements we made in cardiology. But think about what we might have done if we had put those efforts toward Alzheimer's. I think we really could have helped her. I think we could have made a difference."

"That's true, but you can't discount the difference we've made to everyone who has heart issues," Julianna said soothingly.

"I know," Declan replied. He looked into her eyes. "But right now, all I keep thinking about is who in the Costma family suffers from a heart problem. I'm guessing that's the reason they had us focused on cardiology for so many years. If you'll remember, it wasn't our idea. We just learned a lot about the cardiovascular system and got really comfortable with it."

Julianna nodded slowly. She had never really given much thought as to why they initially were charged with working in cardiology. She always had attributed it to the fact that it was a common malady among much of the population. She had never suspected anything self-serving about it, but maybe Declan was right. Maybe heart disease ran in the Costma family and Guardian was hedging his bets by putting his best Scholars on it. The thought made her feel nauseous. She could not stand to think about it much longer. "Just the thought of that makes me sick. Can we please talk about something else?" she asked softly.

"Of course," Declan replied.

Instead, they decided to discuss their plans for the next leg of their journey. Tomorrow, they would head for Springdale, Julianna's hometown, in search of Greta.

Colin O'Connor walked into the meeting of the Warriors feeling overwhelmingly curious. He wondered what could have been so important that the New Regime leaders had called this unprecedented meeting of the Warriors. Never before in Colin's recollection had they ever called such a mass meeting of the Warriors forces. Every Warrior in his geographic region had been summoned to the headquarters for what they were being told was "a very important message from Guardian Costma."

Colin took a seat in the assembly room next to another Warrior, to whom he courteously acknowledged with a nod that was returned, but neither of them spoke. Everyone seemed to be greatly anticipating this message and wondering what possibly could be the cause. Colin looked around the assembly room and thought it looked very cold and sterile. He sat on a standard metal folding chair, and everything around him was either a stark white, drab gray or metallic, with the exception of the Warriors cherry red uniforms. About ten minutes later, a man dressed in the New Regime wardrobe that Colin thought looked a bit ridiculous stepped onto the stage.

Colin recognized the man as Leader Cantor, one of the higher-ups in the New Regime. He rapped the podium with a gavel and authoritatively asked for everyone's attention. The Warriors in the room immediately fell silent and gave him their rapt attention. "I am here today to inform you of an unprecedented situation most disturbing which has arisen out of the Scholars

Compound. It seems two of our Scholars have managed to escape the Compound."

A low murmur rushed through the crowd while Cantor turned to the large screen behind him and pushed a button on a remote control. A badge photo of a smiling young blonde girl filled the screen. Colin could not help but think she must be the prettiest, least threatening fugitive he had seen. "This is Julianna Brenner," he continued. "She is one of the escapees. She has surviving family in the Springdale area and could be heading in that direction. Most recently, she had been working on a very important task assigned directly by Guardian Costma. It is a matter of national security that she be found and returned, alive and well, to the Scholars Compound. I cannot stress this enough. It is *imperative* that she be found."

Cantor hit the remote again and flipped to a new photograph. Colin's eyes grew wide with shock, and he felt his face flush red. Cantor continued, "This is Declan O'Connor." Colin hoped against hope that none of his peers would make the connection that Declan was his brother. He battled feelings of humiliation and tried not to let his reaction give his secret away.

"He is the second escapee," Cantor said. "He and Brenner have been partners for the entirety of their time at the Compound. He also was working on the project for Guardian Costma. He is originally from the Linwood area and may be heading for family located there. In the course of their escape, they attacked and drugged a guard to use her fingerprint to escape through the shipping dock. We are unsure if they are armed, but they are highly intelligent and considered extremely resourceful, which could make them dangerous."

Dangerous was never a word he would have used to describe his older brother. He thought of his last image of his brother. Colin had screamed for him to help, but "dangerous" Declan had stood rooted to the floor, too afraid to move. Colin knew he was out of hope when his brother disappeared from his sight, having never moved a muscle to come to Colin's aid. At first, Colin had blamed him when he was deposited in the Warriors Training Facility without even a chance to say goodbye to his mother. He used that anger to excel in Warrior training, and he advanced quickly through the ranks once he decided he might as well accept his lot in life. As he grew older, Colin had forgiven Declan. He understood how frightened Declan must have been. Besides, did Declan really stand a chance in a fight with two full-grown men? Once Colin realized the answer had been, "Of course not," he was able to let go of his angry disappointment.

Now the New Regime had put a target on his brother and labeled him dangerous. Unless Declan had changed considerably in recent years, Colin found the whole idea almost laughable.

"They are believed to have made their escape in this vehicle," Cantor flashed to a photo of a luxury car. "This car is stored in the dock and went missing the same time. The return of the car, while not of vital importance, also would be most appreciated. This meeting has been called to apprise all Warriors of the situation. Every one of you is being asked to keep your eyes open and be on high alert. While they may be heading for their homes, the real reason for their escape and their intended destination is unknown. They may not have strayed very far at all. No sightings of the vehicle have been reported. The media has been made aware of them, and citizens have been advised to be on the lookout. However, we need every Warrior to be very diligent about this as well. In addition to a small reward being on the table for their captors, Guardian Costma would be extremely grateful for your efforts. Full details have been delivered to your electronic message boxes. Thank you for your service and good luck to you all," Cantor concluded in a business-like manner. Then he quickly walked from the stage, his cape flowing behind him.

Conversation was abuzz all around him, but Colin could not bring himself to join. He stared straight ahead and tried to wrap his head around what had just happened and exactly how he should feel about it.

The following morning, Julianna and Declan prepared to leave Declan's old home and Linwood. Pastor Rollins packed them some lunches of sandwiches, fruit and potato chips for their travels. If they caught the first bus out of Linwood, they could be in Springdale right before nightfall, giving them enough time to locate Julianna's old house while the sunlight still lingered. Julianna hugged the pastor and thanked him once again for his kindness, knowing it had meant the world to Declan to be home again. Declan vigorously shook his hand and thanked him profusely.

"I'm happy I could help. I'm just sorry your aunt did not recognize you," he said with a shake of his head.

"Not a problem at all," Declan replied. "I'm glad I was able to make her happy and let her believe that she spent a day with her son."

"You're a good person," Pastor Rollins told him. "Here's my information." He pulled a business card out of his wallet. "Please keep in touch when you get back home. I'll keep you updated on your aunt."

"I would greatly appreciate it," Declan replied earnestly as he slipped the card in his backpack.

Pastor Rollins dropped them off at the corner where the bus would pick them up. They had fibbed about the direction they were headed just in case anybody caught on and asked questions. Before long, they were seated on a bus again.

The pastor had provided them with some magazines to help their travels pass quickly, so both engrossed themselves in the reading materials, learning as much as they could about the outside world and its people.

Much of what they had been led to believe while they were inside the Compound turned out to be misleading if not an outright lie. It turned out the Workers were not overly supportive or pleased with the leadership of the New Regime. They simply lacked the power or the resources to overcome the New Regime's oppressive rule. The New Regime was a true dictatorship and seemed to control everything from the marketplace to much of the electronic media, but it appeared true investigative journalism still existed in various forms of print media, which is what the pastor had provided to them.

One piece of material even provided an account of how they believed the New Regime was responsible for all the computer malfunctions that happened immediately following the attacks. Julianna assumed this was a conspiracy theory and nothing more because when the internet went down following the attacks, it only made sense to Julianna that it was part of a coordinated effort to cripple the country. She did believe the New Regime had used this to their advantage to step in and enforce their own rules, and people were either too shellshocked to protest or too scared about what may come next that no one protested.

When the lunch hour arrived, the bus made a stop at a diner, but Declan and Julianna stayed on the bus. Julianna passed Declan a sandwich and an apple that Pastor Rollins had provided to them. "Hope you like ham and cheese," she said. "Because that's what you get."

"Well, it's the right price, so I'll eat it," Declan kidded.

If they did not get off the bus, it would help keep their interactions with people to a minimum, so they ate their lunches from their bus seat partially hidden beneath baseball caps and sunglasses. Julianna had snagged an old cap from Declan's room, and Declan liked the way she looked in it. After the quick lunch break, the bus resumed its travels, occasionally stopping to pick up an additional rider or two. The duo enjoyed a peaceful trip watching the passing countryside.

Once again, Pastor Rollins opened his door wearing a friendly smile, but this time it quickly faded when he saw the Warriors standing on his doorstep.

"Can I help you?" Pastor Rollins asked.

"We are looking for Kate O'Connor or any member of her family," one of the Warriors stated in a business-like tone.

"I'm afraid Kate no longer resides here. What business do you have with her?"

"We're looking for her son, Declan O'Connor. He escaped," the other Warrior nudged him at the word choice. "He is missing from a Scholars Compound. He is presumed to be armed and dangerous. It is imperative we find him as soon as possible."

Pastor Rollins knew immediately that Declan had been his houseguest, but he just shook his head. "I wish I could help you, but Kate was taken a while ago to live in a nursing home."

"Do you have the name and address of the facility?" one asked. "If so, I will require it."

"Yes, of course," Pastor said. "However, I should tell you that she probably wouldn't be able to let you know if her son had tried to visit her. Kate suffers from Alzheimer's, and I'm afraid her lucid days are few and far between. I doubt a trip to the nursing home would prove very fruitful for you. I'd hate to see you waste your valuable time."

"Thank you for your concern, but we know what we need to do," another Warrior said as Pastor Rollins scribbled the name of the nursing home on the notepad sitting on a table just inside the door.

Pastor handed the paper to the man with a forced smile. "Safe travels," he said as he shut the door. He leaned against the door and said a silent prayer for the safety of his young visitors.

When the bus approached the first stop in Springdale, Julianna eagerly looked out of the window to see if she could tell exactly where she was. "I think this is it," she told Declan as she excitedly shook his arm. "I think we should get off here."

Declan nodded in appreciation to the driver as Julianna dashed down the steps and through the open door. Once her feet were on the ground, she threw her arms out wide and spun in a circle, giggling with delight. She lifted her knees a little too high as she stomped her feet and cried, "I'm here! I'm here! I'm here!" Then she looked at Declan who was grinning at her. "And *you're* here!" She jumped into his arms and squeezed him tightly. She squealed with excitement. "I can't believe it!"

Declan laughed as he hugged her back. "I hope you know your way home from here."

"I do! I do! Follow me!" She half-skipped and half-ran down the street.

Declan hustled to catch up with her. "Are you going to wait for me?" he teased.

"Come on, slowpoke! Catch me if you can!" she challenged.

He ran up behind her and grabbed her around the waist. "Hold up, silly girl! You don't want to draw attention to yourself!"

Julianna sighed. "Oh, okay. You're right," she agreed. She grabbed his hands and jumped up and down. "I'm just so happy! We're almost there!"

"How much farther?" Declan asked her, holding onto one of her hands.

"It's only two blocks from here."

Julianna felt like she was walking on air as they strolled down the last blocks between her and her home. She recognized many of the houses as she passed them and wondered if she would still know the people who lived in them. Finally, they rounded the corner of Ashley Drive, her old street. And there she saw the most glorious view she had seen in years.

Julianna fought back tears at the sight of the Colonial house, painted white with black shutters lining the windows. It looked exactly like she had remembered, and for the first time since their adventure started, she felt the relief of believing she was safe. For a moment, she stood rooted to the ground, just taking in the sight of the pretty house with its well-kept flower beds and shady trees, and feeling she was home.

Declan looked at her and noticed the emotion on her face, the same he had experienced in Linwood. "Excited to be here?"

CHAPTER 13

Julianna's giddiness returned. She grinned at him. "Excited to be *home!*" she replied. Then she dashed for the winding front sidewalk, leaping over a corner flower bed of tulips. Declan laughed and chased after her. Julianna rang the doorbell and anxiously shifted her weight from one foot to the other while impatiently waiting for someone to answer the door. When her sister swung open the door only seconds later, Julianna almost could not believe she actually was looking at Greta. Greta's initial welcoming smile faded into a look of delighted surprise.

"Julianna!" Greta exclaimed. After an initial moment of awe, she pulled her into a hug so tight that Julianna almost could not breathe. "Oh! You need to get inside!" She pulled Julianna through the threshold and then reached back for Declan's arm. "You too!"

When Greta shut the door, she turned the deadbolt. "You two have been on tv, you know. I don't think anyone in this neighborhood would rat you out, but it doesn't hurt to play it safe."

"What do you mean we've been on tv?" Julianna questioned.

"You've been reported on tv as fugitives wanted by the New Regime. There's a price on your head. I've been worried sick about you. I had no idea what happened to you. What is going on? Oh, you know, it really doesn't even matter. I'm just so happy to see you!" She hugged Julianna again. Then she turned to Declan and extended her hand. "You must be Declan O'Connor."

Declan smiled and shook her hand, "And you must be Greta. I've heard a lot about you."

"Wait! What accusation did the New Regime make against us?" Julianna asked.

"They didn't really specify," Greta said. "The newscast just showed a picture of each of you and said that you were wanted and assumed to be on the run. You must've known something was up by the looks of it." She fingered Julianna's shorter brown hair.

"We didn't do anything wrong," Julianna insisted. "All we did was leave the Scholars Compound."

"I don't care if you had permission or not to leave that horrible place," Greta replied.

"What makes you think it was a horrible place?" Declan asked out of curiosity.

"A place that essentially kidnaps smart kids from their family? And forces them to do the bidding of the New Regime? I was just guessing that it probably wasn't heaven on Earth. Not that it's that much greater out here, but at least we have a little bit of freedom left."

"Greta? What's up?" a voice asked from down a hallway.

"Sam, come here! There's someone I'd like you to meet," Greta called.

A handsome young man of about six feet walked into the room. His eyes bulged slightly at the sight of Julianna and Declan.

"Sam, this is Julianna," Greta said with a note of excitement in her voice. "I'm so glad you two can finally meet! Julianna, this is my husband Sam."

Julianna felt a twinge of pain at the fact that she was not aware that her sister was married. Her mind flooded with questions about what Greta's life had been like since they had last seen each other. Sam extended a welcoming hand in Julianna's direction. She noted the warmth of his smile and the kindness reflected in his brown eyes. Julianna shook his hand.

"It's nice to meet you," Sam said.

"Likewise," Julianna replied.

He ran his fingers through his short dark hair before he turned to Declan and offered his hand again. Once Declan and Sam had been introduced, Greta ushered everyone into the living room. "We have so much to catch up on," she declared. "But first things first. Julianna, I assume you remember where the tunnel is if someone shows up at the house looking for you?" She turned to Sam. "Julianna never forgets anything. Ever!"

"Yes, I remember," Julianna said, almost shyly. She did not want to get into her nagging dreams and feelings of forgetfulness that had plagued her lately.

"Okay," Greta said, turning to Declan. "So if someone knocks on the door, you follow Julianna to the tunnel. You should be safe there."

"You have a tunnel?" Declan asked.

"This is a very old house, and it has secret tunnels that were built within the walls," Julianna explained. "No one would ever know it's there unless they knew to look for it."

"Well, that's certainly handy for us!" Declan said with a smile and relaxed a bit as he took a seat on the couch right beside Julianna.

"Now, tell me everything," Greta insisted. "I want to know all that has gone on with you since you entered the Compound."

"You must know some things already," Julianna assumed. "Some of our discoveries were given plenty of news coverage, I'm sure, and I don't want to bore you. So, I guess, what have you heard about us first?"

Greta noted Julianna's use of the word us, but she was genuinely confused by the question. "I don't know what you mean. I know nothing about what has happened to you since you entered the Compound."

"Really?" Declan questioned. "You mean you never heard of zylothropozine?"

"You mean the heart medicine?" Sam asked.

"Yes," Declan and Julianna replied in unison.

"What about it?" Greta said.

"That was us!" Julianna exclaimed, motioning to Declan and then herself. "We invented that."

"Oh!" Greta cried. "Why, that's wonderful! I believe that's helped a lot of people."

"But you didn't know we invented it?" Declan inquired.

"No, why did you think we would?" Greta asked.

"Because we've been led to believe that we have received the credit for our inventions on the outside. We were told that our families would be so proud of all the good works we were doing," Julianna explained.

"I hate to burst your bubble, honey, but no one from the Scholars Compound ever gets credit for anything. We're told it's a 'new development brought to you via the brilliant minds of the Scholars Compound courtesy of the

New Regime,'" Greta said, employing air quotes and mimicking a voice Julianna had never heard.

Julianna and Declan exchanged a look of annoyance. "I wonder what else we've been told that hasn't been true," Julianna pondered with a frown.

"Probably lots would be my guess," Sam mused.

"So tell me everything," Greta requested again. "For example, how did you two meet?"

"We met at the first meeting on our first day at the Compound. I sat next to him at orientation, and he was nice to me. Luckily, we've been together ever since. We made several important scientific and medical advancements and discoveries. That's where we were ultimately assigned, to the biological-medical wing. Did you know the Scholars Compound is broken down into various wings of services and Scholars are assigned based on interest and aptitude?"

"Ugh! There's that word again," Greta lamented. She said the next word as if it left a bad taste in her mouth. "Aptitude."

Julianna smiled and rolled her eyes. "Anyway, we went through most of our studies together, and because we worked well together at that, they let us continue to work together in the labs. It really wasn't as horrible as you probably believe until recently. In fact, I would say I was pretty content for most of my time there. I had one very good friend and several other friends. For the most part, the guards may bluster every once in a while, but they were never cruel or abusive. The accommodations were nice and clean, especially once I was moved to a private room. It was quiet and peaceful. We were fed, although maybe that was lacking in a bit of variety. I don't think it would've killed them to let us eat a cookie now and then."

Declan laughed out loud. "You and the sweets!"

"Did something happen recently then?" Greta wondered.

"We were asked to work on a project about which Julianna and I had misgivings," Declan answered.

"That's the understatement of the year," Julianna scoffed. "They wanted us to develop a biological weapon of mass destruction for countries considered enemies of the New Regime. They were planning on killing thousands of innocent people in one fell swoop to show the might of Guardian Costma and the New Regime."

Greta gasped, "And you said you would not do that, of course."

"We are not afforded the option of saying 'no' to the needs of the New Regime. We must soldier forward and do as we are told without question," Julianna said in a mocking tone. "For it is all done with the common good in mind. If a few must be sacrificed to save the quality of lives of the many, it is but a small price to pay, according to Guardian Costma."

"You met Guardian Costma in person?" Sam asked.

"Yes, we were summoned to a private meeting with him," Declan explained. "We were told what he wanted us to do and were told it was to remain highly confidential. We were to speak of it to no one. He also made it very clear that the choice was not ours. We were chosen because we had the best track record for quick results. We had been assigned a duty, and that duty must be fulfilled."

"He looks even creepier in person if you must know," Julianna added. "The costume and makeup are really just too much."

"So you decided to run away rather than create such a weapon," Sam supposed.

"Yes, I knew I couldn't live with doing such a thing. But other things had been bothering me as well. We hadn't finished the last assignment we'd been given, which was a pill designed to keep people awake longer and in need of less sleep. I thought the need for that seemed suspicious. Things just suddenly didn't seem right to me," Julianna said with a shake of her head. "I'm not even sure I fully understand why. I just knew I couldn't stay there. And Declan was nice enough to help me and tag along."

"I'd say you made the right choice!' Greta declared. "And not just because you're finally here with me again. But because I don't think Guardian Costma should have such a weapon. I don't think he's the good man he tries to pretend to be."

"Don't think he won't still get such a weapon just because we are gone," Julianna cautioned. "He can assign the job to another team of Scholars who may not have any qualms about performing the task."

"That's true," Sam agreed. "What are you going to do now?"

"I don't have any plans at the moment to try and save the world, if that's what you mean," Julianna said with an apologetic smile. "I agree Guardian is not to be trusted, but to be perfectly honest, I haven't thought much past getting here. I just wanted to get here safely and then take a moment to figure out what's next. I haven't the slightest idea!"

Greta reached out from her armchair and touched Julianna's knee. "You don't need to make any decisions right now. You are safe and can stay here as long as you need."

"Thank you," Julianna replied with a smile. "I'm sorry to just surprise you like we did, but I promise we won't be any trouble."

"Don't you worry about a thing," Sam reassured her. "You're both more than welcome."

"Absolutely," Greta concurred.

"How about you two?" Julianna asked. "Fill me in. How did you meet? What have you been doing since we parted?"

"We met at work. We both work at the local hospital. I work in the lab, and Sam works in radiology."

"We both had an interest in art," Sam explained. "So we started getting together with a group of a few other people from work to talk about art, share our own work, that sort of thing. And one thing led to another."

Julianna smiled. "I'm glad you found each other."

"We did know Greta worked at a hospital, remember? We saw her in the film at the Compound," Declan reminded her.

"Ugh! You mean that awful project in which I was forced to participate and smile and proclaim how great everything is under the New Regime?"

"Yes, but I actually didn't pay any attention to what you were saying or doing in that footage because I couldn't get past actually seeing you in front of me. Plus, I was concerned that you really did not look happy," Julianna admitted.

"Overall, I wouldn't say I'm unhappy," Greta said with a smile. "I'm very happy with my work and family. I've been very fortunate in many ways, but I was trying my best not to look overly enthusiastic in that film. I definitely am not happy with the policies and conduct of the New Regime. I believe in freedom and the values we used to live as children. I do not support the New Regime, but I'm sure, as you know, there are times you really don't have the option of saying no to them."

Declan and Julianna exchanged a look. "Boy, do we know about that! Nothing quite like being assigned a person with whom you have to mate. Plus, I have a feeling your sister would not be so skinny if the New Regime had not been watching her sugar intake all those years," Declan teased Julianna with a gentle elbow to her side.

Julianna giggled and rolled her eyes. "Thank goodness you're such a hottie, or I wouldn't have had a cookie in years!"

Sam and Greta shared a knowing smile at their exchange.

"Well, speaking of cookies, I'm sure you two are getting hungry. I'll just whip up some dinner for us. Would you like to help me, Julianna?" Greta asked.

"Certainly," Julianna replied as she rose to follow her sister into the kitchen. "But I'm not sure how much help I'll be."

"What are you in the mood for?" Greta asked.

"Anything that hasn't been rationed into portions to maintain my ideal weight and likely won't optimize my brain power. If you have something with sugar or a high fat content, it would be great!" Julianna joked.

"What are you talking about?" Greta asked.

"Oh, it's just a reference to our dietary restrictions at the Scholars Compound," Julianna replied with a wave of her hand.

Greta raised an eyebrow. "And you still wonder why I purposely failed that test?"

"No, I get it now," Julianna said. "I mean you were free. Or at least a lot more free than I was. I mean you got to stay here at home, and you got to marry whomever you chose. It looks like you chose well, by the way."

"I just wish there was some way I could have tipped you off before the testing started that you should not do well on that test, but with me at the middle school and you at the elementary, I had no idea how to get to you."

Suddenly Julianna felt eyes on her and turned around to an entry into the kitchen from the dining room. "Who is that?" Julianna asked in surprise when she spotted the child peeking around the corner.

Greta glanced up from the pantry. "That's Starla. She was assigned to us. She's been living with us for a few months now." She turned to the child. "Starla, sweetie, come on out and let me introduce you to my sister."

"What do you mean she was assigned to you?" Julianna asked.

"I'll explain in a bit," she replied as the timid child emerged and took a few tentative steps in Julianna's direction.

"Starla, this is my sister Julianna," Greta introduced. "Can you say hello?"

"Hello," the child parroted.

"Why don't you go play in your room for a little bit before dinner?" Greta suggested.

The little girl nodded and dashed away with her loose, strawberry blonde curls bouncing as she went.

"Starla's parents are in the Scholars Compound. Starla was separated from them recently when she did not test highly enough on her aptitude exams. Did you know they did that?"

"I did," Julianna replied. "But what I don't understand is why she's with you. I thought they tried to match up children with family members outside of the Compound."

"Sometimes, if it's feasible," Greta replied. "But there wasn't anyone willing in Starla's case. Instead, the regional registrar keeps a list of any family willing to take on a child. Sam and I put our names on the list, and we were chosen to take Starla. I didn't want to go into it in front of her because she still is having some difficulty adjusting. At least her parents were able to bring her here and tell her goodbye. In her case, her mother and father did not reside with each other but cooperated on raising her until the point when she was to be displaced. I can't even imagine being told with whom I was to have a baby. And then to have someone tell me I was not allowed to keep my child because they deemed her not intelligent enough for my time? Lord help the person who tried to do that to me!"

"I did not realize they started removing children at such a young age though," Julianna said. "Children develop at different rates. How are they assuming that a child so young won't someday become brilliant? How old is she? She looks like a preschooler!"

"She's only five," Greta said with a sad shake of her head. "Poor dear."

"Do you have any children of your own?" Julianna asked.

"No, I just couldn't justify bringing a child into this world in the state it is in. Sam and I decided not to try to have a baby until something changes. But caring for a child that is already here is a different story. Now we'll raise Starla just like she was our own child, except we'll have to deal with any emotional issues she may have as a result of knowing her biological parents are still out there, but never being able to see them or talk to them again. Don't you find that whole situation just bizarre? Didn't you have an issue with that when you were still in there?"

"Yes, I do have an issue with it. It was one of the factors that pushed me toward running away from the Compound. I had made the Genos List this year, and I did not like my proposed partner. I had no interest in creating a baby with this person."

"Then I'm assuming the person wasn't Declan?" Greta questioned with a knowing smile.

"Of course it wasn't Declan," Julianna answered. "He did not like his pairing either."

"I assume if you had been paired with Declan, maybe you wouldn't have felt such an urgency to leave?" Greta guessed.

"Of course I would have. I left mostly because I refused to participate in a project of mass destruction. Not because I was afraid of my pairing. I just found it greatly displeasing."

Greta bit back a chuckle. "I'm just saying that you would not have found the situation quite so displeasing if you had been paired with that handsome guy sitting in my living room."

Julianna contemplated this. "No, I guess not," she admitted. "But if it were up to me, I'd be off the list altogether. I really don't think the New Regime has any business telling me with whom I should mate."

"You're not really answering my question," Greta hedged.

Julianna looked confused. "Sure, I did."

"What is the deal with you and Declan?" Greta asked directly.

"Oh, Declan is my best friend. He was like my family when I was inside the Compound. He was the first friend I made there and the one person I could trust always."

"And …," Greta led.

"And what?"

"Honey, what kind of a brainwashing job did they do on you if you can't see a great thing when it's right in front of your face?" Greta asked with a shake of her head. "You mean to tell me, in all that time, you have never thought about being more than friends. You've never, say, kissed each other?"

"He kissed me on the forehead once," Julianna reported. "He's hugged me many times. He also did whatever I asked to help me escape. He gave me his jacket when I was cold. He shared his sweets that one of the guards gave him when we were in the Compound. And when we were there, we did something we called Happy Memories where we each had to share something happy about our past to help make sure we never forgot."

Julianna realized she had been rambling when she saw the smirk on Greta's face. "Sounds like he's done a lot for you over the years."

"He has," Julianna confirmed. "But no, we never had a relationship like Mom and Dad or the one I'm assuming you and Sam have because it wouldn't have made any sense. There was no point. For one, such personal relationships are frowned upon in the Compound. Forbidden actually, unless you have been paired, which we were not. If we showed too much closeness and anyone else saw, we could have been separated. I would never risk that. It only would have ended badly anyway once we were paired with others."

"Well, it's a good thing you're free now," Greta said with a sly smile.

"I don't even know what to do with that," Julianna replied honestly. "With being free at all. I'm still trying to get used to the idea that I can eat a cookie whenever I want. This is like a whole new world for me. I can't even begin to think about much else."

"We'll have to work on that," Greta promised. "I'm sure you'll get used to it in no time. Then you can start setting some new life goals. Ones that do not involve being locked away like a prisoner from the family you have left."

After they had finished dinner, Greta noticed Julianna yawning and thought about sleeping arrangements. "Do you want your old room tonight? Greta asked

Julianna. "I have some of my art supplies stored in the top of the closet right now, but other than that, it's as you left it. I didn't have the heart to put all your things away. It would have been like admitting you were never coming home, even once you were past the age where you would've even wanted most of the stuff. Starla sleeps in there now, and she thinks you have fabulous taste in decor."

Julianna smiled. "Thanks for the offer, but I don't want to dislocate Starla. The poor child has been through enough without me trying to reclaim her new bedroom. Besides, I was thinking it would probably be best if Declan and I slept inside the tunnel. Are the cots still in there?"

"Yes, but do you really want to sleep on those uncomfortable old things? You're not a child anymore. I don't think you'd find it as easy to sleep as you think."

"Actually, I think I will find it much easier to sleep when I'm not worried about someone breaking in the door. No one will ever find us inside the tunnel," Julianna reasoned. She turned to Declan. "You don't mind sleeping on a cot, do you?"

"I'm certain it's a step up from the cave floor we slept on, so I'm game."

"Well, if you insist," Greta acquiesced. "But you can at least use the bedrooms to get ready for the night. Julianna, you can use my bedroom and bath, and

Declan, you can use the spare bedroom and the bath in the hallway. Come on, I'll show you."

"Wait!" Declan protested. "Julianna got to see my childhood bedroom. Fair is fair. I want to see hers first."

Greta grinned. "Follow me. I'll show you."

After they had climbed the stairs, Greta pushed open the door to the bedroom which had been decorated with a pastel paint by the name of Petal Pink. Declan was not surprised to see plush carpeting similar to what she had selected for her bedroom in the Compound. Now he realized it must have made her feel a little more at home. Her walls were decorated with a variety of flowers and butterflies, which had been hand-painted. The full-size four-poster bed was covered with a pastel pink canopy that was trimmed with lace. The room had been designed with care, and Declan suspected Julianna's mother, with her artistic tendencies, had gifted it to her beloved daughter. A framed photo on the white dresser caught his eye. He picked it up for a closer look. The photo showed two sisters, hugging each other while they smiled for the camera. The smaller one wore cute pigtails tied with light blue ribbons that matched her sailor dress. "Look at you," Declan said affectionately. "Weren't you adorable!"

Julianna flashed him a smile. "Why, yes, I was as a matter of fact!"

Greta showed Declan the spare bedroom and the bathroom in the hallway. She also offered to supplement his wardrobe with some of Sam's clothing after she sized him up by looking at him. "I think you're close to the same size," she declared and handed him a fresh pair of pajamas.

She took Julianna into the master bedroom and offered up her closet. "Feel free to borrow anything you like," Greta offered. She pulled open a dresser drawer. "Here's something for tonight." She handed Julianna a silky pair of yellow pajamas with a spaghetti strap tank top and short bottoms.

"Thank you," Julianna said.

"My bathroom is right over here. You can help yourself to any of my soaps or shampoo."

Julianna did not follow her into the bathroom; she had stopped at Greta's dressing table and was examining her supply of makeup. She picked up a tube of lipstick and twisted it to see the color. "Is this all yours?" Julianna asked in admiration.

"Yes," Greta answered slowly. "Why?"

"It's just that Scholars really aren't allowed to wear any make-up. No need to make yourself into an attractive distraction," she explained. "I was too young when I went to the Compound. So I've never really worn make-up before. It looks like so much fun!"

Greta gave her a sympathetic look. "Of course. I guess I never really thought about it. You are going to have to try it all out tomorrow. We'll have a great time!"

Julianna smiled brightly. "I can't wait!"

"We've got to make up for lost time. I bet there's lots that you and Declan haven't had the chance to experience, and I'm going to do my best to make sure that you get to try it all out now. Whatever you want."

"How about pizza for dinner tomorrow? Delivered!" Julianna suggested excitedly.

"Sure!"

"And maybe we could play some music and dance. I've never been to a dance before."

Greta's face lit up. "I'll do you one better. I'll send you to the prom."

"Workers are still allowed to do that?" Julianna asked in surprise.

"As long as Workers put in their required hours at their assigned jobs, we are allowed to spend our free time how we like, provided we are not hurting anyone else. Sometimes having the money to pull off such an event is a problem, but people make it work for their kids, even if it's somewhat modified. Maybe the decorations aren't very fancy and the music is provided by someone's parent with a stereo, but they get the job done. High school graduation is a big deal for the Workers. If their children made it that far, it's quite an achievement. It means they will never be taken away to be Warriors or Scholars." Greta smiled. "We need to make a list of everything else you want to do. We'll ask Declan also. We need to do everything we can."

Julianna let a yawn escape, and Greta noticed how heavy her sister's eyes had become. "But I'm getting ahead of myself. You have plenty of time to think about what else you want to do. First, hop on in that bathroom and get ready for a good night's sleep."

Before long, Julianna stood in front of a bookshelf with a flashlight. She hugged her sister goodnight, and Sam pulled open the bookshelf as if it were a door. "You'll probably want to make sure you keep any items that could be identified as yours inside the tunnel at all times, just in case," Sam advised.

"Of course," Julianna nodded. Then she turned to Declan and said, "This way." She flashed the light into the tunnel. Declan followed her, his arms loaded with bedding and pillows. Once they were inside, Sam asked, "You okay for me to close?" When Julianna replied yes, he pushed the shelf back into place to hide the entrance again.

"Cool," Declan said.

"I know, right?" Julianna said with a giggle. "I loved this when we were kids. Greta and I used to camp out in here sometimes. We would pretend all sorts of things in here."

"What an awesome playhouse!" Declan exclaimed as he placed the bedding on one of the two cots which lined either wall.

"My mom put these cots in here for us when we wanted to have sleepovers in here," Julianna explained. She handed Declan the flashlight. "Here, hold this for me so I can see to make the beds." Declan shone a light on the first cot, and she set to work on making their beds.

"How often did you stay in here?"

"Oh, probably a couple Fridays a month," she estimated.

"You were never scared to stay here in the dark?" Declan asked.

"No, we always had some imaginative game we were playing. We would be princesses locked in a tower or crossing the Atlantic in the belly of a ship. That sort of thing."

"Sounds like you had a lot of fun," Declan said.

"We did," she said as she tucked the sheets under the second cot.

"Which one is yours?" Declan asked. "I understand why you letting Starla displace you from your bedroom, but I don't need to take your cot, too."

Julianna smiled. "That one," she said, pointing to the one behind him.

Declan gallantly stepped aside and said, "Please, help yourself."

She hopped onto the bed. "I'm so tired. It's been a long journey." She yawned. "Sorry if you would have preferred the spare room, but I just feel more comfortable hidden in here. Even if the Warriors come in the middle of the night, they won't find us here. Nobody knows about it. Greta and I never even told our friends about it; it was a fun family secret."

As his head hit his pillow, Declan said, "I don't mind at all. I'm with you. I would much rather sacrifice a cushier mattress for a little peace of mind. I think we'll both sleep well tonight."

"Good night, Declan. I'm glad you're here."

"Good night, Julianna. Thank you for having me and sharing your secret place."

"Only with you," she said with another yawn as she curled up and closed her eyes.

His heart smiled. For the hundredth time since he left, Declan was glad he had joined Julianna.

Julianna and Declan both slept later into the morning in the darkness of the tunnel. They rested well until they awoke naturally. Declan woke first and waited for Julianna. "Good morning, Sunshine," he greeted when he heard her stirring.

She stretched one arm over her head and smiled. "Good morning."

"I was hoping you'd wake up soon. How do we get out of here?"

Julianna giggled. "Oh, maybe I should've shown you that last night." She stood and padded across the cement floor, mindful to keep her bare feet on the warm rug her mother had placed on the floor decades earlier. To Declan, she looked like someone who had done this many times in her past. "You just push on the wall right here."

Only then did he notice a small circle of glow-in-the-dark paint placed low enough for a child to reach. Julianna pushed on the spot. Sunlight flooded the dark space as she shoved the door open wide. The smell of bacon hit their noses, and they both smiled widely. "I couldn't even tell you the last time I smelled that glorious smell," Declan gushed.

"Let's go!" Julianna said, already out of the tunnel. Declan followed her to Greta who was standing in front of a frying pan in the kitchen.

"Good morning, sleepyheads!" Greta greeted. "You're lucky I have today off in the rotation at the hospital. Or I would've either had to wake you or left you hungry. I was getting hungry myself, so I decided to get a start on breakfast."

Julianna's mouth watered. "What are we having?" she asked, eyeing what could only be described as a buffet that Greta had set up all over the kitchen island.

"We've got waffles with toppings, omelets made to order, sausage, bacon or, if omelets aren't your thing, any kind of eggs you want. Don't be shy. Start eating!"

Julianna and Declan eagerly loaded up their plates with all sorts of delicious breakfast foods, especially those, like bacon, which they had been forbidden in the Complex. Julianna squeezed a dollop of whipped cream onto her waffle and topped it off with a cherry while Declan smeared his full of jelly.

"Today, you both need to work on your lists," Greta said.

"Lists?" Declan asked. "What lists?"

"You need to sit down and think of all the things you missed out on, and I'll do my best to try to get it for you."

"Mmm," Declan murmured as he bit a crispy slice. "Bacon probably was at the top of my list!"

Greta tossed a couple more slices onto his plate. "There's plenty more where that came from."

"Where's Sam?" Julianna asked.

"He had to work the first shift today, so he left early for the hospital," Greta said.

"How does that work?" Declan asked curiously. "We've learned that things don't necessarily work the way we thought they did. I was curious about how healthcare works."

"I don't know what you've been told, but the care people receive at a hospital is basically the same as it always was. The doctor situation is a bit different. The people who become doctors are not Scholars, but the ones studying to be doctors usually are the ones who almost made the cut. They tested very well, just not well enough. Then they have to take additional courses, but it's really more streamlined because they need to get people trained and in the field. For example, they aren't concerned if a doctor has any college courses in languages or history as long as their science grades are sound. These doctors strictly provide patient care. They may be asked to report findings back to the Scholars Compound, especially about a new drug or procedure. However, they are not permitted to do their own research projects. If they have an idea about a possible advancement, they need to submit that idea to the Scholars Compound. Then you guys would do your thing, I suppose. Most of the doctors with whom I work are actually older and were doctors before the attacks. So I really couldn't tell you if this new way is producing the same quality of doctors as we had prior to the attacks."

"I assume no one is denied healthcare?" Julianna asked hopefully.

"No, they really aren't denied care. The New Regime does not involve itself in the operations of the hospitals. I guess they really don't have much of an interest in it. They release advancements created by the Scholars as they become available for human use, but they don't really trouble themselves with anything else."

"Do you make decent money doing what you do?" Declan asked. "We met a man named Hank who seemed to have come upon financial hard times as a result of the New Regime's economic policies. It seemed like people watch their spending much more closely in general than I remember. Is that really the case across the board?"

"Yes, everyone has to watch their pocketbooks. That is true. I would say that everyone outside of the members of the New Regime themselves have felt a pinch post-attacks. However, Sam and I are lucky because we're in the medical field. The field is a bit immune to economic hardships because people don't really have the option of not getting healthcare. If you need it, you need it. It's not like a new dress or a night out.

Therefore, we've always had steady work, unlike many others. Plus, it helped that I had the house. That took away a huge burden that many people have. Mom and Dad owned the house outright, and when you went away, there was no one else left with a claim on it. Not paying for housing as far as a mortgage or rent has been a tremendous advantage for us."

"Whatever happened to Auntie?" Julianna asked. "Where did she go?"

"The day after my eighteenth birthday, she announced that she had fulfilled her obligation and would be leaving. She took the first bus to Arizona. She will call me on my birthday and send me a Christmas card, but that's about the only time I hear from her. I don't think she ever wanted to be here and only stayed out of some sense of obligation to our parents. We were not very close even when we were living together, but she did provide the basic necessities I needed. She would cook dinner, go grocery shopping, that sort of thing, while I was finishing high school. So that was nice."

"I got the feeling she could not wait to dump me at the Compound," Julianna said.

"You're probably right. You were just one more person to care for. Plus, you would have extended her stay here by four years if she thought she needed to stay until you turned 18."

"Auntie sounds like a very warm and loving person," Declan said sarcastically.

"What other questions do you have for me?" Greta inquired.

"Where's Starla?" Julianna asked.

"She ate while you were still asleep," Greta answered. "She's dressed and ready for her day. Now she's playing in her bedroom."

"I can't believe they start the aptitude tests so early. She seems awfully young to be separated from her parents," Julianna said.

Greta shrugged. "You would probably know more about that than I. I'm just happy she's here."

"I just think it seems a little silly to determine a person's entire future based on a test taken at such a young age," Julianna said.

"Well, you're preaching to the choir," Greta replied. "Take it up with your friend the Guardian."

Julianna shivered. "No thank you! That man creeps me out like no one I've ever met!"

"You're just jealous of how his make-up is always on point," Declan joked.

Julianna laughed and nodded. "Yeah, that must be it!" She picked up a berry from her plate and tossed it at Declan's face.

Declan's eyes grew wide as he said mockingly, "You must put that berry in your mouth. To do anything else would be wasteful and would not optimize your health and brain power."

"True," Julianna agreed. "But have you ever thought about those people telling us about how to optimize *our* brain power? Why didn't they optimize their own?"

"You're right. Why would we listen to them when we are clearly so much smarter than they are?" Declan agreed.

Greta smiled as they continued their joking exchange and was glad to see that Julianna had made it out of the Scholars Compound with her sense of humor intact. Julianna always had been an exceptionally intelligent child from a very early age, but she also had been fun. Greta's best memories were not about how Julianna learned to read by age three. She remembered her mother throwing Julianna a birthday party to which Julianna insisted she invite every girl in her class because she did not want anyone to feel left out. Then, at the party, Julianna entertained the crowd by performing a stand-up routine of knock-knock jokes. Greta thought Julianna had been gifted with her personality as a sort of defense mechanism for her hyper-intelligence, which some people might have found intimidating.

Although, perhaps, their mother deserved much of the credit. Their father had attempted each year to enroll Julianna in a special school for gifted children. Each and every time, their mother had shot him down. She understood that Julianna had a special gift, and she encouraged her husband to provide her with enrichment tools. Julianna was expected to do extra reading assignments and projects at home in addition to her regular classwork, but Anne Brenner also had been very sure to safeguard Julianna's right to be a child. While her father selected advanced reading materials, her mother planned playdates and allowed her to watch cartoons. Anne made sure that, when another child was talking about the latest toy or a popular television show, Julianna could join in the conversation. Julianna may have had an advanced vocabulary and been a genius with computer programming, but she also knew how to play tag and laugh at a silly joke.

"How did you wind up studying medicine?" Greta asked her sister. "I always thought computers were your area of expertise."

"Yes, I do enjoy working with computers," Julianna said. "But I was denied enrollment in the technology wing. So we were put in medicine instead."

"Why were you denied enrollment in any wing? I'm sure you were one of the smartest among the smart people."

Julianna shrugged. "Probably. I don't know why. Maybe because of Dad? It's alright though. I still worked with technology sometimes, just specializing in its application to medicine."

"There was a lot that went on in the Compound that we did not fully understand," Declan confessed. "We really weren't in a position to question them. The expectation was that you would do as you were told."

"That seems fishy to me," Greta said. "But then again, I think most of what the New Regime does is pretty fishy. If he weren't doing anything underhanded, why would he feel the need to hide himself and his upper level officials behind such thick layers of make-up?"

"That's for his protection and to allow him to still mingle with the common folk," Julianna chimed in. The she paused and looked at Declan. "Or at least that's what we were always told." Then she looked at Greta. "But maybe I should make an effort to deprogram myself and not pipe up with a New Regime factoid every time someone asks a question like that?"

"Maybe that's a good idea," Greta agreed.

Julianna and Declan had agreed that they would like to watch as much television as they could that day. To Greta, they seemed like tourists in a foreign land. They were so busy trying to absorb everything they could about this new culture to which they had been exposed. Besides, they thought it would be too risky to be traveling around in public unnecessarily, especially with Greta. Surely, the New Regime would have put a watchful Warrior or two on Greta.

However, the pair found plenty of ways to amuse themselves inside the house. They played a game with

Starla, which actually served as a practice run in case the Warriors arrived. They taught Starla how to hide quietly and patiently in the tunnel away from the "dragons." Starla gamely sat quietly on a cot with a coloring book Julianna had stashed under the cot for the occasion. Later in the day, Starla asked if they could hide from the dragons again. They binged on television programs, especially news programs which they found particularly fascinating since the New Regime seemed to have fashioned an entirely different message to present to the Workers from the one that had been pushed on the Scholars. They played children's games with Starla. Julianna was particularly excited to see a few vintage games that once belonged to her.

"Don't play the memory game with her," Declan advised Starla in a mock conspiratorial whisper. "You'll never win."

They checked out the book collection in the study which had once been Jacob Brenner's haven. Julianna made note of many titles which she planned to read. When they got a little taste of cabin fever, Greta offered to take them for a drive, provided they hide on the floor until they were far enough away from the house and certain no one was following them. As an added measure, Julianna shoved her hair under a baseball cap, and they both wore sunglasses.

CHAPTER 14

When they felt the coast was clear enough, Julianna buckled herself into the middle seat in the back, sandwiched between Starla's carseat and Declan. Declan tried to hide the smile he could not help when Julianna was so close to him. Then Greta gave them a little tour of Springdale, pointing out the many changes that had occurred in Julianna's absence, such as new businesses replacing old ones, new playground equipment at their old school and a subdivision which was built when people began reconstructing after the attacks. She also drove them around the university campus where Dr. Brenner had once taught and researched. The trip made Julianna feel particularly nostalgic. She knew she frequently had made visits to the university with her father, especially during the summer months. While strangely she could not remember anything specific about these trips, the place felt familiar to her, and she knew she had been fond of her time there.

When the sun dipped further beneath the trees, Greta announced it was time to return home. Sam would be arriving soon. "Does anyone have a request for dinner?" she asked.

"Pizza!" Julianna and Declan declared in unison.

"Very well then," Greta said with a knowing smile. She pushed a button on her dashboard and a screen with restaurant names popped up. She selected one with a touch of her finger. Then she clicked twice on the next box. "I got two of our usual order from the pizza place," she explained. "By the time we drive over that way, it should be about ready."

"How did you do that?" Julianna asked. "That's cool!"

"Brought to me by the brilliant minds at the Scholars Compound," Greta replied. "Must have come from the tech wing that denied you. I can set it for restaurants we frequent, and I also can program in a usual order. You can do other things with it, but that's what I just did. It's pretty handy."

Julianna nodded. She realized she knew very little about what the other Scholars had produced aside from what she had gleaned at the lunch tables every now and then.

"Perhaps, we should mention that an over-eager assistant," he said motioning to Starla, "pushed the button twice by mistake. Just in case the New Regime is somehow able to track your orders using that thing and knows you ordered more than usual."

"Good thinking!" Greta exclaimed. "I'll make sure to say something to the server when I pick it up."

Greta made sure she parked away from the large windows of the pizza parlor and entered the building with only Starla beside her. She smiled at the young girl working the counter. "I'm sorry," she said. "But my little cutie here happened to hit the button an extra time to double our usual order." She ruffled Starla's hair as Starla shyly hid behind her leg. "I don't suppose there's any way I could only take half of that order?"

"I'm very sorry, ma'am, but we've already got your order ready," the girl replied.

"Oh, well," Greta sighed with feigned regret as she held out her debit card. "I suppose I know what I'm having for lunch tomorrow."

"Sorry I couldn't help you," the girl said as she ran the card and pushed Greta's order across the counter.

"Oh, it's not a big problem," Greta said with a wave of her hand and a friendly smile. "I'll just keep better track of someone's happy hands. Thanks just the same!" Greta walked out of the pizza parlor, balancing the food with one hand and taking Starla's hand with the other, pushing the door open with her hip.

Greta hoped she had made enough of an impression on the cashier that the girl would remember them if anyone asked questions.

"I think that went well," Greta reported when she returned to the car.

After they grabbed their pizza take-out, the group headed for home. Declan and Julianna ducked to the

255

floor boards again when they got within a few blocks of the house. Greta pushed the button for the garage door opener just as Sam pulled into the driveway also. Sam took a couple of boxes from Declan as they walked inside.

Greta asked Julianna to help her set the table and handed her a stack of plates. Greta grabbed some silverware and napkins while the men flipped open the lids to the pizza boxes and boxes of salad and breadsticks.

As they sat down at the table, Julianna and Declan seemed far too happy to be consuming the long strings of gooey cheese with every bite. They were enjoying themselves too much to give a thought to what was going on across town.

The girl at the counter looked up in surprise as a couple of Warriors entered the pizza parlor. Warriors did not generally frequent the place because, as far as she had heard, they were kept on a strict diet and workout regimen to keep them in optimum physical condition. They would never just stroll into a pizza parlor to grab a slice. The girl stood frozen to the ground, unsure of how she should act.

The large men approached the counter, and one asked, "Have you been working here all night?"

The girl nodded.

"Have you seen a woman named Greta Brenner or Greta Hartford this evening?" the Warrior questioned.

"Um, I … I may have. I don't know everyone's names," she answered, stumbling over her words.

"Check your financial transactions. We have reason to believe she was here tonight," the second man commanded.

"Yes, sir," the girl replied, as she scrolled through a list on the computer. "Oh yes, here she is Greta Hartford." She read the order. "I do remember her."

"What can you tell me about her? Was anyone with her?"

"Yes, a little girl. I remember her because the little girl had pushed the button twice when she placed her order, so she got double."

"Did she order double because she had other people with her?"

"No, she asked if there was any way she could only take half the order. She said it had been a mistake."

"You're sure she had no one with her other than a child. No one in her car maybe?" one of the men inquired.

"I did not see her car, sir."

The men exchanged a look. Then one said, "Thank you for your cooperation." They were gone as quickly as they had arrived.

Meanwhile, Greta asked her husband about his day. Then Julianna and Declan had several questions for him about what he did, how he did it, and if he had used any advancements created by Scholars.

After he had satisfied all their questions, he asked Julianna, "How was your first day at home?"

"Very well, thank you," Julianna said. "We learned a lot from the tv, and we played some games with Starla."

"I think the tour of town was my favorite," Declan said. "Very interesting to see some of Julianna's old haunts. I'm not the least bit surprised that one of them was a college campus."

Sam and Greta laughed while Julianna just looked pensive.

A moment later, she blurted suddenly, "I've been having trouble remembering anything about Dad."

"What do you mean?" Greta asked with a look of concern. "Do you find it too upsetting?"

"No!" Julianna cried, looking pained. "I mean I can't remember him!"

"Oh, that's silly," Greta said with a wave of her hand. "Maybe your memories just aren't as clear as they used to be."

"No, I don't have memories about him. I have … feelings."

"Feelings?" Declan questioned.

Julianna sighed. "I'll try to explain. It's like I cannot recall a single fact, remember a solitary moment, but I feel a certain way when I think about the idea of him. Like today at the campus, I know I went there with him lots. I *know* that, but I don't remember actually going there. Yet, I know that I enjoyed my time there with him because I felt a happy fondness when I was there. I can't explain why I felt that though. Not a single memory comes to mind that would make me feel that way."

Everyone at the table was silent for a moment. Finally, Greta spoke. "Maybe that's some kind of self-preservation. Maybe your mind won't let you remember because it's too painful. I know you couldn't even tell us then, but you may have seen him die."

Her mind flashed to one of her dreams, the one where her daddy suddenly disappeared into the black hole. "Maybe," Julianna said quietly. "I've been having strange dreams that usually involve Mom and Dad in one way or another. Maybe that's the memories working their way back into my consciousness?"

"Could be," Declan said, more as a way to comfort her than because he knew of documented evidence of a similar case.

Another dream came to Julianna's mind. Now she had the opportunity to ask someone about it who was older and might have a clearer memory of it. "Do you remember our trip to Athens very well? Julianna asked.

"I remember bits of it. I have the photographs somewhere," Greta answered.

Julianna perked up. "Do you think I could look at them?

"Of course." Greta wiped her hands on her napkin and arose. Julianna followed suit and tagged along as her sister walked to a bookshelf in the study. She selected a photo album and handed it to Julianna. "They should be in here."

Julianna flipped through the photographs to see if anything sparked a particular memory. She stopped at a photo of her father standing in front of a statue and pulled the photo from the pocket in the album. On the back of the photo, she recognized her mother's handwriting which had scrawled, "Jacob next to Mnemosyne." Her eyes widened.

"This!" she exclaimed. "Do you remember anything about this?"

Greta examined the photo. "That's dad in front of one of the statues we saw there."

"But is this statue of any significance? Does it maybe mean something in the world of art? Does Mnemosyne mean anything to you?"

"Oh!" Greta exclaimed. "That's the statue of Mnemosyne. Sure."

CHAPTER 15

Julianna became anxious and started to talk fast. "What does Mnemosyne mean? Did it mean something to Dad?"

"Mnemosyne was the goddess of memory, and that was the name of one of Dad's projects," Greta explained.

"Which project?"

"I couldn't correctly say Mnemosyne, so I just called it the Rememberer. Does that ring a bell?" Greta asked.

Julianna squinted her eyes and willed herself to remember to no avail. "I know it should, but it doesn't."

Greta raised her eyebrows. "Not at all? That surprises me. Because you know where he hid it."

"Where he hid what?" Julianna questioned.

"You know where our father hid the prototype for the memory control device."

"I don't even know what you're talking about," Julianna replied.

"It played with people's memories. After he was done working on it, he hid it. Only you and Dad knew where because you two had the best memories ever. You were his safeguard; the reason he never wrote it down. Then it could never fall into the wrong hands or something. I remember him telling Mom that. She was not too happy about the project at all, and especially not happy about him involving you. I remember they had a couple fights about it!"

"I don't remember any of this!" Julianna exclaimed in frustration. "How could I have forgotten something so important?"

"That's strange," Greta admitted.

Julianna rubbed her face with her hands. She never had questioned her memory abilities before. Every time she needed to recall an event, she could do so with crystal clarity. She was driving herself mad trying to decipher what was so different about this time. Ever since she first started having those dreams, she felt there was something in her brain just out of her reach, a memory file she could not quite access. Now she had a clue as to what it possibly could be she was forgetting, but that only seemed to make it worse.

"Can you please tell me everything you remember?" Julianna begged.

"Sure," Greta replied. "Umm, I remember Mom and Dad fighting about it. Mom even yelled at him about how he shouldn't even be messing with such a thing.

She told him that being able to do something does not mean that you should. She thought such a device would be terrible in the hands of the wrong person. She asked him to pray about it, but he was just so excited about it that he never really listened to her. In the very end, I don't think they were in the best place in their marriage because of this thing. Most of what I know about that I got from overhearing fights I really wasn't supposed to hear, so my information there is kind of spotty."

"What was his purpose for creating this device?" Julianna asked. "Why would he want to mess with people's memories?"

"He thought it would be a way to help people. He wanted to erase the bad memories for people. For example, if someone experienced a loss through death, he wanted to be able to go in and erase that experience so they did not have to suffer that pain. Mom was against this because she felt that if God allows you to feel pain, it is not without purpose. She believed that taking away all the bad moments also would lessen the value of the good moments. Sort of how she always tried to make us earn any big purchases we wanted because she thought this would make us appreciate it more. I get what she was saying because I do think that is true. I think the bad times make you appreciate the good times that much more. Like if we had been together all those years, do you think we would be having as much joy at this reunion?"

Julianna shook her head. "I guess not."

"I think Mom's biggest issue though was that she felt Dad was trying to play God. She had serious qualms about that."

"How did this machine work? Did it zap you with a laser beam or what?"

"Something to do with magnetic electrodes? I really don't know. I didn't understand it, and I didn't really want to understand it. It held no interest for me back then. That's why I gave it the easy name. Dad was always naming his projects, and I just could not grasp this one. I would pronounce it Project Nesemony, or something like that. I got slightly offended by his chuckle every time I mentioned it which is why I started calling it The Rememberer."

"Do you know where he got the funding for it? I know he usually had people funding his projects. Did Mom have a problem with where he got the money?"

"That I don't know. You would probably have known better than I. You were the one he was always taking with him to the lab."

Julianna stomped her foot in frustration. "I can hardly remember that. Why can't I remember? Why am I having such a hard time remembering my own father?"

Greta put a comforting hand on her shoulder. "I'm sorry you're having such a hard time with this. If it makes you feel any better, I don't really think it matters anymore. He died before anything ever became of it. I'm sure most of his work was destroyed in the attacks. His entire lab at the university was completely obliterated. It's a miracle you made it out." Greta hugged Julianna tightly at the reminder that she was lucky to even have a sister at all. Julianna returned the hug, but her mind was racing with a thousand different thoughts.

Her father had taken a device with such life-altering potential and had entrusted its location to a 10-year-old child. Why had he done that? Did she really see him die and decided to block it all from her mind? If that was the case, how could she unlock those memories now? If she did manage to unlock them, what good, or bad, could come of it? Would she be better off to just accept these blank spaces in her mind?

"What happened that day?" Julianna asked. "Why was I with him?"

"That I don't know," Greta answered. "You weren't with him when the day began. Mom had taken you to school. She dropped you off first, so I watched you walk into the building. He must've picked you up at some point after that and taken you to his office. That's where he was when the attacks started. His building was hit by a plane dropping some bombs. Both of you were inside when that happened. Much of the building collapsed. You were pulled out hours later by rescue workers, unconscious but alive. They took you to the hospital for treatment, and after a few days, you were sent home with Auntie where you eventually made a full recovery. Just in time for the Scholars testing."

"What if this memory issue is due to damage I sustained from my injuries?"

"I suppose that could be, but don't you think it's weird that you only can't remember some of the most recent things about Dad? I mean, you seem to remember things that happened long ago that involved him. You just don't remember right before he died. That's why I think it's probably more like a defense mechanism."

In the meantime, Sam sent Starla upstairs to find pajamas and start getting ready for bed while he asked Declan to join him in the living room. Declan took a seat in a recliner while Sam sat on one corner of the couch nearest him.

Sam said, "I hope your travels here weren't too exciting for you."

"Actually, it wasn't as bad as it could have been," Declan said. "All in all, we've been very lucky. We've met some very nice people who have helped us along the way."

"I'm glad you made it here safely," Sam said. "Have you thought about what's next for you? Any hopes for the future? Or were you too focused on survival to really think about it?"

"To be honest, I was afraid to let myself get too far ahead," Declan answered. "If we had gotten caught, the disappointment would just be too great. I suppose I really should be thinking about our next move. We can't be hiding in the tunnel forever."

"No," Sam said with a light chuckle. "I don't suppose you'd want to do that, but you have some time to consider what you'd like to do next. I'm sure even having options as far as your future is something that's kind of new to you."

Declan nodded thoughtfully. "You know, it really is. We've never had to consider what we were going to do in the future because we always were just told what we were doing next. Since we were children, really."

"I can't begin to imagine what all of this must be like for you," Sam commiserated with a shake of his head. Suddenly, a light outside in the dark caught Sam's eye.

Sam sat upright in the chair with his arms pushing himself out of the seat. "Ladies and gentleman, the moment we were waiting for has arrived," he said loud enough for the sisters to hear him. Greta and Julianna walked out of the study.

"The Warriors are here. Get away from the windows immediately!" Sam instructed Julianna and Declan. "This is not a drill. You need to get to the tunnels."

CHAPTER 16

Greta flew into action and hurried toward the door. "You okay with dealing with them?" Sam asked Greta. "I'll run upstairs and make sure that Starla doesn't speak to them."

"Of course," Greta agreed. "They won't leave until they've talked to me anyway."

"Quick! Into the wall!" Sam commanded as he pulled a book shelf open just wide enough for them to slide inside.

Declan grabbed Julianna's hand and pulled her with him into the tunnel. Sam replaced the book shelf and ran for the stairs. Julianna pulled Declan's hand and led him deeper into the recesses of the tunnel past the cots and into a darker area that she found easily using old instincts. Then she said a silent prayer of thanks that they had thought to make sure to keep all traces of their personal belongings carefully tucked away inside the tunnels.

Greta could hear several sets of footsteps outside the front door. Then someone knocked sharply on the door. Greta, hand already on the knob, waited a beat and opened the door with an expectant smile.

"Hello," she greeted the armed Warriors outside her door.

"Are you Greta Brenner?" one of the three asked.

"Formerly," Greta replied. "I now go by my married name, Greta Hartford."

"We're going to need to search your house," he replied in an authoritative tone.

"Can I ask to what this is in reference?" Greta questioned as she stepped back and waved the men in with her hand.

"We're looking for your sister, Julianna Brenner."

"She doesn't live here anymore," Greta explained, hoping she sounded helpful. "She was taken to the Scholars Compound many years ago as a child."

"Surely, you must have seen the news reports. She's not there now. She left the Compound without authorization, and it is of great importance that she is found and returned to the Compound immediately. It is a matter of national security."

Greta gasped. "Oh no! We really don't watch very much television, so, no, I had not seen any reports. National security, you say? Do you mind if I ask why?"

"Ma'am, I don't really know why. I'm just following orders," the lead Warrior replied. He motioned with his hand for the other two Warriors to begin conducting the search. "As her last surviving relative, you are on a list of people she would likely seek out. Who else is present in the house this evening, ma'am?"

"My husband and my assigned child," Greta replied, wringing her hands and beginning to appear nervous. She could hear her heart thudding in her ears. "Oh my! I just do hope that Julianna is okay. I hope she's not hurt somewhere. I can't imagine her running away. She has always been such a good girl. Why do you think she would run away?"

"I don't know, ma'am. It's really not my concern."

"Oh, but don't you think it should be? Shouldn't you have all the information necessary to successfully complete your job?"

"Ma'am, all I need to know is what your sister looks like and where she may be headed."

"Well, she's a pretty little blonde. Here's her picture," Greta said walking to the mantle and grabbing a framed photo of Greta and Julianna as children. "Of course, this photograph is several years old. I really wish I could be of more help, but, you see, the rules state that I have not been allowed to see her since she entered the Scholars Compound. They do not want me distracting her from her important work, I guess. I really can't give you a more accurate description of her appearance since I have been forbidden from seeing her all this time. I suppose as a Warrior, you understand. You really don't get to spend time with your family either."

"Ma'am, thank you anyway, but I don't need your help. I have a current photo."

Greta gasped and put her hand to her heart. "I don't suppose you'd let me have a peek at it, would you? I'd love to see what she looks like today," she requested as she trailed behind the man who was now searching around her living room.

The man sighed in exasperation and pulled out a small electronic device. He held it out to Greta and showed her Julianna's badge photo, which showed a smiling, perky blonde with warm brown eyes. "Here you go."

"Ooooh! She's so pretty," Greta cooed. "Don't you think she's so pretty? Striking, really."

"I guess," the man replied without much enthusiasm as he opened the hall closet.

Greta continued to distract him with her chatter while the others occupied themselves upstairs, where they would find nothing. "I suppose as far as jobs go, this one really isn't too awful. It's sort of like you're playing a high-stakes game of hide-and-seek!" Greta was fairly certain she saw the man roll his eyes. "Oh dear, but I just don't know what to do with this information. I'm just so worried about my dear sister. I mean, I know we haven't seen each other in forever, but that doesn't mean I've just stopped caring for her, you know? It just doesn't work that way with family!"

"Did you find anything?" the lead Warrior shouted upstairs.

"No," came the reply.

Greta trailed the lead Warrior as he thoroughly searched the kitchen, bathroom, dining areas, and the study. Fortunately, no Warrior ever noticed the book shelf or the other couple of secret compartments used to hide the passages into the tunnels. When they regrouped near the front door, the lead Warrior handed Greta a card that had instructions and a phone number. "If you see her at all, you must call this number immediately."

"Of course, I understand," Greta said with grave seriousness. "And would you please do me the favor of letting me know if you do find her so I can stop fretting over it?"

"I'm sure someone will let you know," the man replied. "Good day to you."

"And to each of you as well," Greta said as she opened the door for them. "Thank you for your service to our country."

As soon as they had walked down the sidewalk toward the van in which they had arrived, Greta shut the door and heaved an audible sigh of relief.

"You did a wonderful job," Sam told her from the top of the stairs.

Greta chuckled. "I've never incessantly chattered like that in my life! But I think it served its purpose. I think I definitely distracted and annoyed him enough that he just wanted to get out of here."

"Do you think it's safe for them to stay here now?" Sam asked.

"I don't know," Greta replied with a frown. "Maybe they won't knock on the door again, but they'll most certainly have the house under some kind of surveillance."

"Maybe we should wait a couple of days and then send them to Abraham's," Sam suggested. "Abe will look out for them and no one would ever think to look for them there."

Greta lit up at the idea. "True! You don't think he'd mind?"

"Of course not! Abe will do anything and everything he can to help the cause. And maybe if they had a little breathing room and time to think clearly, Julianna and Declan could be huge assets to the cause. I was going to broach the subject with Declan before our friends arrived. They have perfect timing."

Greta nodded thoughtfully. "Yes, but we'll wait a couple of days before we do anything. That will give

Abe time to prepare for them as well. We'll also have to come up with a way to sneak them out of the house, sight unseen."

"We have time to think about it. I think we're safe for the time being," Sam said as he pulled open the book shelf.

Julianna exhaled a breath of relief when she saw Sam's face in the light.

"Are they gone?" Declan asked, his arm protectively around Julianna.

"They are," Sam answered. "But I think we need to talk about what we're going to do next now. Greta and I have an idea."

"Why don't we sit in the study? Greta suggested. "Fewer windows."

Everyone walked back to the study. Declan and Julianna sat next to each other on the couch. Greta pulled up an office chair, and Sam just stood, pacing slightly while he spoke.

"We did not want to put too much pressure on you right away," Sam started. "That's why we didn't even mention anything to you. We wanted to give you time to adjust and think about what you wanted in life rather than taking you from one situation where you were always told exactly what to do and put you into another situation where you were expected to do as you were asked all over again."

Julianna looked confused. "What are you talking about?"

Sam knew he was not being very clear, so he tried again. "I think you already know that things you were told inside the Compound aren't necessarily accurate. People out here are not all happy with the actions of the New Regime. In fact, some people are very displeased and think something needs to be done about it."

"Sam and I are two of those people," Greta explained. "We don't think it was right for the New Regime to stroll in and basically overthrow the existing government in favor of their martial law. And what they're doing with the Scholars Compounds and the Warriors Training Facilities is just wrong. They are forcing people to bend to their will and serve them. I think Guardian Costma basically has created a monarchy at best, a dictatorship at worst. I think he has plans to pass on his kingdom to the next generation."

Julianna sat upright. "How did you know that?" she asked in surprise.

"You know this to be true?" Sam asked incredulously.

"We both assumed that was his plan when he assigned his nephew to be Julianna's mating pair," Declan explained with his head down. "Why else would he take his brightest Scholar and pair her with his dimwitted nephew? It made no sense otherwise."

Julianna blushed, for some reason embarrassed by what should have been her role in the New Regime's reign of insanity. "I did everything I could to make him take me off the list," she said in an attempt to justify herself.

"Sweetie, that's terrible!" Greta cried.

"You can just add that to the list of reasons we got out when we did," Declan muttered.

"There are people working together, in secret of course, united in their belief that the New Regime's rule needs to end. We need to get back to a democracy again," Sam explained with passion. "We don't want to put any pressure on you, but we do want to let you know where we stand. In case you think there's no way out aside from living in hiding for the rest of your life, know that there are other people out there who would be willing to fight for your freedom! If we have our way, life won't always be this way."

"Which brings us to how this will affect the two of you," Greta continued. "If at some point you decide to join our fight, we would love it! I think both of you would be a huge asset to our cause. However, in the meantime, we would like to send you in a few days to live with our friend Abraham Beecher. We believe Abraham would have the ability to protect you within his home, and no one would ever think to look for you there. I'm certain Sam and I will be under heavy surveillance from here on out. We need to wait a while for things to die down, but we both think that Abraham's place would be the best place for you."

"I think I'll invite him over within the next day or two to introduce you and make sure you're comfortable with this plan," Sam said. "Like I told you, we don't want to be the ones telling you what you have to do now. But we do want to provide you with all the information we have to enable you to make the best decisions possible."

"I think I want to help you in your fight," Julianna said softly. "I think when I looked in his eyes, I was disturbed in a way that I've never been before."

"Who's eyes? The nephew's?" Greta questioned.

"No, Guardian Costma," Julianna replied. "All the make-up in the world cannot hide what is in his eyes. Cruel insanity would be how I would describe it."

Declan thought of his mother sitting in the nursing facility and said, "I'm with you too. Julianna is absolutely right. There is something fundamentally wrong about him."

"We don't want you making that decision right now," Sam insisted. "You can think about it and see what we're trying to accomplish. Heck, the two of you might even be the leaders of the Freedom Fighters before it's all said and done. But you need to be sure about it. It can't be a knee-jerk decision."

Greta sighed. "I think it's been quite a night. Maybe we all need some rest and relaxation tonight. Why don't we get ready to turn in for the night and discuss this more in the morning?"

"Sounds like a plan to me," Julianna said as she stood to head toward a bathroom and a cool shower. Between the feelings she had dredged up regarding her father and the adrenaline rush from hiding away from the Warriors, Julianna was emotionally exhausted.

"We have nothing positive to report," Leader Cantor told Guardian Costma. "We went to the boy's home. His family no longer resides there. His only surviving parent is in a nursing home and in a mentally compromised state. Our Warriors visited the facility, but she could tell us nothing. The nursing home staff was not much help either. They kept a log for visitors, but nobody really bothered to monitor it. Visitors were not required to provide identification, and most of the names were not even legible. The staff on duty at the time could not really tell us anything, and since we have no idea when they may have been there, we cannot ask specific staff members. Anybody could have been on duty."

Guardian showed no emotion and asked, "What about the sister?"

"We thought we were onto something when the sister ordered double her regular food order at a pizza place she frequents, but it turns out she used a vehicular device and blamed an overeager child for pushing the button twice."

"Greta Brenner has a child?" Guardian asked with raised eyebrows.

"Not one of her own. She has taken in one of the discarded Scholars' children."

"I assume you visited the house anyway," Guardian surmised.

"Of course, we did," Cantor replied. "We had a team of Warriors search the entire residence. We found nothing. Not a trace of them. I have reviewed their personal files. I noted that the boy had a brother who is one of my Warriors. The brother actually has been assigned to Delilah. Perhaps you would like me to talk to him and find out if he knows of any other relatives of places they may have sought refuge."

"No need," Guardian said. "Summon the brother to me. I shall question him myself."

Julianna did not wait for Declan to enter the tunnel. After she had showered and put on the pair of fresh pajamas Greta had provided to her, she shuffled off to the bookshelf and straight for her cot. By the time Declan arrived, he believed she already was dreaming peacefully. Actually, Julianna was not quite asleep yet and had heard him enter the tunnel, but she was too tired to talk to him. She drifted away a few minutes later.

Before long, she found herself as a child, sitting in her desk at her old school before the attacks. She was summoned to the office and felt confused and a little scared when she saw her father. He immediately assured her nothing was wrong with her mom or sister, but she needed to come with him right away. Julianna dutifully followed him to his car.

"We're going to do a very important experiment today, and I need you to be there," he explained. "It's the most important experiment of my life."

Julianna's heart swelled with pride that her dad had selected her for such an important honor. "What are we doing?" she asked.

"You'll see when we get there," he answered nervously. Julianna noticed he did not smile or say it in a way that would have built anticipation. He seemed distracted and upset, and she was starting to feel uncomfortable. She wondered what was wrong with him and if there was something she could do to make it better.

"We must hurry," he instructed gruffly. "We haven't much time."

When her father shakily inserted his key card and pushed open his office door, they were greeted by absolute chaos. The entire office had been ransacked from top to bottom. The filing cabinets had been ripped apart, and paper littered the floor. Glass beakers had been knocked aside and broken. Books had been tossed from their shelves, and some now lay fanned open on the floor. His desk drawers had been pulled open, a family photograph had been swiped off the desktop and onto the floor. Julianna curiously noticed another photo of Greta and her was missing altogether. Yet the oddest thing of all was her dad's reaction. Jacob looked at the destruction of his private sanctum, wearing a strange, almost victorious grin.

Julianna was horrified. She sobbed, "Daddy, what happened? What's going on?"

He put a comforting hand on her shoulder. "Don't worry, Smarty. You know I always have a secret hiding place."

She cried harder. "Oh, Daddy! Why would anybody do this? Why?"

Suddenly, Julianna felt herself being pulled away from her father and found herself looking at Declan's face, dimly light by a flashlight propped on his cot and pointed her direction.

"Julianna. Julianna, are you okay?" he asked with concern. "You were crying and seemed very upset."

After she had a moment to focus, she slapped his hand away from her shoulder which he had been shaking.

"Of course I'm okay," she said, irritated. "Hasn't anyone ever told you it's only a dream?"

Declan rocked back on his heels to put a little distance between them. "I know, but you've been having such a hard time with your dreams lately, and you seemed very upset."

"I was upset in my dream, but I'm fine in the tunnel. I think if I could've slept longer I may have gotten a few answers," she said in a hostile tone. "But now I may never know, thank you very much!" She knew it was irrational and even mean to take out her frustration on Declan, who she knew in her heart had only tried to help her. Still she rolled over and faced the wall, pulling the covers closer around her in a huff, as if the bedding would keep him away from her.

"Sorry," Declan said with soft sincerity as he climbed back into his own bed.

The next morning, Julianna awoke from a dreamless slumber, even more irritated that she had not been able to re-enter the dream world from which Declan had pulled her. If only she had had a few more minutes, she convinced herself, she could have learned why the office had been trashed and about the secret hiding place to which her father had referred. And what about the experiment he had planned, the whole reason he had pulled her from school to start? Suddenly, Julianna sat upright in her bed as her mind connected the dots. Greta had said no one knew why Julianna had been with her father because she had been taken to school that morning with her sister. He had pulled her out of school which had not been part of that day's plan. Had Julianna's dream been about his last day? Was she dreaming about the day of the attacks when he died? The thought made Julianna even more irritated. What would she have learned if she had been allowed to keep sleeping?

She stomped her foot on the rug in frustration and slipped on a pair of slippers. As she opened the tunnel door, she saw that Declan remained in his own cot, sound asleep. She looked at him in disgust as she watched the sheets gently rise and fall to the rhythm of his breathing and muttered, "It must make one very tired to wake other people."

Julianna found Greta in the kitchen and sat down at the table in a huff. Greta noticed her mood right away. "What's wrong with you?" she asked. "Didn't sleep well?"

Julianna scoffed. "Well, I would have slept just fine if someone hadn't awakened me!"

"Does Declan snore or something?"

"No, I was talking in my sleep and sounded upset, so he woke me right in the middle of what I believe to be a very important dream."

"Oh," Greta said with a wave of the spatula in her hand. "So he was just trying to be nice to you."

Julianna frowned at her sister, her forehead wrinkling between her eyes. "No! I'm pretty sure I was dreaming about the day Dad died. I was about to figure it all out. Why he took me from school, why his office was destroyed, what experiment he was about to perform. And then he just yanked me away from it all."

Greta stopped cooking and looked at her sister. "Or the dream could have just been a dream and nothing more. It could have been what your mind conjured from all the talk about Dad last night. Your friend heard you getting upset, so he did what a friend would do. I think you're being a bit unreasonable right now."

"You don't understand," Julianna muttered and laid her head down on the table so she could continue to pout in peace.

It did nothing to deter Greta's lecturing. "It seems to me that Declan has been a very good friend to you and really has expected nothing in return. I sincerely hope you do not give him a hard time about something like this."

When Declan entered the room a short while later, Greta was just getting breakfast on the table. "Good morning, Declan," she greeted with a smile.

"Good morning," Declan returned. He looked at Julianna who still wore a pout and did not offer a greeting. Declan thought perhaps the sisters had had a disagreement. He whispered to Julianna, "Is something wrong?"

Julianna huffed. "I think you know exactly what is wrong with me." She crossed her arms and twisted her body so that he was not in her line of sight. Declan looked bewildered for a moment. Then he bit back a chuckle. "You're not mad at me for waking you last night, are you?"

She sharply whipped her head around and glared at him. "Do you think it's funny?" she asked in outrage. "You of all people *know* what I have been through with my dreams!"

"I *do* know," Declan returned, his voice volume raised a notch. "Which is why I woke you rather than let you continue to be upset. You've told me you've had dreams about people falling into black holes. Most people appreciate being awakened from a nightmare, you know."

"Well, not those who were just about to figure out the answers to so many questions," she shot back.

Declan paused. He had watched Julianna for years and had seen her at her best and her worst. She could garner the attention of everyone at the cafeteria table and delight them with a humorous story. Or she could get angry and tear someone to shreds. Declan felt fortunate she had never turned on him in all the years that he had known her, but maybe Julianna thought her reunion with her sister could give her cause to treat him differently. Declan was not the only person she had anymore. While he had been amused to watch

Julianna take on Henders Costma, there was no way Declan was going to let her treat him in a similar manner.

"I am sorry you're upset," Declan said in a calm matter-of-fact voice. "Yet you must know I had no way of knowing the content of your dream. Therefore, it is unreasonable for you to be angry at me. If you wish to continue to be angry, I can't stop you. However, I also will not sit by and permit you to be nasty to me. I have done nothing that I consider wrong. I thought I was helping my friend, and I deserve no disrespect from you." He picked up his glass and sipped some orange juice. Then he turned toward his hostess. "This looks delicious again, Greta. Thanks!"

"You are very welcome, Declan," Greta returned with a satisfied, amused smile.

Julianna's eyes widened in surprise for a moment before she resumed her glowering. She was not going to give in to him and his reasonableness just yet, even though she may have known he was correct in everything that he had said. She also did not appreciate the I-told-you-so smirk that Greta now wore. Therefore, she stuffed a bite of pancake in her mouth and fumed silently. After a minute, she asked, "Where's Sam?" Perhaps he could be her ally in this room.

"He already left for work," Greta replied. "I have to leave before long. Do you mind if I leave Starla here with you two? I don't want to take her to the child care facility and have her mention our houseguests."

Declan raised his eyebrows. "Oh yes. I hadn't thought of that. Certainly, she can stay here. I'll be happy to entertain her."

Declan almost always used the word "we," and the snub, which she was certain had been intentional, made Julianna purse her lips a little harder, but she said nothing.

"I hope you two will be able to entertain yourselves and a child all day. If you get bored, feel free to clean the attic or organize the basement," Greta kidded.

Declan and Greta chatted amiably throughout breakfast while Julianna continued her silent treatment, telling herself it was a little effective even if they acted like it was not.

Finally, Greta looked pointedly at Julianna, "Well, I'd love to stay and chat with you all day, but I have to get to work. Enjoy yourselves today!" She pushed her chair away from the table, grabbed her purse from a nearby hook and headed for the garage door. "I'll be home around 5:30."

Julianna heaved a sigh. It seemed like a long time to spend in uncomfortable silence, but she was not done being mad yet. She had been so close; she just knew it! The fact that Declan smiled at her before sticking a forkful of eggs in his mouth only fanned the flame of her anger. Her chair clattered as she pushed herself away from the table and stormed into the study. Determined to get something out of this day, she ran her finger along the spines of her father's many books. Then she saw the binders lining a different shelf. As a child, she had never paid much attention to these binders because she was never allowed to touch them anyway. The binders were where her father kept all of his works in progress or unpublished notes. Long ago, Julianna had worked her way through the volumes of his published work in the Compound's library. As soon as she was old enough to understand fully the material, she had devoured his books, hoping to feel closer to her father or that something might spark a recollection of a family dinner conversation. She gladly did anything she could to conjure up a memory of her happy family, especially on the days she felt particularly alone.

She pulled one of the binders from the shelf and blew away some of the thick layer of dust. She coughed a little as she wiped even more away with her pajama top. From the look of it, no one else had read his work in the interim either. She sat in his old armchair and started speed reading. Maybe she could find some clue to help her unravel the mystery of the experiment from that last day. She pushed aside the nagging doubt that Greta might be right. It might have been nothing more than a dream inspired by the talk of the evening. In her heart, she believed that the dream was a message from a memory.

Colin walked into Guardian's personal chambers feeling a lot curious and a bit hopeful. Perhaps Guardian had summoned him to ask him something personal about Delilah. Maybe he was finally ready to give Delilah her due and wanted to suggestions as to the best way he could go about it. These were the thoughts running through Colin's head when he entered the room to find Guardian sitting in an elaborately designed high-back chair that could best be described as a throne, even though this was his personal living space where few were allowed access and airs were not necessary.

Guardian gave Colin a smile that Colin found to be a bit creepy He knew he was not supposed to feel that way, but he just could not help himself. All the training in the world would not have changed the feelings he had when that man was around. Instinct told Colin he should be wary.

"Warrior O'Connor, I understand that your brother Declan is a fugitive from the Scholars Compound. Have you happened to hear from him?"

Declan, Colin thought. Of course, this is about Declan. Why had he been foolish enough to consider Delilah as a subject. "No, sir," Colin responded. "I have not seen or heard from my brother since the day I was removed from my school.

"Were you surprised to find out that he was wanted?"

"Absolutely, sir," Colin replied. "Declan, as I remember him, was always a very straight arrow. I am very surprised to see he would break the rules in such an egregious manner."

"I thought that might be the case," Guardian said with a nod. "I really think he is under the negative influence of his partner, Julianna Brenner. Are you familiar with her?"

"No, sir, I had not heard that name until we were summoned for the announcement."

"I think she may be forcing your brother to go along with her, much to his detriment. I believe, if we can separate the two of them, Declan could work very productively in another Scholars' Compound. I believe Ms. Brenner to be the mastermind behind this, this caper. However, I am worried deeply about your brother's safety right now. I don't know if you're aware of this, but Scholars really are not equipped to be able to survive in the Workers' world. He doesn't have the knowledge or the skill set he needs. This is why I have summoned you. You must know how much I would hate to lose a quality Scholar, such as your brother."

Colin nodded.

"Therefore, I am seeking your assistance. Do you know of any family or friends to whom your brother may go to seek refuge?"

"Our mother. She's all the family that's left. Our father perished in the attacks."

"Yes, yes, but anyone else?" Guardian asked with an impatient wave of his hand.

Colin knew someone must have seen his mother, and he fought back the urge to inquire after her well-being. Such a question would be impertinent. "Not that I can think of," Colin answered. "We really didn't have any extended family, and although he had friends at school, I don't know how he would find any of them today. I don't think any of them were close enough to risk harboring him as a fugitive either."

Guardian's expression soured. "Very well, then. If someone comes to mind, please let me know at once. For your brother's safety."

"Yes, sir," Colin said with a bow.

"You're dismissed."

Declan had not taken Julianna's bait. Instead he had cleaned up the breakfast dishes and sought out Starla. He was sure the child would be in her room, where she spent much of her time. He knew she was still adjusting to her new life and thought the least he could do was play a game or two and make her more comfortable with him.

Later that day, Guardian Costma paced the floor of the living room in his private residence. The opulent quarters featured the best of everything from antique furniture to priceless artwork to up-to-the-minute technology. Yet none of it was helping him to achieve his one goal at the moment. He must find Julianna Brenner. Failure was not an option. Had any other Scholar managed to escape from the Compound, he would have been furious. He would have tried to find them, but by this point, he probably would have determined the search was not worth the resources. Even Declan's own brother had no idea where he had gone. However, this search he could not halt. Julianna was far too dangerous to have on the outside.

Finally, he heard the knock on the door that he had expected. "Come in," he bellowed nervously. "Any word?"

Leader Cantor entered the room. "We have not had any luck asking random people around either of their hometowns. No one recalls seeing them. If they have been to either place, they have done an excellent job of blending in."

"What about the assigned child at the Hartford residence? Did the child say anything?" Guardian inquired, hoping to take advantage of a child's innocence.

"The child would not speak to the Warriors. Evidently, she has not been in the home very long and is still having trouble adjusting. She does not speak much at all," the Cantor explained.

Guardian pounded his fist on an end table. "This is ridiculous! Why can they not be found? Where is my car? The car and two people did not vanish into thin air. This cannot be as difficult as you are making it. I want them found now!" he raged.

Cantor bowed. "We are doing our best," he said before making a quick exit.

Delilah had the unfortunate timing to enter the room seconds later. "Good evening, Daddy. I wanted to talk to you about perhaps being assigned a job. I would like to take on more responsibility. I have grown bored with very little to do."

Guardian turned to her, his eyes flashed with rage. "You have grown *bored*," he repeated incredulously. "I have provided you with all of this," he waved his hands around their surroundings, "and yet you have the nerve to complain to me that you're bored?"

"Daddy, I wasn't complaining," Delilah protested. "I was asking for more responsibility."

"I have set up a situation for you in which you are not required to have any responsibility, and you do not appreciate it in the least!" he shouted. "You have everything a child could ask for, and you are grateful for nothing! You would like a job? Here's a job! Go to your room, lie on your bed and be thankful that you have such a lovely room. Be thankful that you aren't a Worker who has to serve in a job for several hours a day. Be thankful that your father is the ruler of this country and soon will be the ruler of the world. The only expectation for you would be to produce an heir at some point in the next several years. For all of this, you should be grateful, and that is the job to which I am assigning you. You must write me a list of all the things you have for which you should be grateful. Now get out of my sight!"

Delilah turned on her heel and ran from the room, hot tears stinging her eyes before she made it upstairs to her bedroom. She threw herself on the king-size bed, buried her face in a lace-trimmed pillow and sobbed until a soft knock at the door interrupted her.

CHAPTER 17

She sat up and wiped tears away from her eyes with the back of her hand. Although she knew she should not, she could not help but hope that perhaps her father had come to his senses and was there to apologize to her and talk about what she would like to do with her life besides waste away in her gilded tower. She sat up taller on the bed and tried to keep her voice from wavering when she said, "Come in."

Of course, Guardian had not come to see her. It was her loyal, trusted friend, Colin. "I take it your talk didn't go well?" Colin assumed as he entered her room and shut the door behind him for the sake of her privacy.

"No, it didn't," she said glumly, not needing to hide her disappointment from Colin.

Colin took a seat on the bed next to her, and she put her head on his shoulder. "Why does he treat me like that? He acts like he's given me everything in the world, but it's only material things. Why doesn't he want me to learn a skill? Why has he never tested me to see if I could be a Scholar? And heaven forbid he show me any ounce of affection. He wouldn't want me to think he might actually care about me."

He wrapped an arm around her and pulled her close. "I'm sorry," he said sincerely. "I thought maybe he would be happy that you were showing an interest and acting more like an adult."

"Nothing that I do matters to him," Delilah said. "I don't think it ever will."

Colin looked down at his beloved charge. He thought he had hit the jackpot the day he had been assigned to guard over and protect "Princess Delilah" as the other Warriors called her. The Guardian's daughter was a classic beauty with long, flowing waves of auburn hair and emerald green eyes. Many times now he had wiped tears away from her porcelain skin. When she was happy, her smile brightened his world. In the two years he had been put in charge of Delilah's care, he had grown to care about her very much. He saw the wounded child behind the demanding princess the rest of the Warriors knew.

Delilah had been given a Warrior closer to her own age after she had gone through a series of older men who did not understand her, nor care if they did. Colin had been different. The first time she had seen him walk into the room in his bright red Warriors uniform with its gold cords, she had thought he reminded her of a prince. The first time he showed her that he genuinely cared about her feelings, he had solidified their long-standing friendship. Delilah, he found, only wanted someone to care about her. They had bonded over their motherless existence. She confided in him about her issues with her mighty father, and he confided in her that Warriors sometimes got lonely too. He wanted her to get the love and respect she sought. Now he felt terrible because he had been the one to advise her to speak to her father about taking on more responsibility rather than having her potential wither away in the seclusion of her bedroom. Material things were fine, but in Delilah's case, she did not even have anyone with whom to share them.

She lifted her head and sat up straighter. "It's okay," Delilah said sadly. "I wasn't expecting much anyway. Besides, you have your own problems. Have you heard anything about your brother?"

"Nothing," Colin reported. "It seems he and his partner have vanished into thin air. The really interesting part is that, other than your father, everyone seems far more concerned with the partner than with Declan. I haven't really been told why. Just that it is imperative that she be captured and returned to the Compound, alive and well."

"Hmm, that is a bit curious," Delilah mused. "I wonder why."

"I wish I knew. I wish I knew anything about my brother these days," he said.

"It's so ridiculous," Delilah fumed. "Why should you not be allowed to talk to your brother or your mom? Is it not just as much of a distraction for you to wonder about their well-being? Maybe if you had been allowed to see your brother all this time, he wouldn't have gone crazy and be on the lam right now."

Colin nodded. "Maybe you're right. I just hope he stays safe. It is wild to imagine how close in proximity we've been all this time and were never even allowed to say hello. Do you suppose Declan's presence is the reason I was forbidden from ever going to the Compound?"

"Probably, now that I think about it," Delilah replied. Then she giggled through her tears. "But if you ever see him again, tell him I give him credit for stealing my father's stupid car. Boy, was he mad about that!" Delilah had delighted in his anger over the loss of his precious car, and she could not help but wonder if her father would have been half as distraught if Declan O'Connor had walked into her bedroom and had stolen her. *Probably not*, she told herself.

Colin smiled at his favorite friend. "I'll do that if I ever get the chance," he promised. He studied her for a moment. "Are you sure you're going to be okay?"

She smiled bravely and reached out to ruffle his very short dark hair. "I'm sure I'll be just fine. But thank you for caring enough to ask."

"Maybe we should go to the theater later?" he asked as he rose.

"Yes, I'd like that. After dinner?" Delilah stood to follow him to the door.

"Very well then," Colin confirmed. He turned to face her again and opened his arms to invite her into a warm hug. She gladly fell into the strong arms of her constant companion. When he squeezed her, she could feel the well-defined muscles of a Warrior who had spent many years in training and worked hard to maintain his physique daily. She felt safe with him, which is a sensation she had not experienced in years before him.

"See you soon," she said with a smile.

Julianna diligently had been reading through her father's notes, searching them for any ideas as to what experiment he may have wanted to conduct on his final day. As she prepared to start on the third binder, she rubbed her eyes and wondered if there was even a point to what she was doing. So far, nothing in the first two binders had seemed very important. Some of it she could not even comprehend. Some of it had been nothing but random thoughts scribbled in haste, a reminder of a thought to be completed at a future date, and Julianna could not decipher the short-hand or finish the thought for him. Yet, she had the time to spare and could not turn away now.

When she was a few pages into the third binder, Declan appeared in the doorway of the study with a giggling Starla riding piggyback. He hiked the child up a bit and announced, "Starla has a question for you."

Julianna figured he was attempting to use Starla as a buffer and did not return their smiles. "What's that?" she asked.

"Would you like to play with us? We're building a castle," Starla requested through her giggles.

"I would like to help, but I've got a lot of reading to finish," she said. "Maybe in a while."

Declan shrugged and said, "Your loss. Let's go!" As he galloped off, he tried not to let Starla be aware that his heart had just dropped to his stomach when Julianna had turned them down. In the Compound, they had bickered occasionally. They may have disagreed on how to best accomplish a goal or conduct an experiment, but they never got angry with each other. He hated the fact that Julianna seemed to still be upset with him, but he was not going to admit he did something wrong. Even though he hated the feeling, he decided to just leave her alone for a while longer.

When Greta met Sam for lunch that day, he asked, "How were our guests this morning? I didn't come on too strongly last night and scare them, did I?"

"You were not really a topic of discussion this morning," Greta said. "They had sillier problems to address."

Sam gave her a curious look. "What do you mean by that?"

"Apparently, Julianna got rather vocal and upset while dreaming last night. Declan woke her up, and she spent all of breakfast pouting because she thought she was about to solve all the mysteries surrounding our dad. When I seemed to take Declan's side in the matter, I was given the silent treatment as well."

Sam chuckled as he took a bite of his sandwich. "Well, it may seem silly to us, but I don't think it is to her. She's a genius who is missing gaps of her own history. It must be a little disconcerting for her."

"I suppose, but it doesn't mean she needs to be miserable to everyone around her. Especially Declan. She is lucky to have him, and she has no idea. They were so terrified to show each other too much affection. They have no frame of reference as to what a perfect couple is, let alone realize they are one."

Sam laughed again. "True! They do make quite a pair, but they have no idea, do they?"

Greta shook her head. "Do you know they've never even kissed each other? But don't worry! I had an idea!"

Sam jokingly dropped his head and shook it. "Of course you did! And how much work will today's idea make for me," he teased.

"Oh, you hush!" she said as she playfully slapped his chest. "I'm going to do most of the work. I just need you to loan Declan your best suit."

"I will do whatever it takes to make you happy," he said.

For a few minutes, they discussed Starla, her progress since arriving and the decision to leave her with Julianna and Declan. Then Sam asked, "Do you really think Julianna and Declan will join our efforts?"

"I do," Greta said.

"Do you think it'll make a difference?"

"I think it could make all the difference," she said with a smile.

When Greta and Sam got home that night, they found Declan in the kitchen, frying up some pork chops while Starla sat at the counter coloring contently.

"What a nice surprise!" Greta exclaimed.

"I just hope everything turns out well. I microwaved a bag of mixed vegetables, and I have some potatoes baking in the oven. But please bear in mind that I have not cooked anything pretty much ever! I've spent the last ten years eating food in a cafeteria that someone else made," Declan explained.

"Without even trying it, I'm giving you an A for effort," Greta said with a kind smile. She kissed Starla on top of the head. "Where's Julianna?"

"I assume she's still in the study," Declan said. "She headed there after breakfast, and I don't think she's come out."

"She didn't want to build a castle with my blocks," Starla reported, looking up from her coloring page only for a moment. "And she didn't want the lunch Declan made. But Declan says she still likes me."

"Of course, she still likes you," Sam said, patting her head affectionately.

Greta placed her purse on the hook and marched to the study. She found Julianna with papers strewn all around her and a rather crazed look in her bloodshot eyes. "What is going on?" Greta demanded.

"I was reading through Daddy's papers," Julianna explained.

"All day?" Greta asked incredulously.

"Pretty much. I had to stop for a bathroom break and to get a drink, but other than that, I've been speed reading."

"Did you accomplish what you had hoped?" Greta asked with a raised eyebrow and a hand on her hip.

Oblivious to her sister's irritation, Julianna said, "I finished reading everything, but I haven't figured it all out yet. I think it's in one of these notes I can't decode."

"Have you been in here all day as your weird way of trying to stick it to Declan?"

"What?" Julianna said, looking up briefly. "No, I haven't really thought much about him today. I've been trying to figure out what the experiment was. The final experiment. Why he pulled me out of school."

Greta could no longer hold her tongue. "Who cares!" she shouted at her sister.

CHAPTER 18

Julianna sat back in shock and gave her sister a surprised expression. "What?"

Greta stomped over to Julianna and grabbed her shoulders, pulling her to her feet. "Look at you! Look at *this*!" She waved her hand in reference to the mess of papers littered on the floor, chairs and desk.

"I'm sorry about the mess," Julianna apologized. "I'll clean it up."

"I'm not worried about the papers," Greta said. "I'm worried about you. Are you trying to drive yourself mad? You don't remember that last day. You have trouble recalling some aspects of Dad. I understand that you find this a bit frustrating, but I can fill in some of those blanks for you. You have dreams that may or may not be memories. But the bottom line is what does it matter? Knowing what he was working on that last day isn't going to bring Dad back. It isn't going to erase the attacks or keep Mom from dying on that bridge. If you got all the answers you want in the next five minutes, would it change your life at all? I really don't think so!"

Julianna heaved a great sigh and dropped onto a pile of papers in the chair behind her. She put her head in her hands and tried very hard not to start crying.

Greta snatched at papers on the floor and put them into a haphazard pile. "I should've thrown out all of this junk years ago," she muttered. "I definitely would have if I had foreseen this! You've wasted an entire day of your life, of your freedom, obsessing on this!"

She was starting to suspect that Greta was right.

"You could have spent the day playing with your niece and enjoying the company of a really wonderful man, but you were hiding in here digging through ancient papers and trying to figure out notes that make sense to no one but a dead man. Did you think I never looked at them in all this time?" Greta continued to rant. "Of course, I have. I knew what was in here. I knew that it basically was all worthless to anyone but him. I guess stupid nostalgia kept me from throwing it out. I didn't think it was hurting anything, and I didn't really need the space."

At that point, Julianna was not certain if Greta was still talking to her. Julianna was not used to such emotionally charged situations, and she was not sure how she was supposed to react.

"Spending all *day* in here!" Greta continued to rant. "You've been trapped away doing nothing but studying and working for years, and the first chance you get you run right back in here to do it some more. I don't understand it! All day, your … friend, look at that, I'm not even sure what to call him, has been taking care of Starla, fixing meals, and you're in here.

Maybe your day would've been better spent figuring out what to call him. What am I supposed to call him, Julianna?"

Julianna blinked. Greta had been still talking to her, but she had no clue how to respond. Greta clenched her fists and stomped her foot. "Stop being so frustrating! Stop being a Scholar for five minutes and enjoy your life just the tiniest bit. You've been so worried about what Dad was doing. What about Mom? Have you forgotten everything she taught you?"

Whenever she had been in a situation where she was not sure what was expected of her, Julianna defaulted to brutal honesty. "I don't really know what you want me to say. I admit you may have a point. I may be obsessing over this a bit, and I, too, have wondered why. It was something I felt compelled to do. I don't understand why it bothers you so much, but I will stop."

Now it was Greta's turn to look perplexed. Taken aback, she asked, "That's it?"

"Yes," Julianna answered. "But I don't understand all that stuff about what I'm supposed to call him. Why wouldn't you call him Declan?"

Greta paused for a moment and looked at her sister in disbelief before bursting with laughter. "I'm going to get you to figure it out yet!" she declared. "But first, Declan has made us a lovely dinner. Afterward, I have a little surprise for you."

"Sorry about the mess," Julianna said as she started grabbing papers from the floor.

"Leave it," Greta commanded as she grabbed her hand and tugged her toward the door. As they walked out of the study, Greta pulled the door closed tightly behind them and hoped Julianna was sincere when she said she would stay out.

By the time they returned to the kitchen, Sam had set the table, and Declan was pulling a sheet of baked potatoes out of the oven. "I'm not promising the best results ever," Declan gave his disclaimer again. "I looked up some recipes and followed the instructions. That's all, so I hope no one is disappointed by my lack of culinary genius."

"I'm sure it'll be just fine," Julianna offered politely.

Declan was happy that she had elected to speak with him again, but wisely chose not to point it out. While they ate, Sam said, "Greta has been working on a surprise she has for the two of you. So after we're done eating, you both need to head upstairs. Declan, you'll need to go to the guest room, and Julianna will go to our bedroom."

"Why?" Julianna asked. "What's the surprise?"

"If they told you, it wouldn't be a surprise then," Starla piped.

Everyone laughed. Starla smiled bashfully, pleased with the positive attention.

After dinner, Declan reported to the guest room as instructed. Sam handed him a three-piece suit on one hanger and a light blue dress shirt on another. "You need to put these on," Sam instructed. Then he walked to a dresser and retrieved a pair of black dress socks and a royal blue tie. Finally, he pulled a pair of black leather dress shoes from the closet shelf.

"What is all this?" Declan asked as he dutifully began to don the suit.

"Greta has planned a makeshift prom for you and Julianna. Julianna said something about never getting to go to a dance, so tonight is Greta's make-good." Sam gave a good-natured chuckle and added with a wink, "Sorry about this!"

Declan returned his smile and tried not to look too excited. "Well, I've never been to a dance either, so who knows? It may turn out I really like them!"

"At least you don't have to worry about your partner knowing all these dances you don't," Sam said. "I would assume you and Julianna are on a level playing field in that respect."

As Declan buttoned the gray vest, he observed, "It's a good thing we're close to the same size."

"Yes," Sam agreed. "I guess the Brenner girls have similar tastes in men." Declan understood the inference, but he did not question Sam about it.

"Hurry up and finish getting dressed," Sam said as he handed Declan a black leather belt. "In case you didn't know, girls take much longer to get ready, so Greta has assigned us other duties during your wait."

CHAPTER 19

Across the hall, Julianna asked Greta, "So what's going on?"

"You'll see," Greta said as she pushed her bedroom door open. She reached into her closet and pulled out two dresses. One was a silky navy blue dress with a thin silver stripe highlighted with sequins in a curvy line from the plunging neckline to the waist. The floor-length dress was form fitting. The other was a pastel pink confection with a tea-length hemline and plenty of tulle on the flouncy skirt. "Which one?"

"For what?"

"For you, silly," Greta replied. "Which one do you want to wear?"

Since Greta was an inch or so taller than Julianna, she chose the pink dress, afraid the blue dress may be too long. Greta thrust it into her hands and said, "Put that on the bed for now. Next, the shoes. Wait! What size do you wear?"

Julianna wore shoes a 1/2 size smaller than her sister, but Greta said she would solve that problem by jamming some handkerchiefs into a closed toe pair of shoes. With that in mind, Julianna chose a silver pair with a modestly high heel. Greta handed her a pair of iridescent white tights and instructed Julianna to undress. When Julianna started to take the dress of the hanger, Greta shouted, "No!"

She threw a silky bathrobe into Julianna's hand. "We have a lot of prep work to do before you put on the dress. Hair and make-up first. Wear the robe. It won't mess up your hair when you take it off."

Julianna did as she was told and walked willingly to the vanity when Greta grabbed her shoulders and steered her that way. She took a seat on the small bench while Greta fluttered around her. Then Greta wrapped strands of her hair in hot rollers until Julianna wore a headful of heavy pink curlers. While she waited a minute before removing the curlers, Greta gave Julianna a couple bottles of perfume to sample and asked which one she liked best. Greta sprayed Julianna's selection in a mist all around her while Julianna pursed her lips and squeezed her eyes shut.

When Greta removed the curlers, Julianna's shorter hair formed wide, bouncy curls. Greta decorated Julianna's hair with a thin pearl-beaded headband. With her hair dyed, Julianna looked even more like Greta than she had thought. Greta set to work painting her face with blush, eyeshadow, mascara and lipstick, careful not to use too much for someone who had never seen herself in any make-up and using only lighter, natural shades of pinks and bronze that complemented her skin tone. Julianna could hardly believe she was looking at her own reflection when

Greta was done. Giddily, she exclaimed, "You made me look like a movie star!"

Greta smiled broadly, pleased with her own work and Julianna's reaction. "Well, every girl needs to look her best when she goes to her prom."

"What do you mean?" Julianna asked excitedly.

"That's your surprise!" Greta exclaimed. "Your mock prom is waiting for you downstairs." Julianna stood and hurried for the door, but Greta called her back. "Wait! You haven't picked out your jewelry yet!"

Julianna put her hands to her mouth and hopped up and down as she shrieked in a high pitch, "Jewelry? I get to wear jewelry!"

"Of course," Greta answered. She walked to their mother's old jewelry armoire and pulled open the top drawer. "Take a look. Your ears aren't pierced, but you can pick a necklace, bracelet and rings. Help yourself!"

Greta had kept all of their mother's jewelry, and Julianna had her eye on the expensive ones they had not been allowed to touch as children. Their mother had permitted them to play dress-up with some of the costume pieces, but certain drawers were off limits. Now, Julianna gasped as she selected a sapphire and diamond ring, a gold bracelet and a string of pearls. Greta helped her with the clasp on the choker-length necklace. When she was done, Julianna twirled and twisted to examine herself in the full-length mirror on the closet door.

"You look beautiful," Greta said, her eyes misting over. She was so delighted she could give her sister this moment. "Now if you're ready, your date awaits you downstairs."

"My date? You mean Declan?"

"Yes." She took Julianna by the shoulders and looked into her eyes. "When I said I don't know what to call him, what I was implying was that you need to figure out what he means to you in the outside world. When this is all over, when you're not running and you're really free, will Declan be a part of your life? Is that what you want? I'm not saying you need to figure it all out tonight, but I'm saying you really should start thinking about it. I think he adores you, but you need to figure out if you feel the same way."

Julianna scoffed, "You don't know that. You don't know that he thinks of me as more than a friend."

"Granted, it's just my opinion, but I think it's a pretty accurate one."

Julianna's heart beat with anticipation as descended the stairs. The thrill of doing something a normal teenager would do, even if she was a year or so late, was almost too much to take. Until that moment, she had never realized she really felt she had missed out on these moments. Scholars were denied normal rites of passage, but now she had been given a chance to reclaim at least one of those moments.

When she entered the family room, Julianna found the simple decorations, which Greta fretted may look a little cheesy, dazzling to her. Sam and Declan had taken the time Julianna had spent primping to hang some crepe paper streamers, some white twinkle lights that had previously decorated a Christmas tree, a few silk flowers, and a couple other decorations that Sam had dug out of a box from the attic. Music played from a small box which was perched on a shelf on the wall. They even had tossed a white tablecloth over a card table upon which they had placed a few cupcakes, napkins, tiny glass cups, and a punch bowl filled with a red drink. Best of all, Declan stood smiling next to Sam and dressed in fine clothes with his hair neatly combed. She turned to Greta and hugged her, "It's perfect! Thank you!"

"Well, it's not a gym or a banquet hall, but I figured it's better than nothing," Greta remarked as she returned the hug.

Declan hoped his jaw did not drop too far when Julianna entered the room, but he was taken aback by her beauty. He always had considered Julianna to be his pretty little ray of sunshine, but tonight she was undeniably gorgeous. Greta's make-up work only accentuated Julianna's naturally attractive features, like her high cheekbones and full lips. She approached him and pulled out her skirt into a little curtsy. "You look very handsome tonight," she said.

He smiled goofily at her until Sam nudged his arm. "You forgot this," Sam reminded. Sam handed Declan a plastic case which he popped open to present Julianna with a white rose fashioned into a wrist corsage. Declan widened the stretchy silver band, and Julianna slid her hand through it. She admired it from afar before holding it to her nose to smell the sweet scent.

"Thank you," Julianna said with a smile.

Sam put an arm around Greta, and they both smiled at the couple in the living room before they started to quietly tiptoe out of the room. Declan spotted them, "Hey! Where are you going? Aren't you going to dance?"

"We've already been to proms, and we're both really underdressed," Greta explained. "But you two have fun!"

"Are you sure?" Julianna asked. "You both did so much work."

"It was no trouble at all," Sam said. "Enjoy yourselves. We've had a long day."

When Sam and Greta had slipped away, Julianna had nothing left to do but face Declan and deal with the way she had treated him all day. "I'm sorry I snapped at you about waking me," Julianna said humbly. "I know you were trying to look out for me." She added, "Just like you always do." Her head remained downcast, but she lifted her eyes hopefully to meet his.

"It's okay," Declan said. "I wouldn't have done it if I had known you were getting some answers."

She smiled gratefully at him. He held out a hand to her. "May I have this dance?" She placed her dainty hand in his, and he pulled her closer as he wrapped his hand around her waist. She tentatively placed her left hand on his shoulder as they began swaying to the music like they had seen people do in old movies.

"How did your day go?" Declan asked. "Did you find anything?"

Julianna shook her head. "No, and I don't want to talk about it now." She had decided to take Greta's advice and figure out how she felt about Declan outside of the restrictions of the Compound. Declan thought not discussing her quest in the moment sounded like a great plan, and they danced the rest of the dance in silence.

The next song was a fast-paced number. Declan whirled Julianna away from him without letting go of her hand. Then they both laughed at themselves as they performed every silly dance move they had ever seen. They were breathless by the time the song ended, so Declan suggested they try the punch.

Declan ladled some of the red juice into a glass cup for her. She accepted the cup and took a small sip before she asked, "You guys didn't spike this, did you?"

"I assure you, it's just juice," Declan said with a laugh.

"Well, I understand from some old movies I've seen that a girl can't be too careful," she teased. "I wouldn't want to fall down and sleep in the front yard or swing from the dining room chandelier." She thought for a minute. "Or maybe I would. I've never really thought about the option. Have you ever thought about how much there is in the world that we can choose now?"

"A little. If I think on it for too long, it becomes a bit overwhelming. I'm still trying to decipher the facts of the real world from the fiction we were fed inside the Compound. I'm still a nerdy Scholar at heart. I need all the information before I can make a good decision."

Julianna smiled. She was hoping to get some information for decisions about her future as well. "What kinds of decisions have you entertained?" she asked. "Have you considered what you would like to do outside of the Scholars Compound?"

"I really haven't given that much thought," he admitted. "I really liked our work inside the Compound. I was happy doing it, so I suppose I would like to find something similar I could do on the outside as a Worker."

"Hmm, me too, I suppose," Julianna said. "What sort of job do you think that would be? All the research is done inside the Compound. Maybe we could pass for teachers or something. I know it's not exactly the same, but it'd probably be something we could do well."

"Maybe," he said noncommittally. "What decisions have you been thinking about?"

"So many," she answered. "What I want to be when I grow up, who I want to be with, where I want to be, how I want to live my life."

"Those are some pretty big ones," Declan pointed out.

"I know," she said. "And I haven't really figured any of them out. But the biggest decision I want to make tonight is," she paused dramatically, "which flavor of cupcake to eat. Chocolate or vanilla?" she asked him with a sweet smile.

"Chocolate," he answered. He smiled at her as he accepted the cupcake. As his fingers brushed against hers, Julianna could not ignore how much she liked every time he touched her and how she looked forward to the next time their skin would meet.

"You look beautiful tonight, in case you didn't know," Declan said.

She smiled shyly and bit her bottom lip. "Thanks, you clean up pretty well yourself, too," she replied as she gave his chest a gentle shove.

As they polished off their sweets, the perfect up-tempo song came on, one to which they could really move, but also let him hold her and move close to her. He asked if she would like to join him on the dance floor again. She held out her hand for him. As they danced, he noticed a tiny dab of frosting on the corner of her lips. "Oh, you have a little something there," he said as he gently wiped the spot away with his finger.

"Thanks," she said as the next song, a slow ballad, started.

Declan's heart was racing as he made the decision to pull her even closer. He hoped he was not playing with fire. He hoped that she still wanted to spend time with him even though now she was not forced to be with him. The thought that she would move on without him was one on which he found it too painful to dwell. He had figured out quite a while ago that he loved her and wanted nothing more out of life than to be with her. His love is what had compelled him to follow her and leave everything he knew because he was not prepared nor willing to live a life without her. He knew he should tell her all of that, but he just did not know how to say those words. Plus, a part of him was terrified she would reject him. As long as he said nothing, he at least still had his dreams.

Julianna liked the way she felt when he held her close. She liked it so much that she dared to move closer to him and rest her head against his chest as they swayed to the music. Declan took in a deep breath, and she felt his chest move. In his arms, she felt safe and warm. She thought she might even feel loved, but she had no idea how she was supposed to know if she was right. Who was she to judge if she felt love? For the girl who was used to knowing all the answers, she knew nothing about this particular subject, nor could she just look it up. Was she sure she loved Declan? Or did she just think so because he was always there and she had never had another option? She had trouble imagining someone better in her opinion than Declan, but was that just because she had not really met anyone else? Maybe I shouldn't be so hasty, she told herself. Or maybe he doesn't care if I love him or not. Maybe he's my best friend and that's it.

Now that she had set her mind to really thinking about their feelings, she found it to be nearly as confusing and frustrating as her dreams. If Julianna could not figure out her own feelings, how was she supposed to understand his? She tried hard to think about if she had had these feelings before they left the Compound. She knew she had wished he would be paired with her in the Genos Ceremony, but did that mean she loved him or was she just most comfortable with him? She tried to never think about it much before because she would not be able to do anything about it one way or another. Protecting their partnership was far more important than daydreaming about a romantic relationship.

Declan debated with himself what it meant that Julianna had moved closer and rested her head on him. Was she feeling what he was feeling? Was she just comfortable with him in a completely platonic way? What should he do? Should he kiss her? He was very unsure of himself.

The song had ended before either of them had decided anything. Julianna pulled back and smiled sweetly at her potential suitor. "That was nice," she said.

Declan brought his mind back to the present. Another well-timed, fast-paced song let them burn off some nervous energy for a few minutes. When her face was flushed red again, Declan suggested, "Take a break?" They walked to the sofa for a brief rest.

"Know what?" Julianna began. "You never really told me much about what happened during the times you would sneak off with Britta. Did you two dance together?"

Declan snorted "No."

"What did you do? Why did you never really fill me in?"

"For one, it was embarrassing," Declan admitted. "I did not feel anything for her. I liked her well enough, but I was not attracted to her in the least. Plus, I felt bad about using her like we did. But to be honest, I think she was using me a bit, too."

"How do you mean?" Julianna asked.

"She knew from the beginning that nothing was going to come of our relationship. It's not like we were going to get married and ride off into the sunset. Yet she kept pursuing me. I think she enjoyed the sneaking around, and that was the attraction for her."

"From the way you said that, I take it you did not enjoy the sneaking around?"

"No! I thought it was very nerve-wracking!" he exclaimed. "Think of the chance I was taking. If we ever were caught, it would be my whole life at stake. I would get shipped off somewhere."

Julianna giggled. "That's a little dramatic. Getting shipped off somewhere isn't exactly a capital sentence."

"It would be if I couldn't be with you." The words popped out of Declan's mouth before he had much time to think about them.

Julianna looked a little surprised, but her expression faded away into an irrepressible smile. "So you never answered the first part of my question. What exactly did you two do? Where'd you go? How'd you avoid getting caught?"

"We'd move from place to place within the Compound with Britta acting as my guard escort. To be honest, nobody really questioned us. She knew her way around and when other people would not be present. I think she knew every secluded corner in the

Compound. I saw places I never knew were there. I started to think maybe I was not the first Scholar of whom she tried to take advantage."

"You didn't tell me any of that before," Julianna admonished. "Why were you holding out on me?"

"I already told you. It was embarrassing," Declan repeated. "It was embarrassing for me to behave that way."

"What did you do that was so embarrassing to you?" Julianna pressed.

"I kissed her for one," he admitted.

Julianna tried not to look a little hurt. "You kissed her?"

"I guess, more accurately, you could say she kissed me. In the end, I was having trouble fending her off from wanting to do more than that. I thought she was a little aggressive."

"Was that your first kiss?"

"Yes," Declan said. "I wasn't much of a ladies' man when I was 12. I was pretty much a nerd back then, too."

"Was it weird?" Julianna asked.

"Very," Declan admitted. "For one, I was doing something we had been conditioned not to do. And for two, I didn't have those kinds of feelings for Britta. But I just kept reminding myself that I was taking one for the team. I was doing it for us."

Julianna could not look at him when she asked her next question. She looked at her lap and asked, "What about Sarah? Did you kiss her too?"

"Sarah? No, we were just talking. She was a bit handsy, always thinking she needed to touch me, hold hands with me, that sort of thing. But she never tried to kiss me."

"And you never tried to kiss her?"

"Of course not!"

"Well, then technically, you've never kissed anyone. You've just been kissed," Julianna reasoned.

Declan found her response curious. Had she been jealous of Britta and Sarah? Did she want him to kiss her? He was used to her straightforwardness, which was something he always had admired about her from their first meeting. This time though, she was anything but straightforward. He was going to have to guess at what she was thinking.

"Would you like to dance again?" he asked.

Julianna rose and tried to discreetly wipe her sweaty palms on the skirt of her dress. He quickly pulled her close again and tried to work up the nerve he would need. Maybe this time, it was his turn to be straightforward, he considered. Could he live with himself if he did not take the chance? As the song continued, he knew he was running out of time to make a decision. By the time the song played out its final notes, he took a deep breath and gathered up all his courage. He let go of her right hand and gently lifted her chin up until their eyes met. Then he slowly moved toward her until their lips met. Julianna did not protest. She slipped both of her arms around his neck and kissed him back.

When they parted, she gave him a giddy smile. "It's about time," she teased. "For a while there, I thought you were going around kissing everybody but me!"

Declan asked incredulously, "Don't you know you're the only girl I've ever wanted to kiss?"

She smiled demurely, stood on her tiptoes and stole another quick kiss. "I'm glad," she said matter-of-factly, back to being her usual honest self.

They may not have had their plans sketched out for their lives twenty years from now, but Julianna finally realized that they did not need to do that. They just needed to try to enjoy the moment in which they were living and not worry about tomorrow for a change. The pair danced several more dances before finally deciding to call it a night.

Before Julianna headed to a bathroom to trade her delicate pink frock for some practical pajamas, she turned to Declan and said, "I had a wonderful time tonight. Thank you!"

"Believe me when I say it was an absolute pleasure, my dear." He bowed gallantly and softly kissed her hand.

She curtsied and then hurried off. Declan smiled as he watched her go. Then he returned to the spare room to get ready for bed.

The next morning, Greta was giddily anxious to hear about how the "prom" had gone. If Sam had not been there to stop her, she would not have been able to resist the urge to peek last night and see how things were going. When Julianna finally wandered upstairs to find the shower, Greta practically pounced on her. "Get in here!" she commanded, pulling Julianna into her bedroom. Once Greta had closed the door, she asked, "Well?"

Julianna raised her eyebrows expectantly. "Well, what?"

"How did the prom go?"

"Oh! It was lovely! I can't thank you enough. You have no idea what it was like to go back and recapture some of those moments I always felt I'd missed out on. I had a perfectly delightful evening." She kissed Greta's cheek. "You and Sam are the best!"

"That's great, but how did things go with Declan?" Greta persisted.

"He had just as nice a time, I'm sure. We danced and danced."

"That's wonderful, but that's not exactly what I was looking for," Greta hinted.

Julianna finally caught on to Greta's questioning. "Oh! You want to know if I decided what to call him?"

"Yes! What are you going to call him? Do you know?" Greta asked excitedly.

"No, I don't know what I would like to call him," Julianna answered. Greta's shoulders slumped slightly. Julianna smiled broadly and added, "But I did like it when he kissed me!"

Greta squealed and playfully shoved Julianna. "Give me the details!"

"Well, I wanted him to kiss me. Then he did, and I liked it very much. However, I decided I don't need to decide to call him anything other than Declan right now because I have time to explore my options and figure out how I feel about him. I don't need to make a rush decision. I can't imagine enjoying being with someone as much as I enjoy being with Declan, but then again, I really haven't been exposed to many other people. So I think it's best to take it slow, have fun and don't close myself off to any options just yet.

It's like I have a mess of all these emotions inside of me now that I never allowed myself to feel before. I need some time to untangle them."

Greta raised an eyebrow. "That sounds very practical and mature of you," she said drily. "How did you feel when he kissed you? You said you wanted him to."

Julianna sighed. "I don't know. How do you know if you love someone like that? How do I know I won't find someone I like even better once I'm exposed to other people? There's so much to consider!"

"Well, let's think about it for a minute. You said he kissed you?"

"Yes, after we talked about him kissing other people. He didn't kiss that prissy little Sarah, thank goodness. He did kiss Britta, but that was only part of our plan to escape, so I can let that slide, I suppose."

"Wait a minute! You're jealous!" Greta exclaimed.

Julianna considered this and said, "Maybe. I just thought that Declan should be the first person to kiss me, and I'm glad that he was."

"But you wish you were the first person who kissed him. You're jealous," Greta explained. "It's okay!"

In many ways, Julianna had been a very wise and mature ten-year-old child. Greta remembered she had seemed old for her age then. Now, she seemed stunted in the area of social development. To Greta's observation, it seemed she had not changed much at all. She was still very wise and mature, but some things, especially those involving personal relationships were far out of her wheelhouse. Greta silently vowed to do everything she could to help Julianna navigate these uncharted waters, and Greta was very much a fan of Declan.

"Listen, I'm not saying you have to marry the guy," Greta stated. "All I'm saying is to think about what you want and make sure you don't let a good thing slip away."

Julianna smiled at her sister. "That's exactly what I intend to do."

Sam greeted Declan at the breakfast table. He folded the newspaper to see his young houseguest. "How was your evening?"

"It was very nice," Declan answered. "Thank you for putting that together for us."

"You're welcome. Greta was really excited by the idea. She is looking forward to giving you and her sister even more of those experiences, so consider yourself warned!"

Declan chuckled. "That's fine with me. I guess I didn't really think I was missing out before. Now, I'm looking forward to whatever is next." He poured himself a bowl of cereal and joined his host at the breakfast table. "Anything interesting in the news today?"

"This is a mainstream paper, so if you want to hear about how wonderfully the New Regime is doing, here you go," Sam tossed the paper in Declan's direction. "I keep my eye on that paper and compare it with a couple of independent publications."

"That seems like a lot of work," Declan kidded.

Sam smiled. "Actually, it is. Not only is it more reading, which I'm sure wouldn't be a problem for you or Julianna, but you have to be careful about which underground papers you're reading. Some of them are just looking to incite drama for the sake of selling copies. They have just as little journalistic integrity as the mainstream papers which basically serve as publicity pieces for the New Regime."

While they discussed media options, Greta, carrying Starla, and Julianna walked into the kitchen. Greta set Starla on a chair with a booster seat, and Sam grinned at the little girl whose hair was done up in pigtails tied with pink ribbon. "Good morning, sweet girl."

"Good morning," Greta answered in jest. Greta tried to be discreet, but she watched like a hawk as Julianna sat down next to Declan. Greta could not wait to see Declan's reaction and note if the dynamic between the two had changed at all. When Julianna sat down, Declan looked her way and smiled as he greeted her in the same familiar way. "Good morning, Sunshine."

Julianna beamed a smile at him, relieved that Declan had not suddenly gone weird on her. "What are you eating?" she asked him.

Much to Greta's disdain, the two went on as if nothing had changed between them. Declan knew he was sure of what he wanted, but he also knew Julianna. He knew she would have to come to a decision in her own time and trying to force her hand would not end well for him. He was content to wait for her to figure it out. Greta, however, had decided to work even harder to point out to her sister what was right under her nose.

Julianna's day was much more pleasant than the previous one. Instead of reading old scribbled notes until her eyes were bleary, she decided to spend the day playing with Declan and Starla. They built with blocks, played hide and seek, had a tea party joined by some dolls and stuffed animals, danced silly dances and dressed up as a king and two princesses. Throughout the day, Julianna took note of how imaginative and creative Starla was. When presented with a problem, she would come up with some unique and funny solutions. Nothing about her seemed slow, and Julianna found herself curious to know how they had scored Starla on a test to determine she was no longer worth the New Regime's time and resources in the Scholars Compound. She knew Starla would have taken a different test than the one administered to her and Declan when they were older, and she wondered how the New Regime thought it could accurately gauge a child's intelligence at this stage. As far as creative play, Julianna thought Starla was brilliant, but they must not have counted that for much.

At one point, Declan said to her, "I'm glad you decided to join us today."

"Me too," Julianna replied with a grin. "I'm really having fun."

"I was thinking we should surprise Sam and Greta with dinner ready for them tonight," Declan suggested. "You know, as a thank you for their efforts last night."

Julianna smiled at the thought of her mock prom and dancing close to Declan. "That's a nice idea, but do you think it's safe? What if by some strange chance a take-out person happens to recognize one of us? Should we send Starla to the door? Wear a mask?"

Declan looked at Julianna like she was silly and laughed at her expense. "That's not exactly what I had in mind. I thought you and I could make dinner."

Now Julianna looked as if he were crazy. "We don't know how to cook. We've always had food put in front of us and people told us to eat it, whether it be our parents or the Compound dietary department."

"Did you miss that I cooked dinner last night?" Declan asked. "I know you were busy in the study, but I believe you did come out to eat. I just looked up a recipe and followed it. We can read and follow directions. It's not that hard. The trick is to find a recipe in which you understand all the words, and then look around the kitchen and make sure all the ingredients are there. It's really fairly simple."

Julianna still looked doubtful, but she shrugged and said, "I guess it couldn't hurt to try."

"It might be a skill you want to pick up," Declan suggested. "Since we no longer eat what the dietary department provides." As an afterthought, he added, "I'll help you make a cake."

Julianna gave him a sideways look, held out her hand across her body and said, "Sold."

Declan laughed as he shook her hand.

Later, as Declan watched Julianna in the kitchen, he thought he may have finally found her Achilles' heel. Cooking may have been the one thing at which Julianna most definitely did not excel. Her speed reading did not serve her well in comprehending recipes, and she often found herself in a bind by not considering the next step to come. At one point, he caught her before she threw in double the ingredient because she could not remember if she had added it. She did not fasten the lid on the food processor, which delighted Starla who clapped at the show, but resulted in quite the mess for them to clean up. Her hair was a mess from trying to brush it out of the way with ingredients on her hands. When he looked at her, he thought about how adorable she looked with a dot of flour on the tip of her nose and some cream cheese smeared across one cheek. When Julianna happened to catch his eye, she glowered and said, "This is a dirty, disgusting job."

He laughed. "Well, you're almost done now. Then we just need to clean up before Greta and Sam get here."

Julianna groaned. "Oh no! We have to clean up too?" she whined. "Will this torture ever end?"

With Declan's help, she was able to tidy up the kitchen before Greta arrived, though she was not very confident in how the food may taste. "Don't worry," Declan assured her. "I was nervous yesterday, too. But it turned out just fine."

Julianna and Starla set the table in the dining room, and Julianna showed Starla how to fold the napkins into pretty shapes, like Anne Brenner had once taught her. When Greta and Sam came home, Declan led them into the dining room. Julianna and Starla popped up from behind the table and shouted, "Surprise!"

"You did all this?" Greta asked. "Thank you!"

"Very impressive," Sam complimented.

When they sat down to eat dinner, even Julianna was impressed at how well the food had turned out.

They talked about how everyone had spent their day, and then Sam turned the conversation to his friend and their future. "You remember when I mentioned I had a safe place for you two," Sam reminded. "I've invited our friend Abraham over this evening so everyone could meet. He's looking forward to meeting you, and you can feel free to ask him any questions you like."

"Of course, we're not trying to kick you out," Greta added. "So if you're uncomfortable with anything, we're not going to force you into it."

"Absolutely," Sam agreed.

Julianna and Declan looked at each other. "I, for one, am very interested in learning more and hearing what Abraham has to say," Declan remarked.

"Me too," Julianna said.

"Great! He'll be here after dinner," Sam said.

After dinner, they retired to the living room and waited for their guest. Julianna was curious to see what this man had to say to them. Greta noticed that Declan sat right next to Julianna on the sofa, but she said nothing. Sam saw Greta focusing on the pair as she gnawed thoughtfully on her bottom lip and whispered into her ear, "I have to draw the line at a mock wedding."

She smiled and lightly elbowed him in the ribs. She just wanted her sister to have someone in her life like Sam was to her. Her concentration on the subject at hand was interrupted by the chime of the doorbell.

"I'll get that," Sam offered as he patted Greta on the knee and rose.

Sam opened the door and greeted the man he called Abraham. "Come in please," he welcomed. "Why don't you join us in the living room?" Sam shut the door and added, "I have some friends I'd like you to meet."

Julianna sized up Abraham as he walked into the living room. The older gentleman looked to be in his 60s and of African descent. He stood well over six feet tall and wore his graying hair closely cropped. He took long strides as he approached them. Julianna thought he moved with confidence, and she supposed she had no other option than to trust him.

"Abraham, this is my sister-in-law, Julianna Brenner, and her partner, Declan O'Connor," Sam introduced. "They are Scholars."

Abraham raised his eyebrows. "Are they now? And how did they get here?" he asked, his curiosity piqued.

"We escaped," Julianna answered.

"They have some very interesting information from inside the Compound," Sam reported. "I think they could be of great value to the cause."

"I'd like very much to hear what you have to say," Abraham said.

"We would like very much to hear more about the cause and your plans as well," Declan replied.

Abraham examined the duo a moment. Then he sat back and looked at Sam. "Are you sure they can be trusted?"

"I am," Sam replied with unwavering confidence.

"Very well then. Let's share," Abraham said.

Julianna and Declan told Abraham about their daring escape. Abraham seemed highly entertained by the fact that they had stolen Guardian's car and sunk it in the bottom of a lake. They told him about Project Much Death, and they answered everything they could about the inner workings of the Scholars Compound. Declan added tidbits he had learned from Britta. As much as the Scholars had to learn about how the world really functioned, the Workers knew even less about what really happens to the Scholars after they are taken from their families.

"Okay," Julianna said. "We told you everything we know. Now it's your turn. Tell us about the cause. What are your plans? What's the end game?" Julianna quizzed.

"Our end game is to remove the New Regime from power and to re-establish a democracy that works for its people," Abraham explained. "We want to set in place a government based on the principles of the original founding fathers. Guardian Costma and his police state need to end. He is not a stable man, and we cannot have him continue to steal the brightest minds away from their families and put them to work for his own selfish purposes. He came to power by playing on people's fears, but many people are no longer afraid. Many people are ready to reclaim their lives as they once were. The lives they deserve."

"How do you propose you would accomplish that?" Declan inquired.

"We have some brilliant minds of our own on the outside. Did you never notice when they built the Scholars Compound that they took only the children? There are plenty of highly intelligent older adults who are working for our cause. We are still discussing our possibilities and weighing our options, but we would love to have a couple of brilliant minds like you to join our team, especially when you have so much useful knowledge from the inside. The only thing that is required of you is that you believe in our cause. You would like to see the country return to the values it once held rather than the values of the New Regime. What do you say?"

Declan and Julianna exchanged a look. "I would say that we're with you," Julianna answered. "But as it is, we are being hunted as fugitives. I don't know how useful we might be to your cause, but speaking for myself, I believe in it. I want freedom."

"I agree with Julianna wholeheartedly. We can't live as we wish as long as the New Regime remains in power," Declan added.

"Wonderful," Abraham exclaimed. "We are happy to have you. Now the first thing we have to do is to get you out of this house without you being spotted. The New Regime will have Warriors watching this place until they catch the escaped fugitives, I'm sure. Once we get you out of the house, you will come to my property. You will be safe there, and you will have more freedom of movement. There we will begin filling you in on what we know about the New Regime. You can sort out the facts from the fiction you may have been given in the propaganda films. We are hoping you'll also be inspired to come up with some ideas that will help the cause, but even if you don't, you are welcome to take refuge there for as long as you need."

"Thank you," Julianna and Declan said in unison.

"And Julianna, I once worked with your father. He was a brilliant man. I did not want to tell you that upfront because I did not want that fact to bias your decision in any way. However, I am looking forward to chatting with you about him." He stood and offered Julianna and then Declan his hand.

After they both shook hands, Sam escorted Abraham to the door. "I have an idea on how and when to get them out of here, but why don't we give her a couple more days with Greta first?" Sam told him.

Abraham nodded. "I'll be in touch."

After the door closed behind Abraham, Declan remarked, "He seemed like a really nice man. It is very kind of him to offer harbor to us fugitives. Won't it be wonderful to be able to spend a little time outside again?" Declan asked her.

"Yes," Julianna replied, but she seemed a bit distracted. She looked at Sam. "So he knew Dad?"

"Yes," Sam said. 'That's actually how I met him. Through Greta."

CHAPTER 20

"Greta, you knew him from when he worked with Dad then?" Greta nodded.

"I take it you have no memory of him at all?" Declan asked. He put a comforting arm around her shoulder.

"No, but that's okay," she said. "Maybe I will once I've spent a little more time with him."

When Declan and Julianna retired to the tunnel that night, Julianna fell asleep quickly, but the dreams had returned. She was a young child, standing inside her father's office at the university. She heard him saying Mnemosyne repeatedly, almost as though it were a chant, and he seemed to be in a trance. Then Guardian Costma, dressed in full costume, barged into the office with a sinister grin. Guardian chased Julianna around the office as her father finally snapped out of it and screamed in protest. Just as Guardian reached a long arm out to grab her, she screamed. Suddenly Julianna was awake and sat upright in her cot.

Although she had broken out into a cold sweat, she must not have screamed out loud because Declan still slept soundly in the cot across from her. She mindfully slowed her breathing and lowered her head to her

347

pillow again. She stayed quiet and restless until she heard footsteps outside of the tunnel and knew it was okay to get up.

She plastered a fake smile to her face and greeted her family in the kitchen. She put on a cheerful act and made it through the morning until Sam and Greta left for work. Knowing her sister did not seem happy with her previous efforts to decode her dreams, she just remained silent. This dream seemed to validate Greta's theory that they were just nightmares, her brain misfiring information during the night. She had never seen Guardian Costma, especially not in the full costume, before the terror attacks. It made no sense for him to be in her father's office. Yet, this nightmare had disturbed her more than any of the others.

When Declan suggested she and Starla join him to watch some mindless cartoons, she jumped at the idea. She hoped a distraction to take her out of her own mind would help erase the wicked feelings left over from her nightmare. They snuggled together on the couch with Starla in between them. She tried to concentrate on the silliness displayed on the television screen, but her mind kept wandering back to her child-like screams.

She stood and walked away to be alone for a while, grateful that Declan knew her well enough to just smile understandingly as she stood to move away. She decided to head to the attic. Since she had been home, she had spent time checking out various parts of her old house, noting what had changed and being comforted by what had remained the same. Yet, she had never set foot in the attic. The walk-up attic was accessed by opening a door in the second floor hallway. A set of stairs took her to the full attic with its bare wood floors and boxes stacked neatly around the attic. They seemed to be in some kind of order though Julianna knew not what the order was. She only knew that she had the feeling that she had enjoyed spending some time with her father in this attic.

Julianna paced the attic floor, thinking hard about her past and hoping the atmosphere would trigger the escape of some sort of trapped memory. When she stepped on one floorboard, it creaked loudly. The noise made her stop. It seemed familiar for some reason. She rocked her foot back and forth on the board, trying hard to think back to another time she had heard that noise. Suddenly she had a vision of the floorboard being popped open. She leaned over and dug her nails under the board. The loose plank came up enough for her to stick a finger underneath and remove it. A small, hollowed space was revealed. She saw a white envelope with the name Smarty written on the outside in a handwriting that Julianna recognized from her past in a way that made her feel warm and nostalgic.

"This was one of his secret hiding place," she whispered to herself. "This was Dad's secret hiding place."

She remembered him using that place to hide only the most important papers for research that was a work in progress. He used the secret compartment as storage for his most valuable ideas and work so that no one could access the most crucial components of anything before he was ready to reveal it. She knew he had scrawled the name on the envelope, and she remembered that Smarty was his pet name for her. He had left her this letter in a secret place about which only Julianna knew. Even her mother did not know about the floorboard. But Julianna had forgotten it. Julianna, who never forgot about anything in her life, had forgotten something as important as this. "How could I have forgotten?" Julianna asked herself in a whisper.

She removed the letter, replaced the floorboard and opened the sealed envelope. She wondered if she had known the letter had been there at one point and just had forgotten about it too. When she unfolded the letter, an old photo floated to the floor, and a key fell in her lap. She began reading, and she had her answer.

Dear Julianna,

If you are reading this letter, my attempt to erase your memory must have failed on some level. It was never my intention to involve you in any of this. I now realize that I have done something horrible in that I created something which I had no business creating. I tried to become too powerful by aligning myself with the wrong people. I told myself that it was to build a better life for our family, but I now know that I was only lying to myself. You should never let someone convince you to go against your conscience for either their selfish reasons or yours. Your dear mother tried to warn me about associating with such people and trying to mess with things that should be left up to God, as she put it. My hubris would not allow me to listen to her reason.

Now I write this letter and will hide it for you to find only if you can, only if my attempts to put things right somehow go awry. This letter is a little insurance policy. I know you are too young to do anything to fix this now, but maybe someday, you'll be able to use this information I have provided you to help repair some of the damage that I have done. Please do not feel that you have to take on this responsibility if you do not have the power or ability to do so. I am the one who created this problem - not you.

Here are a few things you need to know. If you are experiencing partial memory loss relating to me it is because I used Mnemosyne, my memory altering device on you. I did this for a very good reason and as a way to protect you. I wanted this so badly that I was willing to wipe out all of your memories of me in order to accomplish it. If this did not work correctly and something has happened to me, you may come looking for this letter. Therefore, I offer you this confession. I created this device and did so with the financial backing of a man named Gary Adams. Gary posed as a friend and investor who wanted to better the world. I thought he embraced an idea of a better way of life in which people could co-exist peacefully without feelings of sadness or bitterness. The memory altering device could be used to erase painful or unpleasant memories, or it could alter memories to give people a more pleasant association when they were recalled. Your mother was adamantly opposed to such an invention from the onset. She thought that one's mind and memories are exclusively a person's own, the only thing that could not be taken away or tampered with by another. She thought it would be too easy to abuse and believed that suffering serves a purpose. Now I understand that she was right on both accounts.

Because of your genius memory and because even in the beginning stages, I recognized the potential for abuse of such a device, I kept my research and prototypes top secret. The location of the research was so secret in fact that I refused to even write it down. Only two people in the world knew the location - you and me. I used your exceptional memory to serve my purposes. I thought this would keep Mnemosyne more protected than if I were to enter the location into a computer or even a notebook. I did not anticipate that this would put you into any kind of danger. I never should have mentioned to Gary that I had given you the coordinates of the location as a back-up plan.

Of course, I did this before you discovered the anomaly in the grid while you were working on a computer at my lab. Unfortunately, Gary happened to be present that day as well. You came to show me what you had found and asked how you should fix it; like the good girl you are. I was proud that you were intelligent enough at your young age to even be able to identify such a thing, but Gary showed an intense interest in your discovery. He asked us everything he could about how this could be "a bad thing." You explained how it could be used to lock down services across the internet and that it should be addressed right away.

Instead, he took the knowledge you had given him and armed another one of his associates with the information to help make him capable of wreaking havoc across the web. This led me to a disturbing discovery. I learned that Gary and his cohorts were planning to launch a domestic attack on this country as a way to quickly come to power. This attack was to involve disabling internet services to disrupt everything from communication to energy to financial services. They plan to throw this country into chaos as a means to completely change our world for their selfish benefits. I know I have to do something to try to stop them. I feel that I played a role in making them prepared to carry out such a plan. I believe they can do it, but I hope I am successful in my attempt to thwart them.

I learned their true desire for the memory device was pure evil. They wanted to use it to alter the memories of everyone in the country. They wanted to erase the ideas of democracy, capitalism, and freedom as we know it. They wanted to mass produce the prototype and use the technology on a grand scale. I refused to participate and would not hand over the technology, but I have not yet destroyed the prototype; I need to use it on you first to protect you from Adams. No one else knows how to re-create the technology, not even you.

The research is still in the secret place which only can be accessed by the enclosed key. Please keep this close to your heart and don't let anyone else have access to it. You also must make certain the prototype has been successfully destroyed. It is my wish that this piece of my work be completely obliterated with my humble apology for ever creating such a horrific piece in the first place.

Although I had not had the chance to complete full scale testing of the device, I will use it on you so that I can erase any knowledge of anything associated with the device in order to keep you safe from these awful people. If you don't have the knowledge to give them, you will be of no use to them. Whatever you do, please do not trust Gary Adams. You may somehow remember him as a nice man for whom you used to have a fondness, but he is a mortal danger to you. Please stay as far away from him as you can and seek out the protection of others if necessary.

I love you dearly, and I hope you are safe and happy.

Love,

Your Dad

Julianna picked up the photo from the floor. It featured two men in suits, smiling and shaking hands. She instantly recognized one as her father, but she recognized the other one as well. She flipped the photo over and read the names penciled on the back. Jacob Brenner and Gary Adams, it read. She turned the photo back over to stare into the cold eyes of the man sporting a phony smile and standing with her father. Her father may have known him as Gary Adams, but she knew him as Guardian Costma. She dropped the photograph to the floor as if it had shocked her hand.

Her head was spinning. For years, she had worried about what might happen if "the terrorists" ever won. Little did she know that they had. She and her father had played a role in the terrorist attacks, and those attacks had not been engineered by a foreign enemy as nearly everyone believed, but by Guardian Costma and the New Regime. And she, Julianna Brenner, was one of the only people in the world who knew this. What was she to do now? Did she have the power to stop him?

AUTHOR BIO

 Kim Frauli lives on a farm in rural Illinois with her husband, three children, and a menagerie of animals. She spent several years in marketing and communications for non-profit organizations, including serving as editor-in-chief of a hospital's health magazine. She took a break from full-time work to focus on family and volunteer work and became involved in education. She has served as a PTO president, board of education member, reading tutor and youth sports coach, in addition to chairing various events.

Website: kimfrauli.authorreach.com

Made in the USA
Middletown, DE
13 March 2018